Obsession

by

Sharon Buchbinder

Obsession

Cover Art by *Kim Mendoza*

The Wild Rose Press, Inc.
PO Box 708
Adams Basin, NY 14410-0708
Visit us at www.thewildrosepress.com

Publishing History
First Faery Rose Edition, 2013
Print ISBN 978-1-61217-867-7
Digital ISBN 978-1-61217-868-4

Published in the United States of America

**"Who are you? Who is that giant?
What did you say to him?"**

The pony-tailed man flashed a grin, the smile reaching his sky-blue colored eyes, giving him an appealing boyish look. "The big guy's name is Tio. I told Tio to truss Raul up like the pig he is and to bring him to Isabel Ramirez. She'll know *exactly* what to do with him."

"Who are *you*?"

The movie-star-handsome man stopped, bent down until he was eye-to-eye with Angie.

"I found your passport tossed onto Raul's desk, Angela Edmonds from the U.S. of A. I like that name. You *look* like an angel."

She shook her head and the street twirled. "I'm no angel." She steadied herself on his well muscled, naked arm. Rather than creeping her out, the skin on skin contact with her rescuer reassured her that he was a real human and not an angel conjured up in fevered religious delusion and desperation. "You sound like an American. You haven't answered my question. What's your name?"

"Torres." Still holding her ID, he strode to the driver's side of the car, hopped in and flashed a dazzling grin. "You could call me your hero because I'm taking you to see the woman who can help you find your son. My name is Alejandro Espinosa Santoyo Torres. But most people just call me Alejandro."

Praise for Sharon Buchbinder

Author of the Paranormal Romance Guild
Best Mystery/Thriller in 2012

"Sharon Buchbinder does it again. *OBSESSION* is a gripping mystery with interesting characters and twists that will keep readers turning pages until the fast-paced end. This is the type of story that will stay on your mind long after you've read the last page."

~*Joya Fields, author of* Beneath the Surface *(4½ Stars, Top Pick, RT Book Reviews, available from The Wild Rose Press, Inc.)*

"*OBSESSION* is a roller coaster ride of emotions, from devastation to elation and back again. As Angie Edmonds searches for her kidnapped son, she faces danger at every turn; corrupt and ineffective law enforcement, drug cartels, and the psychotic cult leader who thinks her son is the chosen one. Somehow in the midst of this miasma, Angie also finds love."

~*Tamara Hoffa, author*

Dedication

To my husband, Dale,
who fills my life with love and romance.
To our son, Joshua,
who taught me the truly important things in life.
And to all the mothers and fathers in the world
who would lay down their lives for their children.

Acknowledgements

Once conceived, a novel grows over time with love and lots of hard work. *OBSESSION* is the result of over two years of research, writing and revisions. Without the assistance of a kind, caring, and candid support group, this book would not be here today. I would like to take this opportunity to thank my alpha reader, cheerleader, and husband, Dale Buchbinder, for reading the first draft and every draft thereafter, typos and all. My Maryland Romance Writers (MRW) critique partners were instrumental in helping me to hone my craft and hit my deadlines. I was most fortunate to have two of the best beta readers in the world, Joya Fields and Tamara Hoffa. And, finally, I am very blessed to have Amanda Barnett in my life. She is an awesome editor who believes in my work and polishes my diamonds in the rough to brilliance.

While *OBSESSION* is a work of fiction, the story is set in real world situations. As of this writing, drug cartels continue to rule with iron fists in many areas of Mexico. The Sierra Madre remains an arduous terrain largely populated by the Tarahumaran people and goats. People still flock to cults and delusional, charismatic leaders, despite the lessons learned from Jonestown. And, sadly, human trafficking, a thirty-two-billion-dollar-a-year business, occurs in everyone's backyards. For those readers who wish to learn more about the cartels, cults, human trafficking, and the Sierra Madre, following is a list of books and movies I used in researching this novel.

Cartels

Langton, J. (2011). *Gangland: The Rise of the Mexican Drug Cartels from El Paso to Vancouver*. John Wiley & Sons. Kindle Edition.

Longmire, Sylvia (2011). *Cartel: The Coming Invasion of Mexico's Drug Wars.* Macmillan. Kindle Edition.

Cults

Gifford, Dan & Gifford, Amy Sommer (Producers) & Gazecki, William (Director). (2003). *Waco: The Rules of Engagement*. USA: New Yorker Video.

Graham, William (Director). (2008). *The Story of Jim Jones: Guyana Tragedy*. [Motion picture] USA: Alpha Home Entertainment.

Grimberg, Sharon (Producer) & Samels, Mark (Director). (2007). *Jonestown: The Life and Death of Peoples Temple*. USA: PBS Home Video.

Layton, D. (1998). *Seductive Poison: A Jonestown Survivor's Story of Life and Death in the People's Temple*. New York, NY: Anchor Books.

Reiterman, T. with John Jacobs. (2008). *Raven: The Untold Story*. New York, NY:Tarcher/Penguin.

Sherrick, Edgar & Regan, Judith. (Producers). & Young, Roger. (Director). (1996). *The Siege at Ruby Ridge*. (CBS Mini-Series). USA: MGM DVD.

Human Trafficking
Amritraj, Ashok, Landesman, Peter, Leger, Robert, Sylvest, Lars, Ortenberg, Tom, Hamson, Nick, Wimer, Michael, (Producers) & Kreuzpaintner, Marco (Director). (2007). *Trade.* USA: Lionsgate.

Bales, K. (1999). *Disposable People.* Berkely, CA: University of California Press.
EuropaCorp, M6 Films, Grive Productions, Canal+, TPS Star, All Pictures Media, Wintergreen Productions (Producers) & Morel, Pierre (Director) (2008). *Taken.* France, USA & UK: 20th Century Fox.

Focus Features, BBC Films, Astral Media (Producers) & Cronenberg, David (Director). (2007). *Eastern Promises.* UK, Canada & USA: Universal.

Muse Entertainment Enterprises (Producers) & Duguay, Christian (Director) *Human Trafficking* (Life Time TV Mini-Series). (2005). Canada & USA: Echo Bridge Home Entertainment

Red Light Films & HBO Cinemax & Sundance Institute Documentary Film (Producers) & Zana Briski and Ross Kauffman (Directors). (2004). *Born into Brothels.* USA: HBO Cinemax

Cohen Media Group, Harwood Hunt Productions, Off Hollywood Pictures (Producers) & Hunt, Courtney. (Director). (2008). *Frozen River.* USA: Sony Pictures Classics.

Scion Films, Canana Films, Creando Films (Producers)

& Fukunaga, Cary (Director). (2009). *Sin Nombre.* Mexico & USA: Universal.

Shelly, L. (2010). *Human Trafficking: A Global Perspective.* New York, NY: Cambridge University Press.

Sierra Madre
Anderson, A.E. (1994). *Ethnic Tourism in the Sierra Tarahumara: A Comparison of Two Raramuri Ejidos.* (Thesis). University of Texas at Austin. Retrieved from http://www.planeta.com/ecotravel/mexico/chihuahua/anderson/anderson.html

Biggers, J. (2006). In the Sierra Madre. Urbana & Chicago, IL: University of Illinois Press.

The California Native. (2003). Copper Canyon Companion. Los Angeles, CA: The California Native.

Warner Brothers (Producer) & Huston, John. (Director) *The Treasure of the Sierra Madre.* USA: Warner Video.

November, One Year Ago, Maryland Eastern Shore

Angie Edmonds' screams echoed through out the sparsely furnished room as another contraction ripped across her abdomen. Wincing from the glare of a naked light bulb, she tried to shake off wet strands of hair that fell into her eyes and clung to her neck. As the pain receded, she loosened her white knuckled grip on the damp sheets and squinted at her watch.

How could it only be a minute's respite between the tortuous agony?

For over twenty-four hours she'd been pushed to the edge, then pulled back with increasing frequency. Her arms, legs, belly—everything—felt as if they'd been rolled over by a tractor. She wondered how much more the baby—or she—could take. If her judgment hadn't been so awash with pregnancy hormones, maybe she wouldn't have fallen for her mother's invitation for a "quiet family dinner." She should have known better. If *only* she'd said no, she'd be in Baltimore, near healthcare providers who didn't practice barbaric home deliveries.

As her stomach began to harden and the urge to push down forced its dominance over her body, she grabbed her father's callused hand.

"Something. Wrong. Call. The. Doctor." She squeezed words out between gasps for air.

"Pleeeeease." The last word came out in a shriek.

He jerked his hand away. His gaunt, sun-weathered face twisted with disgust as he leaned in close to Angie's head. His heavy circular pendant struck her brow, narrowly missing her eye.

"Your Momma's the best midwife on the Eastern Shore. She ain't *never* lost a baby. *God* is on her side."

A pain-free moment. Then another. Angie blew rapidly through pursed lips. The still rational part of her mind wanted to beg him to bring a doctor for the baby's sake, if not hers. "I beg—"

"Women were *meant* to suffer in childbirth."

As if on cue, pain exploded in her belly. Angie arched her back and clutched the sweaty bed sheets.

Her mother whispered, "The baby is breech, Father."

He turned and roared at her mother, "Do *something,* you stupid woman. That child belongs to *me*. I don't care if you have to cut her open like a pullet. Get *him* out alive."

"Yes, Father." Angie's mother answered in the aged way by giving her husband the title of father.

Barely able to catch her breath as the throbbing cramps receded, Angie focused on the sound of his heavy work boots as he clomped out of the bedroom, taking his threatening presence away from her side. She was only thirty-two, in the prime of her life, it wasn't *fair*. Where was God when she needed him? Arms and legs trembling uncontrollably with a mixture of exhaustion and fear, Angie prayed her mother wouldn't be forced to carve her up to rescue her child.

"If I can't turn the baby, he'll die." Her mother grabbed Angie's hands with her large work worn ones and yanked. "Stand up."

"My legs. So weak—" A swift, hard contraction took her off guard, knocking the wind out of her. She threw her head back and fought to catch her breath. *Remember the mantra. Puff, puff, blow.*

Iron hands circled her wrists. "Get up—or so help me God, I *will* use that on you." The butcher knife glinted on the nightstand, a stark reminder of her father's command.

Angie heaved herself up. Her legs shook, but held her weight. *She had to do what her mother said, stay alive at any costs, no matter how painful. If she didn't survive, the baby would be left in the care of these two lunatics. She had to hang on for him.*

"Put your back to the bedpost." The older woman grabbed the knife and placed the steel tip against her sweat drenched nightgown.

"Mama—no—please don't—"

Metal entered cloth, shredding her last hope of survival. She was as good as dead. Angie closed her eyes and wailed, "Mama, no!"

The fabric ripped and cool air hit her naked belly.

She blinked. Her mother set the knife down. Half of Angie's nightgown puddled on the floor, covering her bare feet. Hot tears ran down her cheeks. She wasn't going to die—yet.

The older woman kneaded Angie's stomach, massaging and twisting the womb, attempting to move the baby's head into a downward position. She whispered, alternating between begging God for help and urging the child to come out. After an eternity of wobbly legs, wrenching contractions, prayers, and constant belly massage, the baby shifted and her mother shouted, "Thank you, Lord!"

Eyes burning with tears of pain and gratitude, her breath coming in short, searing gasps, Angie attempted to swing her right foot up onto the clammy sheets. Halfway up, her weight-bearing leg gave way. She collapsed onto the cold floor. Lead-limbed, she couldn't even think about moving.

So tired. She closed her eyes and slipped away from the pain, away from the sounds and pungent smells of the room, into nothingness. Silence enveloped her like a thick wrapping of cotton batting. Suddenly alert and pain free, Angie opened her eyes and watched the room fall away beneath her. She seemed to be floating upward. The hardwood floors gleamed in the early morning light peeking through the windows. Her mother stood over her inert body, her mouth working— but no sounds coming out. Her father burst into the room, his face twisted into a snarl of rage. Heart heavy, unable to gaze at the scene anymore, Angie turned away and found herself in a long, dark corridor.

At the end of the black tunnel, a blinding light shone. A large, shadowy figure emerged between the darkness and the light. As she watched with wonder, glittering white wings unfurled, and a creature of awesome beauty shimmered and formed before her. Neither male nor female, the intangible, but unmistakable *Divine Messenger* had skin like fine white marble and piercing azure eyes.

Was she having a delusion like her father? Had his ravings finally turned her brain to mush? Despite her trepidations, she wanted to believe—someone, something—that would make her suffering worthwhile. She drew closer to the towering creature. Unable to resist his mesmerizing gaze, she reached up and touched his pale cheek. It was warm—wet. He, it, this being was *real*. Her heart rejoiced. There *were* angels. Despite her father's dire predictions, she had *not* been thrown to the dark realm. She was going to heaven.

Was he crying? Why? Was he sad or happy?

He grasped her shoulders in his strong hands, turned her, and pointed to the silent tableau below.

Her father and mother lifted her flaccid body and dropped it onto the bed.

Dead. She was dead. Angie closed her eyes. The realization filled her not with fear and dread, but with peace and relief. Every molecule of her being rejoiced. Her earthly trials were over. No more pain. No more captivity. No more beatings when she tried to escape. Safe at last from her obsessed, delusional father. She sighed—and a thought jolted her back to the moment.

The baby. Was he dead, too? Where was he?

Below, her mother worked with frenzied movements, a bloodstain spreading across the bed sheets. Then she pulled the limp-limbed, mottled gray, blood-slicked infant out.

Angie mouthed the words, *"Save him, dear God, please save him,"* but no sounds came out.

A membrane covered the child's face. Her mother snatched up the knife and cut a hole in the sac. With swift, sure movements, she swung him by his feet and slapped his back. Thick white mucus flew out of his mouth. The baby took a deep breath, flushed pink, and flailed his arms.

Her mother's stern expression was erased by a smile of joy. Holding the child as if he was made of glass, she placed him on the bed, tied and cut the umbilical cord, then cleaned him. She left his face for last. With slow, careful motions, she peeled the rest of the gauzy membrane off his nose, eyes, cheeks and ears and placed it on a nearby towel. She then held the child out to his grandfather. Lips tight, a frown creased her father's brow as he examined the baby's hands, feet, and abdomen before tracing a crescent-shaped mark on the child's right side. At last, a radiant grin burst across his face. He held the baby up in the air, his lips moving as he danced around the room. Angie noticed her body lay pale and still, ignored by her parents. She had served their purpose, her body a vessel for their grandchild's life. Sad to be tossed to the side like road kill, but grateful her baby was safe, she turned back to the angel. She was at peace and prepared for her journey to the next level—but he shook his head—and vanished.

The black tunnel became a tornado, its force sucking Angie down to earth, pulling her back into her body. Heart racing, jumping in her throat, breathless, utter panic at being trapped, held hostage again, overtook her. She wanted to be free of this thing, this heavy weight, the burden of her past life. *No, no, no.* She wanted to be with the angel. The soft silence was shattered by her mother's exultant voice "—the Chosen One!"

Angie blinked. Her parents stood at the side of her bed, eyes pinched, hands clutched, fervent prayers being raised on high. What happened? One moment she was content to stay with the angelic being—the next thing she was back to reality.

Why couldn't she stay with the angel?

Her newborn son sucked noisily at her breast, and a

fierce swell of protectiveness washed over her. She clutched her baby closer. Her job was here—with her son. *No one* was going to hurt him. Angie counted his perfect fingers and toes and touched his impossibly tender cheek. Bright red hair crowned his head in an exuberant soft thatch. A rush of euphoria overwhelmed her. Hot tears of joy streamed down her face.

She was alive, alert, and oddest of all, *pain free*.

Angie kissed the top of her son's head and reflected on her fantastic dream. The pain of childbirth must have induced an altered state, one where her father's religious tirades took over her subconscious and ran riot with her imagination. There was no tunnel, no light, no angelic being. Only the cold, hard reality that she *had* to get her son away from her father and his cult.

Sharon Buchbinder

Chapter One

Angie Edmonds stood in the open doorway of her Rodgers Forge townhouse and glanced beyond the two men in black on her doorstep. No reporters, no roaming news vans. Good. The last thing she wanted was for the media to get wind of this story. She could just hear the screaming newscaster: *Crazed Cult Leader Escapes From Maximum Security Prison, Kidnaps One-Year Old Grandson.* She nodded, motioned for the agents to come in, and closed the door behind them. These guys were here, in *person,* to give her news.

Not a good sign.

The pulse in her temple tapped like a hungry woodpecker, portending a hellacious migraine. She pressed an index finger to the side of her head.

"Where's my son?"

FBI Special Agent Warren and ATFE Special Agent Benson exchanged anxious glances. Warren said, "We *think* he's in Mexico."

Her vision telescoped and threatened to shut down completely. She staggered back and clutched at the wall with her left hand. The faux grass wallpaper rasped against her fingertips, the tiny paper cuts bringing her back to reality and the present. She could not fall apart when her son needed her.

After Jake's dangerous birth, it was a wonder he

8

was alive, happy, and extraordinarily healthy. A wretched childhood with her obsessed, delusional father ensured that as soon as she discovered the *real* world outside her father's religious cult that she'd go a little wild. Before Jake, she had sampled every forbidden fruit, including a long series of sexy but emotionally cold one night stands with strangers—and a red hot love affair with cocaine. But *everything* had changed when she found out she was pregnant. She wasn't *that* woman anymore. She was Jake's mommy now, a new and improved version of herself—thanks to a lot of help from her program and from Dan, the father of her son.

Feeling like a boxer on the ropes, she pushed herself away from the wall, shook her head to clear away the tunnel vision, and glared at the agents.

"As soon as I reported my one-year-old son stolen from the day care center, I *told* you my father would try to get out of the country. Why didn't you *stop* him?"

"We followed established protocol." Teeth gritted, Benson, the ATFE Agent monotoned, as if he thought removing all emotion from his speech would keep a crazed mother calm. "We've been investigating the owner of this ranch, a known member of the Recreationist Cult, for over a year. We tracked all weapons and ammunitions sales to him and tried to get search warrants for probable cause. But the judges in that county said they wouldn't have anything to do with another Waco."

Fists clenched, jaw clenched tight, Angie's muscles thrummed with the tension of her restrained rage. "And?"

Warren cleared his throat and picked up the story. "Using extensive calculations, the joint task force was able to ascertain *exactly* how many guns, rounds of ammunition and explosives the cult had stockpiled in the ranch house, barns, and outbuildings." He paused, looked up at the ceiling and sighed.

Angie's stomach rolled. She said nothing.

"There was a truck labeled 'Water'." Benson continued the story, his voice somber. "It was, in fact, filled with aviation fuel. The owner of the ranch shot at the Texas Rangers' helicopter, trying to lead them away from the plane. When the chopper closed in on the tanker, he blew it up."

She struggled to envision where the little plane had been in relation to the truck-turned-giant flame-thrower. Her teeth clenched and unclenched in sync with the contractions of her arms and legs. Control, that's what her martial arts training had drummed into her. Fight only when you must. Find the calm within.

"Where was the plane when the explosion occurred?"

"We don't know for sure." Benson glanced at Warren. "They didn't get a tail number, but we do know a small plane matching the description of the one with your son in it crossed the border into Chihuahua."

Her stomach plummeted in free fall. *Not again.* Last year her crazy father, Reverend Edmonds, had kidnapped her son as a newborn, claiming the child was the Chosen One, the one who would heal the world, as prophesized in the Book of Enoch. After an ordeal and manhunt, the so-called holy man had been imprisoned in Baltimore's most secure penitentiary, the super max, a prison within a prison. He escaped by feigning a heart attack. Then he and her mother had bee-lined to the daycare center, and with the unwitting assistance of a temporary receptionist, abducted her son—again.

"I'm sorry." Warren shook his head. "I know it's not what you wanted to hear."

As Angie listened to the gray-haired man apologize, she fought to keep her palms at her sides and her feet planted on the ground. This was not a good time for her to be arrested for assault. She bit back the words she really wanted to spit out: "incompetent bureaucrats" and "gutless morons." The lawmen had underestimated her father and enabled him to escape with Jake under the cover of a martyr's pillar of fire. How very Biblical. Her father must be so pleased. He'd see this as yet another sign that God was on his side, instead of the truth—his followers were no better than demon worshippers.

"Ms. Edmonds, we're doing everything in our power to find your son." Warren wiped sweat off his red face. Benson shuffled his feet and looked away.

"So you've contacted the Mexican government?" She stared at Warren, not blinking. He glanced down. *He was hiding something.* What? What could be so awful that he wouldn't share it with a terrified mother of a kidnapping victim?

Warren exchanged furtive glances with Benson. A long silence filled the foyer. At last he looked her in the eye and said, "Yes."

Her empty stomach yawed and pitched. "What aren't you telling me?"

"They said they'd look into it, but the drug wars and murders in Juarez and elsewhere are consuming most of the police force's time and manpower."

Rage bubbled up, plucked at her sanity, and threatened to overcome her restraint. This wasn't happening. Her only hope of recovering her son stood in front of her, telling her they couldn't help. Was everything reduced to an accountant's calculations of time and labor costs? How about factoring in a little compassion?

"No," she shouted. Warren jumped back, as if he expected her to attack him. Keeping her hands balled into fists at her side, she took two steps closer and got into his personal space. His sweaty face was so close to hers, she could smell his pungent perspiration mixed with the odor of minty mouthwash. "*You* are going to Mexico. *You* are going to get my son. Do you understand me? *You* are going to do your job!"

Gray eyes wide, his face now crimson, the FBI agent shook his head. "Once they made it into Mexican airspace, they were beyond our reach. It's a private kidnapping. We're working with the State Department. I *swear* we're doing everything we can."

Useless. They were completely, utterly, useless. "Get out of my house." Warren tried to press a business card into her palm. She let it flutter to the floor. "Leave me alone." She slammed the door on their retreating backs.

How could drug wars take precedence over her baby? Was she never going to see him again? What had she done to deserve this? She'd paid her dues, made her amends. Where was the justice? Where was the humanity? Where was a divine intervention? Nowhere. If there was going to be an intercession on her behalf, the time was long past. The only thing she could rely on was herself—and her connections. The discovery of her son's abduction at the day care center had sent her into a tailspin. *Enough.* She'd had enough of being jerked around by her father and the authorities. She had to *stay strong*, channel her hopelessness and helplessness into anger—and action.

She picked up her phone and choked back a sob. "They're in Mexico."

Dan, her ex-lover, and Jake's father, gasped. "What happened?"

Angie filled him in about the firefight at the ranch and the loss of the Texas Rangers. "They won't go after them. Said they're working through the State Department."

"What about a press conference? Get the media involved? Beg for Jake's safe return?" His voice rasped with emotion.

She took a deep breath before responding. Dan still didn't understand how the cult worked. "First off, I don't want to escalate my father and his followers' insanity. We need them to believe we're defeated, that he's smarter than we are and have given up."

"Jake could be an adult before we see him."

"As long as he's with my father and mother and the cult, at least there's a chance we'll see him again *alive*."

"What are you talking about?"

"Kidnapping and holding wealthy victims for ransom is rampant in Latin America. Even if you pay off the kidnapper, there's no guarantee the victim will be set free."

"I thought that was only in movies—"

"Based in reality. If we call a press conference, some thug is going to hear that the son of a rich American physician is being held by a cult leader. How long do you think it will be before some creep decides he wants to make some quick money? We might as well paint a target on Jake's back."

Dan choked back a sob. She knew this was hitting him hard, too. He loved Jake as much as she did.

She plunged onward. "I'm going after him. I can't just sit here in Baltimore and wait."

"I'll go with you."

"No. Not happening." She wiped a tear off her cheek. "You need to stay with your wife."

He started to protest. "No—"

"Sarah's about to explode. If you aren't here for that baby's birth, you'll never forgive yourself."

"If something happens to you and Jake, I won't forgive myself, either."

She chewed on her lower lip. "I have a plan. But I'm going to need Sarah's help."

"Anything."

His voice was as tight as piano wire. She needed him to stay calm, not snap. Using her closing argument voice, the one she used to coax, cajole, and win over juries, Angie shared her thoughts. "Juarez is a war zone. My father wouldn't take him there. He'd never endanger the Chosen One."

Dan cleared his throat. "So, where?"

She closed her eyes and concentrated on memories of her father's ravings. "He's been ranting about building a fortress in the wilderness for twenty years."

"That's half of Mexico. Drug lords control entire provinces, totally outside the law."

"Exactly. And your wife knows the one person with longer arms than the law."

Dan sucked in his breath. "Holy crap. You're right."

"We're going to fight fire with fire. Tell Sarah to

find Isabel Ramirez. Call in every favor she has. We need the biggest, baddest drug lord in the country to help us. If I can't get Jake back with her help, then I'm going to die trying—and take my father with me to hell."

****

Angie tapped the GPS for the hundredth time and tried to keep an eye out for landmarks, signs, anything that would tell her she was in the right village. At last she spotted the cheap dive with a battered sign, *El Hombre Loco*. A thrill of recognition ran through her exhausted body. A week of preparation and forty-eight hours of non-stop travel had finally brought her to the bar where she was supposed to meet Isabel's underling. True to her word, Sarah had called in every favor owed her and even thrown in a few threats of sending a certain incriminating DVD to the Mexican press. Sarah had sent a photo of Angie to her former colleague, so there'd be no mistaken identity and no suspicion of undercover *federales*. Dan had even hired a Spanish speaking chauffeur for Angie, but the man had fled the car at the sight of the border patrol in Fort Hancock, Texas, saying he was never, *ever* going back to a Mexican prison. "Hellholes," he had shouted and leaped out of the car.

She was on her own. All Angie had to go on was a name. Torres. Might as well be Smith or Jones. Without a physical description to guide her, her imagination ran wild. Was he short and beady-eyed? Tattooed? Smelly? A giant muscle-bound thug? In her practice as a defense attorney, she'd met every size and shape of alcoholic and drug addict in Baltimore. Despite the lucrative fees offered, one of the few categories of miscreants she'd refused to *ever* defend was drug dealers. Now her key ally in this battle to rescue her son was the supreme drug lord of Mexico. Angie felt like *Alice in Wonderland*, her world turned upside down.

She pulled over to the curb and parked the car. Angie tried to take the keys out of the ignition, but her hands shook and tears blurred her vision. Overcome by shaking sobs, she put her head down on the steering wheel and bawled like a baby.

Baby, baby, baby. Her baby, her one and only reason for staying clean, for being alive, taken from her. Doubts filled her mind. Could she do this? Was this the right way to go about finding him? She *had* to find her son and get him away from her lunatic father, if it was the last thing she did.

Someone pounded on her window and shouted in Spanish. Her heart jumped erratically, and she swiped at her eyes. *Why was that cop yelling at her?*

Unsure of which piece of paper he needed, Angie rolled down the driver's side window and thrust her license at the scowling Mexican police officer.

He glanced at her Maryland document and waved it away. *"El pasaporte y la visa."*

The passport and visa slipped out of her hand, fluttering to the ground.

"Sorry, I didn't mean to do that." She attempted to open the car door, only to have it kicked back into place. The rental company was not going to be happy with that dent. She coughed and squinted at the sun's glare. "What's the problem?"

Clearly not happy that he'd had to bend over and pick up her now red-dust-coated paperwork, he rattled off a barrage of Spanish, waving his arms back and forth, spitting as he spoke.

Her high school Spanish was too rusty to keep up. *"No comprendo."*

The officer responded by pulling out a notepad and scribbling. He showed her a number.

"Five hundred dollars?"

He grinned. *"Si. Dinero.* Cash."

She'd been warned this might happen and instructed to bargain. She opened her wallet and showed him a one-hundred dollar bill. "This is all I have."

His eyes narrowed, and his smile turned into a scowl.

As she reached out the window to hand him the cash, he motioned at her to get out of the car.

"No comprendo."

He pointed to hood of the car. "Stand by there."

The rat-faced cop obviously understood and spoke better English than he'd let on at first.

He slid into the driver's seat and turned his back to her, obscuring her vision as he rummaged in the glove compartment.

He gave a triumphant shout. "Ha!" A plastic bag containing a white powder dangled between his fingers. "You bring drugs into my country?"

"No, no. I don't know where that came from. It's not mine." Where did that come from? Had that idiot driver left his stash in her car? Or did the cop just plant it there? She closed her eyes and took a deep shuddering breath to beat back the panic bubbling in her chest. She didn't have time to screw around with the police, even if it was a shake-down. She had to find Torres, get to Isabel, and rescue Jake. All the rest was bullshit. She wiped the tears off her cheeks with the heels of her hand. *Just pay the jerk and be done with it.* "You want more money? I'll give it to you."

"Assume the position." Cobra quick, the cop was out of the car. He twirled her around, forced her against the hood, kicked her feet apart, and pinioned her hands behind her back with his big rough ones.

Her head spun. What was happening? She was a lawyer. She'd dealt with thousands of American cops. Her voice shaky, she tried to reason with him. "There's been a mistake. Those aren't my drugs. I have no idea where they came from. *Honest.*"

"That's what they all say." He leaned his hips against her butt, an unmistakable bulge pressing against her.

Her skin crawled as if a thousand cockroaches were tap dancing on her body. Bile rose in her throat. Having her son kidnapped by her crazy father wasn't enough of a punishment, now she was being held for something she didn't do by a horny, corrupt cop. What else could go wrong?

His breath rasped close to her ear. "You are under arrest." And with that, manacles clicked into place on her wrists. He ran his hands up and down her chest, lingering a long time on her breasts.

She shuddered at his touch and bit her tongue to keep from screaming at him. He had already made up his mind that she was guilty. She had to find a way to get through to him.

Then he patted down her legs and ankles, sliding his hands up to her buttocks and pressing hard on her crotch. "No weapons."

As if she carried a Smith and Wesson in her bikini

panties. His touch made her skin crawl. She needed a bath.

"You come to the station. Now."

This wasn't right. She leaned hard against the car and dug in her heels.

"Isabel Ramirez said I was to meet someone named Torres at *El Hombre Loco*. He'll be looking for me."

He pried her off the car and whirled her around to face him. He gave her a yellow-toothed grin. "Some paperwork. Then we go to see *Professora* Ramirez."

Angie tried to shake out of his iron grasp. "Isabel Ramirez said to speak *only* to Torres. I'm meeting with Isabel Ramirez." Wasn't this guy even a little bit intimidated by Isabel's name? Sarah had said she ran everything in Chihuahua. Had their info been wrong about the drug lord's power?

Rat face rattled off a string of Spanish words, his face contorted with anger, and he pulled out his sidearm and pointed it at her chest. Spit flew out of his mouth. At last, in English he said, "I am Raul, chief of police. I am in charge here. You are under *my* arrest."

Frozen in place, Angie glanced around the empty streets. A black tabby slunk between red stucco buildings, and a dust devil swirled further down the road. *Odd. She could have sworn there were people on the street before. Where did they go?*

She couldn't tear her gaze away from the huge black handgun. He could have felled elephants with it. Why would anyone need a gun that ridiculously big?

He kept the weapon trained on her as he reached into the car and pulled out her purse, then he motioned for her to walk ahead of him. They walked two deserted blocks to the small building labeled *Policia*. It appeared only Raul the Rodent was on duty. Her lawyer's mind quickly cataloged the station. One desk, olive drab metal; one holding cell, empty; two doors to God only knew where. Behind her, she heard a deadbolt lock snap into place.

Were the thugs so bold that he had to lock the police station to keep the criminals out?

He dragged her through an unmarked door. The sight of a chair with manacles attached to it caused her breath to catch in her throat. Despite years of using drugs, she'd never been detained in a police station as a perp in her life. How ironic that her first arrest was a *false* one. She turned and found Raul way too close for comfort. Sweat slicked his brow.

He shoved her shoulder and pushed her further into the windowless chamber, smaller than most bathrooms she'd used, even in Mexico. The tiny space reeked of the cop's acrid body odor and garlic-laden halitosis.

"What—?"

The cool metal of the chair bumped into her bare legs. Her hands were cuffed, but her legs were free. She tried to slide to one side, using an evasive move from karate, but he moved faster than she thought possible. He slammed her into the wall, unsnapped one end of the cuffs and slapped it onto a metal bar bolted on the wall with a clang. She yanked at the manacles. The metal dug into her wrist, and a thin crimson line trailed down her arm and snaked under the sleeve of her white blouse.

Still trying to use her one and only connection in Mexico, Angie repeated, "Isabel Ramirez isn't going to be happy about this."

He gave her a slow, lecherous grin, undid his belt

and tossed his trousers and holster onto a hook on the wall by the door. His dingy white boxer shorts did little to hide his erection. A musty smell that spoke of poor personal hygiene filled the tiny space, fighting for dominance over his bad breath.

Her stomach lurched, threatening to bring up hours old eggs and coffee. Angie yanked at the metal cuffs to no avail. Her gaze darted around the hot, smelly room. No windows, door locked. All she had going for her now were her wits and a good set of lungs. She tried reasoning with him. "You don't want to do this. The Ambassador won't take kidnapping and rape of an American citizen lightly."

He laughed and slapped her so hard her teeth rattled. Tears welled up in her eyes and rage filled her chest. She literally saw red. "You think you're going to get away with this?"

Raul ripped her white blouse open. Buttons flew across the room and pinged as they hit the metal table. His filthy hands touched her breasts, his dirty fingers yanking and pulling at her brassiere, until the front clasp broke.

"*Muy bonitas.*" He licked his lips and twisted her nipples so hard she yelped in pain.

The thug hee-hawed like a jackass, his erection tenting his dirty drawers. Unable to watch, she closed her eyes and bit her lower lip hard. She welcomed the pain, embraced it, made it the focus of that moment in time. At last her mind cleared and she could step outside of her body and think.

This wasn't her first time at the sadism rodeo. Thanks to Daddy Dearest, she'd been tied up, starved, and beaten before. She'd learned how to dissociate her mind from her body, separating her true self from the woman tied to the bed with ropes. Determined never to be a victim again, Angie had undertaken a rigorous training program of martial arts and down and dirty street fighting. She could almost hear her instructor snarling at her. "Are you going to let this smelly pig torture and rape you? Or are you going to use your discipline and training to protect yourself?"

There *had* to be an opportunity for escape. She played everything back in her mind in slow motion freeze frames from the moment she entered the interrogation room to the second he snapped the handcuffs to the metal rod. *His pants. They touched the ground. If she could slide closer to the end of the metal rail, she might be able to reach a trouser leg—and that humongous gun.*

She opened her eyes and stared at the beast attacking her. More depraved than any drug addict she'd ever met, this so-called cop clawed at her waist band and fumbled with the metal buttons of her jeans. His filthy ragged nails scratched at her soft belly. She'd rather be torn apart by wild animals than have this senseless brute paw at her skin. She wouldn't cry out, wouldn't give him the pleasure of watching her weep and wail in pain. He was not going to get away with this. She worked up a glob of sputum and spat into his sweaty, panting face.

"Puta!"

This time she was prepared for the slap. She blocked his hand with her left forearm and ran across the wall, sliding on the metal rail toward the door. He slapped at her arm and shoulder, finally connecting with the side of her head. Her ear rang with the force of the blow—but she was two feet closer to his pants.

As she twisted away from his grasping paws, she thought she heard a muffled pounding. Hope combined with desperation, filling her lungs. Her voice boomed like an opera singer. "Help me!"

Cursing, Raul struggled with her pants, tried to yank them down, but she kept her butt glued to the wall. He stepped back, pulled his hand back to slap her again and in the split second just before he brought his palm back down, she blocked his hand with her arm and snap-kicked at his crotch.

Raul shrieked and fell to the floor, his groin clutched in his hands. Fearing he'd grab her leg, she resisted the urge to kick him in his buck teeth.

The pounding grew louder. The door. Someone was at the door.

"In here! Help me, please!"

His pants and the attached holster were within reach of her fingertips, if she could just get her arm to the other side of the door. Hugging the wall with her back, she stretched her right arm as far as she could— despite the pain of the metal grinding into her flesh. Leaning as far left as physically possible, she flailed at the pants—and missed.

She glanced at her enemy and screamed. "If someone's out there, please get in here *soon*. He's gonna kill me!"

Raul was up on his knees, grunting in pain and swearing.

Angie focused on the pants, reached again, got a piece of cloth between her second and third fingers. Millimeter by millimeter, the cloth *finally* came into her grasp.

Raul roared as she yanked the pants off the hook. The holster and sidearm flew across the room. A stream of putrid curses, only half of which she understood, poured from his lips like venom. If he got his hands on her, he'd kill her first, then rape her.

As clear as if he stood next to her, Angie's martial arts instructor's voice spoke to her. "Use your environment to your advantage." She faced her abuser.

Face twisted with rage, the cop rushed at her with a roar.

She grasped the metal railing with both hands, swung her legs up and connected with his chest. He stumbled backwards and fell over the metal chair. She sucked in huge gulps of air and tried to gauge his next move. Her body shook, and the manacles rattled on the metal bar. How much time had she bought? How soon would the vermin be back up on his feet and at her throat?

The center of the door exploded, spraying chunks of wood throughout the room. An enormous hand reached in and unlocked the door.

Raul's spew of invectives stopped, and his voice suddenly stripped of rage, turned apologetic. *"Tio, no! Lo siento, lo siento!"*

The biggest man Angie had ever seen in her life broke down what was left of the door. Bald head shining, a mask of rage twisting his face, the Goliath took one step into the small room and grabbed Raul by the throat. A flood of Spanish poured out of the giant's mouth as he shook the cop like a rat. Her would-be rapist's eyes bulged, his florid face turned purple, then blue. Just as Angie was positive the colossus was going to kill the man, someone barked out a command from behind the wall of muscle.

"Alto, Tio!"

The huge man dropped Raul face down on the floor. The cop turned his head, his face now bloodied, sputtered, and regained his normal florid coloring. With his underwear half off and his chubby, sweaty butt crack showing, the man looked like a skid row bum. Still, he managed to spit out one word before he passed out. *"Puta."*

The giant shrugged and stepped outside of the room.

A tall man with a dark, well groomed beard and ponytail strode through the door and locked pale eyes with Angie. Without saying a word, he found Raul's pants, dug out a key, and uncuffed her.

Legs buckling, Angie fell against her rescuer's chest. Uncontrollable tremors overtook her. His hands hovered in the air over her shoulders, heat from his body suffusing her breasts.

Her breasts!

She regained her balance and stepped back. Flushed with acute awareness that her breasts were exposed, Angie crossed her arms over nipples, and tried to stop shaking, to no avail. The stranger removed his shirt, fixed his gaze above her head, and helped her slide her arm into one, then the other sleeve. He buttoned the oversized shirt, taking great care to avoid touching her skin. Perhaps more than anything else, those small acts of kindness which allowed her to keep her dignity intact, broke through her walls of defense and made hot tears spring to her eyes. Trembling, Angie stood several inches shorter than the man, and felt a bit like a child. Unable to lift her gaze to his eyes, she focused on the deeply sculpted muscles of his naked chest. Covered with a vee of dark hair tapering down to the waist of his denim jeans, his well-toned abdomen spoke of years of training. It also bore evidence of his violent lifestyle. Alongside a large scar, a tattoo of *Santa Muerta*, a skeleton draped in robes and carrying a scythe, grinned at her.

"Th-th-thank you." Her voice came out in a hoarse whisper, and her teeth chattered.

Saying nothing, the stranger took her hand, and they both stepped over the unconscious police chief.

Angie was tempted to kick the slimy creep while he was unconscious, but she could barely lift her feet to walk out of the room. Her muscles quivered, and she had to fight off the urge to lean against the one sane person she'd met in this hell hole.

The giant stood outside what had been the door to the interrogation room. A fire extinguisher lay on its side next to the threshold. Piles of shattered wood were strewn throughout the station. The man with the pony tail jerked his thumb back toward the interrogation room and spoke in rapid Spanish. The giant nodded, grinned, and rubbed his hands, glee dancing on his face.

Her rescuer held her elbow. The warmth of his large hand seeped through the cotton shirt and infused her with a sense of security. His calm, quiet demeanor told her he was in charge, and she was safe with him. She blew out a long breath and allowed him to lead her through the demolished office and out onto the street. In the middle of the dusty road, a small crowd clapped and cheered. If she could have raised her hands, or her voice, she would have been there with them. Right now she just wanted to know her liberator's name.

"Who are you? Who is that giant? What did you say to him?"

The pony-tailed man flashed a grin, the smile reaching his sky-blue colored eyes, giving him an appealing boyish look. "The big guy's name is Tio. I told Tio to truss Raul up like the pig he is and to bring him to Isabel Ramirez. She'll know *exactly* what to do with him."

"Who are *you*?"

The movie-star handsome man stopped, bent down until he was eye-to-eye with Angie.

"I found your passport tossed onto Raul's desk, Angela Edmonds from the U.S. of A. I like that name. You *look* like an angel."

She shook her head and the street twirled. "I'm no angel." She steadied herself on his well muscled, naked arm. Rather than creeping her out, the skin on skin contact with her rescuer reassured her that he was a real human and not an angel conjured up in fevered religious delusion and desperation. "You sound like an American. You haven't answered my question. What's your name?"

"Torres." Still holding her ID, he strode to the driver's side of the car, hopped in and flashed a dazzling grin. "You could call me your hero because I'm taking you to see the woman who can help you find your son. My name is Alejandro Espinosa Santoyo Torres. But most people just call me Alejandro."

Chapter Two

Zeke Edmonds admired the panoramic view from atop a flat rock that rivaled the size of those at Stonehenge. Positioned at the pinnacle of a cave-riddled, terraced ridge of the Sierra Madre, the aerie enabled him to see for miles in every direction. Half a dozen turkey vultures circled in a sapphire-blue sky speckled with cotton puffs of clouds. Below, just as he had seen in his visions, a sparkling river undulated like a thin silver snake. His legs quivered with fatigue, his breath came in short puffs, and his pulse pounded in his ears—but his soul rose above his physical distress and sang with ecstasy.

This was no aura, no harbinger of his seizures and spells. No. Pure unadulterated joy filled his heart and dizzied his mind. He gazed at the rugged landscape and thanked the good Lord for giving the congregation's planning committee the wisdom to settle here. No one would ever find them, not even the evil spies of the United States government

"Brother Aaron," he waved to a muscular middle-aged man and indicated that he should join him.

Aaron clambered up onto the rock and snapped off a smart salute. "Yes, Sir."

"You're not in the military now. I'm your spiritual leader."

With a horse shoe of hair remaining on his balding head, Aaron reminded Zeke of a monk—his monk—willing to do whatever it took to prepare for End Days. A former colonel with the US Army Corps of Engineers, Aaron had proposed situating the colony in the Sierra Madre.

"Tell me about this beautiful place."

As if reporting to his superior officer, Aaron rattled off details. "Four-thousand feet above sea level. One of the most rugged, remote, and inaccessible areas in North America. Isolated from cities likely to be bombed in a nuclear war. Other than the Chihuahua al Pacífico Railroad and the *Gran Vision* paved road, there's been so little development, the Army Corps of Engineers' maps from the Mexican and Civil wars are still useful."

"Water and food?"

"In the rainy season, we collect water in barrels and store it in cisterns. Apples, beans, corn, and squash. Our agricultural committee brought some cultivars and seeds they thought would be suitable for this part of the world. We've been living off our own plantings for the last six months." He held his hands a foot apart. "Brother Nathan grew the biggest butternut squash I've ever seen."

"What's the secret?"

"Goat manure." Aaron grinned. "We use portable corrals, pasture them where we plan to plant, and let them fertilize plots of land."

Zeke guffawed. "Where did you get a notion like that?"

"From the Indians."

Aaron loved to play practical jokes on new recruits. Did he have the balls to try to put one over on his spiritual leader?

"Indians? You pulling my leg?"

"Nope. They're around, but you won't see them much. They're not fond of outsiders. *Chabochis* in their tongue." He waved his hand toward the panoramic view. "Some live in caves without electricity or running water."

"Threat potential?"

Surprise crossed Aaron's face. "They're shy. Call themselves the Rarámuri—the runners. I've been told they can chase a deer to death."

Zeke unclenched his fist and smirked. "We ain't fawns, and we ain't running away."

Aaron glanced away and took a deep breath. "There was one among us who did."

"Who?"

"Brother Jim."

"What do you mean?"

"He'd been acting a little—weird. I caught the man whipping his back with a knotted rope. I took it away from him, told him that wasn't the way of our community. He said he only listened to you, not me. I figured he'd get over it. Next morning he was gone."

"Do the others know about this?"

Aaron nodded. "We think he wandered out into the desert and died."

Zeke blew out a long breath. "Well, I'm here now, just in time, it seems. Doubt is contagious. Our congregation is like a group of children. They need us to be strong and give them firm guidance, not boogey men to fear." He dismissed the man with a curt nod.

Time to stir up the troops and put on a show. He knew just how to do it, too. Zeke spread his legs on the altar and raised his arms to the heavens. A thousand followers flattened themselves on their stomachs on the ground, their arms outstretched in surrender to their leader, their father, their Lord and master. He liked the sounds of that: *their Lord and master*.

"Dear God, we come to you in humble awe of your goodness to us. Thank you for this beautiful citadel, which we will defend as your people did at Masada. We pledge our lives and souls to you and will serve you as you have asked."

The air was so crisp, the silence of the crowd so profound, that the *c*hicka-dee-dee-dee-dee of a black-capped chickadee shattered it like crystal. Over the birdsong came the unmistakable wail of a baby. The child was the *real* reason everyone had sold their homes, handed over their life savings to the church, abandoned jobs, and in some cases, their families. The congregation pinned their hopes and dreams for a better world after End Days on the youngest Caulbearer. It was time to introduce Jake to his followers.

"Bring me the little one."

Miriam, who'd been standing on the sidelines holding the child, climbed two steps on the ladder and handed him up to Zeke.

Jake wailed and cried, "Mama, mama, mama!"

Zeke held the child on high. "I command you all to look upon the Chosen One."

Heads lifted, gazes locked onto the infant, and people wept.

"Did I not prophesize this to you? Did I not say he would be born with a caul? Did I not say you would know him when you saw him and you would shout with joy?"

An elderly woman, drawn and pale, beseeched him, "Father, help me, please. I have cancer. I'm in so much pain, please. Heal me."

How awkward. His usual tricks weren't set up yet. Miriam always assisted him with the healings, bringing cancer-ridden victims to the front of the church. Using the old magician's trick of distracting the crowd with his wife's ecstatic movements, Zeke would pound on the petitioner's back, shouting for the cancer to come out. Miraculously, the stricken would cough the "tumor" into Zeke's hand. Miriam would then parade the rotten chicken livers around the church to show proof of the Reverend's "cure." Unprepared and out of poultry parts at the moment, he'd have to improvise.

"You may approach."

The old woman struggled to her feet and wheezed her way to the base of the rock. "Lung cancer, Father. Years of smoking and sinful living caught up with me." Tears rolled down her cheeks leaving tracks in the red dust on her face. "I've repented. Please help me."

Zeke handed the child back to Miriam and climbed down from the altar. He placed his hand on the woman's forehead. "Sister Rose, I feel your pain. I'm not sure I can help you at this late date. My time in prison weakened me."

Miriam held the wriggling baby to her chest. "Father—"

Through gritted teeth, he said, "What is it my good wife?"

"The Chosen One." Miriam nodded toward the ailing woman. "Let Sister Rose hold him. He's such a comfort."

Lock jawed, he forced a smile onto his face. "Yes,

of course, my *darling*."

Miriam placed the squirming child into Sister Rose's open arms. Tiny arms and legs stopped flailing. The child placed his hands on the elderly woman's pale cheeks and began to pat them. Enchanted by the baby's touch, Sister Rose leaned her forehead onto the child's, closed her eyes and smiled. Her labored breathing slowed, the wheezing receded, and splashes of pink bloomed on her face. Her eyes flew open.

"The pain. The pain is gone."

Hysterical cries rose up from the crowd, and hymns of praise broke out in the crowd.

The woman held the baby close and rocked. Jake giggled. "Thank you, thank you, Lord for taking away my pain." She held the child up and turned in a slow circle. "The prophesies were true. He is here."

Miriam reached over to retrieve Jake, but Zeke grabbed the child. Opportunity was knocking, and he wasn't about to let it pass by. "Yes, you've heard my prophesies, now you've seen the miracle. Sister Rose is healed, saved by the Chosen One."

A wave of murmurs rolled over the crowd, swelling to a crescendo of praises.

"Return to your dwellings and prepare to celebrate the sacraments for the initiation of the Guardian of the Mothers of the Twenty-Four." He paused and stared pointedly at Brother John. "Fast and prepare for the greatest event of your life."

The Lord had given him the Chosen One, and now Zeke had proof of the child's powers. Nothing and no one would be able to stop him.

****

Miriam stood at the side of Jake's crib, covered

him with a pastel quilt, and smiled. He reminded her so much of her little brother, Abram. She'd been ten years old when he'd been born, and she thought he was *her* toy. She'd fed him, bathed him, changed his diapers, and been responsible for all his needs. Sorrow pierced her breast at the memory of how she'd gone in to wake him up one morning and found him cold and gray, dead in his crib. The sudden death of the baby she felt was her own had very nearly driven her mad with grief and guilt. Years later when she'd been unable to carry babies to term, she often wondered if it was God's punishment for not taking better care of Abram. Her heart ached for babies, and her arms felt empty. No matter how much the midwife and doctors told her it wasn't her fault, she still felt as if there should have been something she could have done to conceive a child.

When Angela had been born healthy and hearty, she'd rejoiced. However, the sweet taste of joy had turned to sawdust in her mouth when her adult daughter had rebelled and turned against the church and her family. Miriam's fault, Father had said. Spare the rod and spoil the child. She'd been too lenient. At last, Miriam had been given a chance to redeem herself. After she'd shown Father the Chosen One's true powers today, he had taken her aside and entrusted her to select the Mothers of the Twenty-Four.

Whispers of doubt slithered through her mind. What if she chose poorly? What if the women were infertile? What if Father couldn't impregnate the women? Would Father be able to keep his followers if he failed to produce the Twenty-Four babies needed to fulfill the prophecy? Utopian visions needed to be fed to keep them alive and well here in the wilderness. Would Jake continue to produce the needed miracles to keep the dream alive?

Miriam shook her head. What was she thinking? Father was a prophet. He *knew* the future, would lead them to their destinies. No room for skepticism now. It was time to put her faith into action. Time to prepare the ground work for the future. And, in spite of the sharp pangs of her own petty jealousies, it was time to help Father in his quest for fertile young women.

Miriam nodded to Sister Rose, who had not left Jake's side since her healing. "Will you be okay to stay with him?"

"Oh, yes, thank you, Mother, I feel so honored to be allowed to be alone with the Chosen One. You know I'll protect him with my life."

"We're safe here. No need to repeat your vows." When they'd been in the United States, every member of the congregation had sworn blood oaths, sealed with a tattoo, to protect Father, Miriam, and the Chosen One with their lives. "The biggest enemy this child has here is hunger. Just make sure he's well fed if he awakes."

After a wrong turn into a bathroom equipped with an overhead tank to flush the toilet, Miriam followed the signs to the Women's Quarters, aided by a string of lights along the walls. Unlike the spacious cave she now lived in, this area hosted living spaces for the female members of the congregation, separate from the males.

A congregant fell on her knees and bowed her head when Miriam approached. She knew pride was a sin, but a thrill of pleasure ran up her spine at the gesture of respect. It felt wonderful to have someone look up to *her* and obey *her* every command. She smiled and offered the woman her hand.

"Save that for Father. Please rise, Sister Anne." She hugged the woman. "It's wonderful to see you. You're looking well."

"How may I help you?"

"I understand you were in charge of the committee responsible for identifying potential Mothers of the Twenty-Four. Were you successful?"

The woman's averted gaze betrayed her nervousness. "We found a boarding school and an orphanage for the Indians, not far from the village on the next ridge. The graduates are the right age, eighteen."

"Can you tell if the women are healthy?" She couldn't bring herself to ask if they were attractive. Just the fact that they were younger—*much* younger than Miriam was hard enough to handle.

Sister Anne licked her dry lips and answered with her Chicago twang. "Seem to be. The girls are dark-skinned, pretty."

Pretty. Why did she have to say that?

"Are they obedient? Smart? The Mothers of the Twenty-Four have to be both."

"The ones we've met at the trading post are very shy. They stared at us, giggled. When the nuns spoke, they snapped to attention." Sister Anne frowned. "In fact, they're so obedient to the nuns, I don't think we'll be able to induce the girls to serve Father of their own accord."

"Did Father ask you to *think*?"

The woman flinched as if struck.

She hadn't meant to be so sharp. This dark place,

these caves, the thought of Father with younger women—she pushed the image out of her mind. "I'm sorry. I'm tired and my tongue is taking liberties."

The woman nodded. "It was hard for me to adjust, too. You'll get used to living underground. The caves are cool in the summer, warm in the winter."

Miriam sighed. "Back to the girls. Where do they get jobs after they graduate from school?"

"There aren't any jobs here. The silver mines dried up ages ago, leaving ghost towns. Women weave baskets and sell them to tourists. Some move to the city of Chihuahua to work as maids."

"What if we told them we had jobs and wanted to hire them?"

"If they come to work here and don't return to their village, they'll have the authorities all over us."

"Tsk, tsk. Ye of little faith. We need young women to assist us with educating our children and with child care."

"Father said we weren't allowed to marry or have babies, that it was selfish."

"We will have children. Twenty-four of them."

"But—"

Miriam held up her hand. "Enough. I'll take care of the nuns and getting the girls here. Your job will be make sure they *stay* here."

Chapter Three

Angie winced at the sound of rocks hitting the underside of her hired car and wondered how she'd explain the dents and dings to Rent-A-Ride. Should she start with the sinister and surreal story of the rat-faced psycho-cop? Or would they be more likely to believe that she allowed a complete stranger to drive the vehicle on a side-of-the-mountain dirt trail with a stomach-sickening drop two inches away from the tires? On second thought, she hadn't paid for a second driver. Better not share that story. A giggle percolated up from her belly and shook her shoulders.

"You okay?" The man in question shot her a questioning look. "Want to talk about it?"

She shook her head. Speaking about the assault and near rape would only give psycho cop more power over her. Neither he nor her father deserved free rent in her psyche. *Both* were going to pay.

"Raul is a disgusting rat bastard. Should have his nuts cut off. I'd do it, but that pleasure belongs to the boss lady."

She bit her quivering lower lip. As a child, her father's oft-repeated, "I'll give you something to cry about" had forced her to suppress tears—or risk more severe punishments. Even now as an adult, without his threats and fists to enforce them, crying was an anathema to her. Instead, much like a basketball pushed underwater too long, her emotions would explode to the surface in the guise of mirth. With the exception of Jake's abduction, whenever she'd been in out-of-control situations, a snicker would lead to a guffaw, then a tee-hee-hee, and before she knew it, uncontrollable hiccupping fits of laughter would kidnap her body. One time a client had insisted on taking the stand to defend himself. Once there, he'd protested his innocence loud and long, called the trial a joke, and donned a big red clown nose. Completely taken off guard, Angie had laughed so hard, she'd fallen down. The judge had fined her a thousand dollars for contempt, despite the fact she'd no idea the pot-head was going to pull the prank. Just recalling the look on the judge's face was enough to put her over the edge. A little snort escaped. Too late. No going back now. It was a good thing she was sitting down.

"Something wrong?"

"No." She stuffed her fist in her mouth in a vain attempt to suppress the sound of her giggles.

"It's okay, you can cry." He reached over and patted her hand. "You're safe with me."

Of *course* she was. Hadn't she just been rescued from a psycho cop by a Mexican drug lord named Alejandro? Wasn't this same man now driving her battered rental car on a road so close to the edge of a thousand foot drop that she could see the gravel rolling down the cliff? And weren't they going to meet a woman who allegedly had killed seven people? Safe? She never felt safer in her life. Angie exploded in gales of laughter.

"What's so funny?" His gaze flicked between her

face and the treacherous road.

"N-n-nerves." She snorted and lost it again.

For a heartbeat, Alejandro stared at her as if she'd completely lost her mind, then he returned his attention to the road. "I've never really heard contagious laughter before today." He chuckled. "Isabel's gonna have a good time with you."

The car rocked, and it sounded as if metal and stones rained down on the roof.

"What now?" If it weren't for bad luck, she'd have no luck at all. "A rockslide?"

Alejandro shook his head. "One of Isabel's pet goats."

The creature bleated in confirmation.

"Goats? As in goats with *hooves* are on the roof of my rental car?" When had her life turned into a Fellini movie? What was next? Naked women and circus dwarves? The four-legged stowaway tapped overhead, as if excited to be heading home. She envisioned the creature looking much like a dog on the stern of a boat, feet dancing, eyes closed, ears flapping in the wind, tail quivering with excitement. "I can't take it back with hoof marks. I'm going to have to set it on fire and throw it off a cliff."

"We can arrange that."

Alejandro turned right onto a gated gravel road lined with pine trees and low-lying shrubbery. *No Trespassing* signs warned people in Spanish and English of punishment, fines, and imprisonment. There were worse things. Like Raul and his special room. She thought about the big man who'd helped rescue her from the hell on earth.

"Where's your giant friend?"

"Tio had some business to attend to in town. He's meeting us here with our police chief." Alejandro made a face as if someone had just farted. "About time Isabel put him in his place."

Angie licked her bruised lips and gingerly touched her swollen cheek. Eager to confront her attacker with two armed men at her side, she wondered how Raul would respond. Would he grovel because his boss found out? Would the creep fast-talk his way out of attempted rape, blame her, point to the obviously planted bag of drugs? Would Isabel relent because she needed cops and politicians in her pocket? Or would she give the man some equally rough justice? One could only hope.

Alejandro pulled the car into a huge circular driveway. In the center stood an enormous three-tiered copper fountain topped with a winged cherub taking a watery piss. Exuberant growths of bright red geraniums fought for space with Bird-of-Paradise plants and an array of greens that she couldn't identify. An expansive brick walkway invited visitors to the front door, a door that appeared to be hand-carved mahogany. A balcony on the second floor with wrought iron railings called out for hot coffee at sunrise. The biggest surprise was that everything, right down to the Moorish style mullioned windows, was done in good taste—except the cloven hoofed pet.

"You're not like any of the drug dealers I've ever met before. What's a nice guy like you doing in a place like this," she waved her hand at the villa, "with goats?"

He pulled the key out of the ignition, turned, raised his sunglasses, and winked.

Her breath caught in her throat, and her stomach

tensed—but not from giggles. Handsome, charming, breath taking. And a drug lord. She was *not* falling for a drug dealer. No. Way. Not *again*.

As if reading her thoughts, he gave her a long, sexy smile that went all the way up to piercing azure eyes. Pinned by the intensity of his scrutiny, her boneless arms refused to move. Almost otherworldly in color and intensity, his bright blue gaze and slow non-verbal assessment reminded her of someone she'd met long ago. Who? Where? The man had to be the devil incarnate. Maybe the goats were *his*.

He reached over and placed his hand on her shoulder with care. The gentle touch and warmth of this chivalrous man's hand on her shoulder warred with the hard, cold knowledge that he worked for one of the biggest cartel bosses in Mexico. Alejandro tipped his head toward the mansion and spoke in a low rasp. "Here, at this house, no one is what they seem. Remember that. It could save your life."

****

Alejandro climbed out of the VW Beetle and confronted the goat.

"Hey, Guillermo," he shouted and waved his baseball cap at the animal. "Get off, you furball." Guillermo the goat, aka "Billy," was a black shaggy thing the size of a German shepherd. Billy turned his face toward Alejandro and shook his head and short horns.

"Don't you give me that who-died-and-left-you-boss look. Get down."

Billy raised his nose in the air and clattered from the roof, to the front windshield, to the hood of the car. Then, as if to demonstrate who was *really* in charge, the animal performed a tap dance worthy of a Broadway hoofer. Alejandro pushed the arrogant beast off the car. The creature pranced over to the center of the driveway and began to graze on the red flowers alongside the fountain.

"Stupid goat." He glanced at the woman through the windshield. Dammit. Of all the drug cartels in all of Mexico, why did this gal have to come to Isabel's? And why did she have to be so damn—*winsome*? Under that kick ass exterior, the woman had a childlike quality and sweetness that reached into his chest and squeezed his tough heart. He shifted his gaze to the munching goat. He *had* to stop thinking about her that way. She was a momentary bump in an otherwise smooth operation. There was *no room* for romance in his life. His weekly visits with the lovely Natasha satisfied his needs. What more could an undercover agent want?

He shook his head. It was the damn mother card. Hooked. Again. First the sex-trafficked Natasha, who really *did* have a daughter being held hostage by an organized crime ring in Moldova, now Angie, who had a baby being held hostage by an organized religious cult. Since when did criminals and cults become organized? Had they all gone to business schools for MBAs? What was the world coming to?

He sneaked a glance at Angie. Why, oh why, did she have to be a redhead, too? Her long copper colored hair was the erotic equivalent of waving a red cape in front of a horny bull. Add the gorgeous breasts that he tried to pretend he didn't see in the craptastic jail, her battered but still beautiful patrician face, and her warped sense of humor—and he was ready to slit his jugular. As if feeling the heat of his gaze through the glass, she looked up and gave him a teary, lopsided grin with perfect teeth. His heart lurched. He pressed his eyeballs to crush an image of grabbing her and pulling her into her into a passionate kiss on her full red lips. If he didn't stop, he'd have a hard time explaining his hard-on. He heard the car door slam shut.

"Are you okay?" The object of his obsession stood in front of him, a concerned expression creasing her forehead.

"Fine," he lied with a smile. "Just a bit of headache. I hate that drive."

"Here I thought you had nerves of steel." She grinned. "I was terrified we'd fall off the side of the canyon."

"There are worse things to be afraid of." The front door yawned open. "Like the people inside that house."

A man's massive frame filled the entryway.

Angie took a step back and bumped into Alejandro. "Who is that?"

"That, my friend, is Tio's little brother, Pepe."

"Are there more like that where they come from?"

"Dozens." He took her by the elbow with care. "It's okay, his bite is worse than his bark. Time for you to meet the boss lady. You're gonna *love* her."

Angie straightened her shoulders and shook her arm out of his clasp. "I'm a bad ass girl, too. Don't you ever forget that."

"How could I? Even in handcuffs it was obvious you were putting the hurt on that jerk. I have no desire to tangle with you." Except in bed, he added to himself. *Stop that. No sex with the women on the job.*

As if hearing his thoughts, she quirked an eyebrow at him and shook her head. "Let's go see my new BFF, shall we?"

Pepe shouted in Spanish.

"What'd he say?"

"He said, 'Get your asses in here.' Such a class act, that guy." Alejandro swept his baseball hat off and bowed. "You first, milady."

She spun on her heel and marched ahead of him. As if to add icing on the delectable confection named after angels, her luscious behind swayed hypnotically before him, begging for his attention. He sighed and enjoyed the view. Thank all the gods by whatever names they go by, the baby would be here soon, safe in his mother's arms. Then she'd be on her way. The tingling he felt from head to toe told him if he spent too much time with her, the combination of her physical beauty, grit, and passion could damage more than his heart. The last time he'd felt this way about a woman, she'd blown his cover. The thought of *that* debacle cooled his libidinous thoughts.

He crossed into the cool hallway and smacked Pepe on the back of his head. "*Cállate!* Shut your mouth. Your balls are falling off your tongue."

Pepe roared with laughter, picked Alejandro up in a bear hug and squeezed him until he was breathless. Garrulous and profane when excited, the big man rattled on in Spanish, "Tio called and told me about your adventure. Now I wish I'd gone with you to meet the *senorita* instead of my brother. He has *all* the fun."

"When he gets here with Raul, I bet you'll have some fun, too."

"How did that asshole get to her first?"

"She arrived half a day early. Must have driven all night and day." Alejandro nodded at Angie who stood nearby and tapped her fingers on her crossed arms. "Angelita wants her baby back and she wants him *now*."

Pepe's smile faltered. "Couldn't find a trace of him in any of the missions, towns or villages in the entire State of Chihuahua." He gave Alejandro the details of the network's inquiries and ended with a sigh. "No crazy cults, no white babies."

Alejandro's stomach dropped. Who was going to have to tell her the bad news?

Isabel's commanding voice cut through the air. "Pepe, I need you. Where are you?"

The big man shrugged. "We've got company." He pointed at Angie and spoke in English, "Taking you to meet the boss lady."

A flash of hope lit her green eyes. "Is my son with her?"

"Sorry. No. We're still searching for him."

Tears filled her eyes and spilled down her scratched cheeks.

Alejandro put his arm around her slumped shoulders. "It's a large state, a lot of territory."

She looked into his eyes, her gaze imploring. "Tell me the truth."

He nodded. "Pepe said they've searched all the populated places in Chihuahua. No cults, no white babies."

"Everywhere? Are you sure?"

"They've checked the villages along the railroad and the highway. Nothing."

"What about the Sierra Madre? My father *specifically* prophesied about a fortress in the mountains."

Pepe man shook his head. "You'd have to be a goat or a madman to get in those places."

"My father's a psychopath. He can do things you would *never* think possible." She headed down the hall. "If you can't figure out a way to search those mountains and canyons, I will. I'm taking this up with your boss."

Alejandro ran after Angie, Pepe lumbering behind him. They all screeched to a halt in the living room. Alejandro gagged. Something smelled like hairy armpits mixed with a porta-pottie on a sweltering day. Fists on her hips, Isabel stood behind a large wicker sofa. "About time you got in here," Isabel directed her comment at Pepe. "Angie, I'm Izzy." Her wild black curls danced around her head as she spoke with jerky, wild gestures. "I went for a ride on my favorite horse, Nightrider. This—this *thing*—jumped out of the bushes on the side of the path, waving a machete and looking like something from a bad parade for *Día de los Muertos*—Day of the Dead. He terrified Nightrider. The poor animal reared up and almost threw me off his back. If Pepe hadn't shot this lunatic, I don't know what would have happened next."

The Latina turned and pointed at the floor.

"Can you tell us who the hell this is?"

Pinioned with ropes at the wrists and ankles, the man's head lay at an awkward angle, a hefty blue tattoo exposed on the side of his neck. A large blue cross inside a circle matched the pendant lying on his scrawny chest. Alejandro circled the prisoner and pulled his shirt over his nose in a futile attempt to avoid the stench of sweat and urine drenching the air around the filthy man. Bones tenting beneath his pale skin, Alejandro could not only count the man's ribs, but his vertebrae. Covered with red peeling skin, bug bites, and scabbed over wounds, the man's back gave mute testimony to a litany of abuses, the least of which was severe sunburn.

His stomach knotted when he realized what the stripes meant. Flogging. Alejandro crossed his arms and stroked his beard, puzzling out the possibilities. That left either penance *or* punishment at someone else's hands. Who would have done that to him? His gaze travelled down his back to the knotted, blood-stained rope tied around the man's waist as a belt for his shredded denim shorts. He shuddered. Those wounds were self-inflicted. But fresher ones, bruises and abrasions dotted his arms, legs and ribs.

The red haired woman gasped and her eyes widened. "That's one of my father's followers."

"Glad you know who he is. I couldn't get a thing out of him, even with my favorite steel toed boots."

"Is he alive?" Angie touched the poor wretch's arm.

The man shrieked. "Nononononononono."

"Still breathing." Izzy grinned. "He thinks you're going to kick him."

A reasonable fear, Alejandro thought.

Angie glared at Izzy. "What'd you do to him?"

"He's been on a time out." Isabel smirked. "In a hot box."

"He's *useless* to us if he dies." Angie sat on the floor and lifted the scrawny man onto her lap.

How could Angie stand the stench of the man? Alejandro gagged every time the fumes wafted toward him.

She pointed at Pepe. "You. Water. *Agua. Now.*"

While Pepe raced out of the room, she worked at the ropes without success. The redhead looked up at Alejandro with an exasperated expression.

Without a word, he knelt down, pulled out his pocketknife and sawed at the ties until the man's hands and legs fell loose.

Pepe returned with a case of water and handed her an open bottle.

Lifting the man's head, Angie began to pour small amounts into his mouth. At last, he began to swallow, first in tiny sips, then great gulps.

"Okay," she spoke in soft voice, "easy, Brother."

His eyes flew open. Confusion washed over his dirt-encrusted face. He stiffened and croaked, "I work for great and glorious Almighty, the Messiah of End Days, the Chosen One—and our Father!"

Angie flipped copper strands of hair out of her eyes, and gave the poor wretch a gentle smile. Alejandro felt as if he was watching *La Pietà* come to life.

"Father sent me to rescue you," Angie whispered.

The man sighed, "Father."

"Do you know who I am?"

A smile cracked his parched lips. "Mother. Chosen One."

"Yes, exactly." She gave him some more water.

His brows furrowed. "Apostate."

"I repented. Come to take care of my son."

His eyes lit up. "Father happy?"

"Yes, Father is so very happy. And so is Mother Miriam."

"Ahhhh," he sighed and closed his eyes. "Good."

She waved Pepe over. "Get me a wet towel."

Sharon Buchbinder

Pepe flew out of the room and returned with a basin of water and a pile of towels.

Alejandro glanced at Isabel. She hadn't said a word since Angie sank down on the floor and began giving orders. Arms crossed over her ample cleavage, the Boss Lady's stance gave little away. He wished he knew what she was thinking. He shuddered at the idea of crawling around in her mind. *On second thought, never mind.*

The mother of the *Chosen One* dabbed at the pathetic man's face. The towel grew dark red with a mixture of dust and blood. She tossed one filthy cloth after another onto the red tile floor until the man's head and neck turned from dark red brown to pink scrubbed flesh.

He smiled up at his rescuer. "Thank you."

"Father says thank *you* for your love, faith, and loyalty..." She paused.

The man watched her with an open mouth, clearly in awe.

Who wouldn't be? Alejandro thought. Not only had she saved his life and freed him from his bonds, but she looked like—well, an angel.

Angie began to stroke the disciple's brow. "Father told me to come here and save you, said you'd lead us home."

The mesmerized man nodded assent.

"There's just one thing." Angie paused. "You *must* tell me so these people will let us go."

"Any—anything for Father and the Chosen One," the man rasped.

She held his chin in her hand and forced him to look her in the eye. "Where's the gold?"

50

Chapter Four

Zeke sat on his raised chair in the middle of the great hall and smiled down at his congregation. He felt right at home. The women had placed bright colored, native, woven tapestries on the walls and festooned the tables with corn stalks and pumpkins. Hanging on the wall at his eye level was an enormous blue and white replica of the tattoo each man and woman wore as evidence of their blood oaths to him. Zeke had told Aaron a normal stage with a microphone and podium would do, but the admiring engineer had insisted on setting a more regal tone, saying it befitted a man with the wisdom of Solomon. Decorated with repeating patterns of the congregation's five pointed star within a circle tattoo in blue and white, the throne towered eight feet tall and four feet wide, sufficient space to accommodate seating another person at Zeke's side. A bright blue cushion filled with scented stuffing protected his bony derriere from any discomfort. He leaned back, closed his eyes, and basked in his followers' adulation.

It was good to be Zeke Edmonds, formerly Carl Logan, fugitive-at-large from the Texas Rangers. If *only* that young woman hadn't resisted his pastoral attentions after the Sunday School picnic, she'd still be alive today. Stupid bitch. It was her own fault. She flirted with him like a brazen hussy, even let him know her parents were going out that night, that she'd be all alone. Then she'd acted as if she was a nun when he visited her at her home that evening. He'd been the wronged party, not her. Good thing he'd been wearing gloves that night years ago. The authorities had never connected the man in Baltimore's inner city prison to the one the Rangers sought. No worries now. Here in the Sierra Madre, he was safe from snoops and prying eyes.

If his parents could see him now, they'd be stunned. *Doubters.* After their *untimely* deaths, not only was he able to purchase a car, but also establish a hefty bank account. When his troubles with the law occurred, he'd closed the account, and taken a bus cross-country, thousands of miles out of the reach of the Rangers, into the bowels of Baltimore.

At the inner city bus station, in her modest Amish dress and *kapp*, Miriam had appeared to be a creature from his religious visions. But when the cloud of diesel smoke cleared and she stumbled on the step, he realized she was meant to be his. She was his angel, made flesh and blood. A little bird, lost and lonely, fallen down from the heavens into his hands. That night, he'd performed the marriage ceremony himself. After spending time in the Baltimore City Library researching the area, he had decided to establish himself in a small town on the sleepy Eastern Shore of Maryland. Chicken farming and religion were the main businesses of the town, and with Miriam as his strong helpmate, he quickly became a captain of *both* industries.

He sighed. Life was good. He opened his eyes. When would he have his virgins? This space was perfect for the ceremonies. Aaron had created a pleasing environment for dining, worship, and initiation rites. *Here*, high in the isolated mountains, Zeke was king, high priest, *and* the god of fertility. He stroked his thigh and fantasized about the ripe young women. He motioned to a female congregant placing sheaves of corn around the base of the throne.

"Yes, Father?"

He smiled and spoke in a low voice. "I need to speak with you in private. I need some assistance with an urgent problem." Zeke stared deep into her eyes. "Can you help me?"

The middle-aged blonde-haired woman with freckles and wide blue eyes, blushed. "It would be my honor."

He stood. "Meet me in my quarters in ten minutes." Zeke tingled with anticipation. She probably wasn't a virgin, but she'd do for now.

****

Miriam trudged after Sister Anne, wondering how many more miles they had to go to reach the orphanage. Anne had said it wasn't far from the village on the next ridge. What she *hadn't* said was that the village was miles up and down steep inclines of the interwoven mountains and canyons. Miriam wasn't afraid of hard work. Her hands were as large as a man's, and God knew she had the stamina of a bull, but this terrain demanded the feet of a goat. She laughed out loud at the mental image.

Sister Anne stopped and looked at her with an expression of concern. "Mother, are you okay?"

"I could use a rest, if you don't mind. How about there?" She pointed at a small cabin nestled in a field below them. Wisps of smoke rose from the chimney, and goats grazed in a nearby corral. "The sun is setting. Let's go see if they'll take us in for the night."

The other woman frowned and shook her head. "No, you can't do that here. We wait to be invited in. They say 'only ghosts knock at doors'. Let's sit over here, on this pile of wood. I have some *pinole* we can eat while we wait."

Miriam took a cup of the ground corn mixed with water, sipped, and grimaced. "This could use some milk and sugar."

"You'll get used to it. Sugar is only available at the trading post. We have little money for luxuries here." She smiled. "That's okay. We are rich in our own way."

"It's not as if we need to worry about keeping up with the Joneses. When we came through the train stop, women and children lined the streets, selling baskets and little dolls to the tourists. Where do they get those layers and layers of colorful clothes?"

"They trade for the fabrics. Have you seen the men in their loincloths?"

Miriam shook her head. "You mean like Tarzan?"

Sister Anne giggled. "No, not that kind. Sort of like a skirt tied in front, with a shirt and *huaraches*— sandals. The haircuts—well, let's just say the men look like someone put a bowl on their heads and used it as a guide."

The door to the cabin opened and light outlined a small figure *"Hola!"*

"Hola!" Sister Anne called out in Spanish.

"May we sleep in your cabin tonight?"

Time had left its indelible stamp on the old woman's wrinkled features. She nodded at Sister Anne, stopped in front of Miriam, and looked her up and down. "*Es su Madre Menonita?* Is your mother a Mennonite?"

Sister Anne shook her head. "*No, no es Menonita.* Not Mennonite. Recreationist. Over the ridge." She pointed in the direction from which they'd come and flailed her arms. "Windmills?"

"*Ahh. Si, si.*" She patted her chest. "*Mi nombre es Maria.*" The old woman motioned for them to follow her.

Miriam whispered to Sister Anne, "How does she know about Mennonites?"

"They came from Canada in the early 1900's," the other woman responded in normal voice. "Looking for religious freedom, just like us. Keep to themselves, except to sell their dairy products."

Nostalgia for Pennsylvania's green pastures and milking cows washed over her. She wondered what had become of her best friend, Leah. Had she married a good Amish man? Did she still go to quiltings and singings? Was Leah happy?

Once Miriam married Zeke, he'd allowed her only one letter home to her parents, telling them she was married and would not be returning to the Church. The letter might as well have been her suicide note and obituary rolled into one. For the sake of their souls, and for her own good, if she had returned home, she would have been shunned.

The old woman pointed to a pile of blankets in a corner of the smoky room. Miriam rested her aching joints and worn out bones on the rough floor of the hovel, listened to the wind sweep over the roof, and looked back at herself as a young woman in Lancaster.

Little did she know then that she'd someday sorely miss her good bed and warm quilts. She dashed an errant tear away, lest the other woman notice.

"This is an extraordinary place, Sister Anne," she whispered. "Just as Father foretold, we're among friends in a land of peaceful living. Everything is going according to his plan."

****

Sister Ellen, the freckle-faced blonde, was suitably impressed with Father's large living quarters. He showed her the shower and bathroom, and attempted to hustle the woman past the nursery to his bedroom.

"Is this the Chosen One's room?" She paused in the doorway. A mobile with birds and butterflies dangled over a blue and white crib.

"Yes, but as you can see, he's sleeping." He pulled at her arm. After shooing Sister Rose away, he'd rushed to prepare for the younger woman's visit. It had been months since he'd felt this virile. Truly it was a sign from above.

Jake chose that exact moment to wail. Zeke groaned.

"Oh, the poor baby. Let me see what he needs."

He bit back a diatribe and choked out, "Sister Ellie—"

"Ellen." She flashed him a quick grin. "I know, there are so many of us and only one of you. Diapers?"

Zeke shrugged.

"Never mind, here they are." She leaned over the crib, exchanging Jake's wet diaper for a clean one. He admired the woman's fine bottom.

"Aren't you the handsomest baby I've ever seen. Look at that cute little dimple when you smile." She lifted the baby, turned and faced Zeke.

A gray-haired hag with rotting teeth, a milky eye, and drooping tits stood before him, exuding the odor of rotten cheese. He gagged and staggered back. "What have you done with Ellen?"

The gruesome thing frowned. "Father, I'm right here."

He twirled around, looking for people hiding in corners, waiting to leap out, point their fingers, and laugh at him. "Who put you up to this? Bring Ellen back. Now."

The drooling old crone shifted the baby to her other hip. "Father, are you ill? Shall I call the doctor?" She stroked the child's hair with long bony fingers and filthy yellow nails.

Zeke considered the hideous old woman's question. *Was* he having one of his seizures? This was *not* the Lord speaking to him. On the contrary, this was a witch, much like the one King Saul consulted to call up the ghost of the Prophet Samuel. This had to be a hoax. Was Aaron behind this? If so, he'd *pay* for his trick.

Trembling with rage, he shouted, "Where is Ellen?"

The repulsive creature shook her head, and maggots fell out of her greasy mop of hair. "I'm Ellen." She took two steps closer to Zeke.

He raised a fist. "Do *not* come any closer. I swear I will strike you down."

"Father," she croaked and the stench of methane and sulfur hit his nostrils, "please, you need to lie down, take care of yourself."

"Stop calling me father, you abomination—you—

you *witch*!"

She stepped back and placed the baby in the crib. "I'm getting help."

Zeke closed his eyes and leaned against the rock wall. His fingers brushed the rough surface, anchoring him in the here and now. The hag brushed past him and wrapped his senses in a putrid miasma. Gut muscles clenched, bile filled his throat and mouth. He shuddered, blinked, and saw Ellen's long blonde hair and lovely ass as she ran down the corridor, away from him and the waiting bed.

Chapter Five

Alejandro Espinosa Santoyo Torres glanced around Isabel's air-conditioned home office and admired her sense of style. Attention to modern technology flowed with the villa's traditional Mexican stucco walls and dark leather furniture. Colorful marketplace oil paintings arrayed on the walls over the cherry wood desk and between matching book shelves, bore the signature of Lola Getz or Lara Spencer. Based on the ATFE background information he'd memorized before taking this assignment, Alejandro knew Lola/Lara was one of the rare non-criminal relatives in the extensive crime family. A well-known artist, she had escaped a kidnapping attempt in Mexico a few years ago and now lived in upstate New York with her cop husband and a young son.

Beneath one of the more abstract pieces of her art, a laser printer/fax/scanner/copier stood alongside a large fireproof filing cabinet, a hungry maw waiting to be fed its evening meal of corruption. At the end of each nine to five workday, it was Alejandro's job to back up and safeguard digital and hard copies of every money-laundering transaction conducted by the Mendez family. In the unlikely event that any of the government officials in the Mendez family pocket decided to go legit or find new business associates, the safe held plenty of blackmail material on their powerful partners.

If the patriarch of this Mexican mob had applied his fist and wits to a legitimate corporation, he might have rivaled Donald Trump's wealth. Instead, his assets exceeded the Donald's, as well as the Gross National Product of most African nations and several European countries. Alejandro shook his head. Anyone who believed crime didn't pay was a fool, an idiot, or both.

A burst of laughter attracted his attention to the idyllic scene outside. Under the glaring Mexican sunshine, Ramon Mendez's grand-daughters, twin three-year-old girls, Ruby and Sherry, and his five-year-old grandson and namesake, Ramon, splashed in the Olympic sized turquoise pool. The little boy wore the solemn mien of a funeral director and paddled around the perimeter of the pool in his blow up canoe while wearing a bright orange life jacket. Alejandro turned away from the window and stared straight ahead, oblivious to the numbers on the computer screen before him.

His nephew, Esteban, would have been eleven years old this year. He should have been running around a pool, laughing and playing in the sunshine—instead of lying in a graveyard next to his mother. Alejandro's step-brother, Luis, should still have his hands instead of *hooks*. Jaw clenched, his hand curled into a fist and pounded the top of the desk.

Hooks, for God's sake. Hooks!

A life sentence for a surgeon who had saved lives with his manual dexterity and technical abilities. The desk shook with the force of his pummeling. His relatives had received *no mercy* from the head of

Mendez crime family, Ramon Mendez. Justice was blind, deaf, and corrupt. Alejandro's implacable fury raged and roared for revenge. The offender *had* to be struck down.

Meantime, Mendez, the wily old bastard, was nowhere to be found. Alejandro had volunteered for this risky assignment just to have access to the crime boss. The thug was going to get as good as he gave. While he had no desire to go after children, the score *had* to be settled. Mendez would be missing the same body parts as Luis—and more when Alejandro was finished.

Howls of laughter erupted from the girls, jarring him back to reality. *Patience, Alejandro, patience.* Stay under the radar, remain calm, and keep everyone in the dark, especially the United States Bureau of Alcohol, Tobacco, Firearms and Explosives. If his ATFE handler knew his *true* agenda, he would be back in Texas before he could say his real name. It was a good thing the news about Luis hadn't hit state side. Otherwise the Bureau would have yanked his butt out of Mexico and destroyed all the groundwork he'd built over the past six months. Six months where he had proved his trustworthiness to Isabel as a crooked accountant.

The mahogany door to his office crashed open. The massive moron, Tio, lumbered over to the couch and threw himself onto it. The sofa squeaked as if in protest. *"Que pasa?"*

If you only knew, Alejandro thought. He needed to shift gears, put on his game face. *"Nada.* Just trying to clean up the books a little, make them pretty." He waved his hands over the computer like a magician. "Presto, chango!"

Tio threw his head back and laughed like a braying donkey. "If I'd gone to school, instead of hooking up with a gang, I bet I could have been good with money, too."

"You, my friend, are a very talented bodyguard. Don't let anyone take that away from you. Not even *Professora* Isabel Ramirez."

The man of muscle hee-hawed. "That's so funny, man, as if anyone would *ever* cross the boss. She'd cut their balls off and hand them to them. She may look hot, but that bitch is cold."

"La doctora?" Alejandro put his hand on his heart and feigned shock. "She's a saint. She saved me from that lunatic, Raul."

Tio brayed again, slapping his thigh. "Man, the look on your face! I wish I had a camera. Oh, wait! I have a phone. Hold that thought." Tio whipped out his cell and snapped a photo. "That one is for the books."

Alejandro probed, digging to see what else the big jackass might divulge. Maybe he knew where to find Isabel's venomous father, Mendez. "She may be a sharp businesswoman—but I've seen her with her kids and Sean. She's also a loving mother and wife. She's crazy about her family. I bet she misses her father and mother."

Tio shook his massive head and lowered his voice to a hoarse whisper. "Rumor has it she offed her own father and mother." He drew a finger across his throat. "Heard she did it with her own hands."

Alejandro's heart skipped a beat, seeming to stop at the news. Hands cold, he clenched and unclenched them into fists. Could that be true? Isabel had told Alejandro her parents had moved out of the country to lay low and avoid the phony crackdown on crime that occurred around each election. The elections had been over for two months, and they weren't back. So, where *were* Ramon and Marta Mendez? And why didn't Isabel ever speak of them, except when someone new had the impertinence to ask.

"Tio, do you *really* think she murdered her own parents?"

The heavy wooden door slammed open, and Isabel Ramirez stood in the entryway, her emerald green eyes narrowed.

Oh. Shit. Had she heard them talking?

He took a deep breath and waited.

"Alejandro. Just the man I've been looking for."

Deep. Deep. Deep Shit.

"Tio, you can leave." She waved him toward the door. "I need to speak with Alejandro. Alone."

Tio whispered, "Nice chatting with you, bro'."

Alejandro nodded. Sweat rolled down his back. Did she know? Was she on to him?

He mentally enumerated the ways he could escape. He had to stay in control of his emotions. Show no fear despite the effects of the huge rush of adrenaline that coursed through his body, priming him for flight or fight. After sorting through the least-likely to the most-likely-to-survive scenarios, he decided the best tactic was to take Isabel Ramirez hostage. As soon as he'd been trusted to wander the mansion unaccompanied, he'd concealed handguns in strategic locations. One was under the desk where he sat. He'd probably have to hurt his big buddy, Tio, in the process, but collateral damages were unavoidable.

Isabel plopped on the sofa. "I want you to work

with Angie."

Alejandro paced the cool office and tried to block out the sounds of children galloping in the hallway. Memories of his young nephew, Esteban, shouting, "Close your eyes, Uncle Josué and start counting...*uno, dos, tres*..." blended with the chatter of Isabel's kids, alive, well, and laughing.

He needed to focus on what Isabel was saying. To avenge little Esteban's death and his brother's maiming, he had to stay sharp, pay attention, and act like he was an obedient underling. When he opened his mouth, however, his emotions spoke before his brain could rein in his tongue.

"I'm an accountant, not a foot soldier. Why me?"

He locked gazes with her, a risky, aggressive move. What was so important about this American woman that Isabel would put her day-to-day cartel business on hold and send her sole financial wizard off into the wilds?

In her short, low-cut black dress, Isabel looked as if she was ready to go out to a nightclub—if there'd been any safe ones in the province. Stepping out of her fortress into a dimly lit bar would only invite rival cartel bosses to line up to take turns trying to rape, kill, and dismember her—and not necessarily in that order. In their *machismo* minds, it wasn't bad enough someone had captured Chihuahua out from under their noses in a relatively bloodless coup. No, the cherry on top of the cake for these thugs was they'd been bested by a *woman*. The Latina adjusted her ample breasts, tossed her black hair over her shoulder, and leaned back.

Her eyes bore into him, and she spoke in a low

husky voice, forcing him to move closer to hear. "You were also a Green Beret in the US Army. If you want to rise in the ranks and become one of my Lieutenants, you have to do what your boss tells you to do."

Her legs fell open, and his gaze automatically followed the movement.

Shit shit shit! She wasn't wearing any underwear. He knew this move. He'd seen her use it thousands of times on unsuspecting males, from dementia addled old men to testosterone addled adolescents. The Pavlovian effect was so uniform, it was cartoonish. And, sad to say, it wasn't lost on him either. The region below his belt shifted and rose to the occasion. *Shit.*

Isabel smirked. "Something wrong?"

He squeezed his eyes shut and tried to will the after image off his burning retinas. *Think, man, think and not with your little head.* Do the numbers. One, she wasn't *really* his type. He preferred redheads. Like Angie. Two, she was married to a strapping stud muffin. Three, most important of all, she was his boss, and he never, *ever* screwed any woman on the job.

"Alejandro, are you ill?"

He shook his head to clear the fog of hormones. "No, not at all. Just trying to understand the assignment." *And stay out of your non-existent pants.*

He averted his eyes from her dark triangle and stared out the window. "If it's not too impertinent, why would you send me, of all people, off on this potential wild goose chase?'

She shrugged and crossed her legs.

Thank God that distraction was gone.

"I have a debt to pay to an old friend. She called it in. And, as a mother, my heart goes out to Angie. Who wouldn't want to help her save her baby from that lunatic?"

"I agree. I would love to see the child back with his mother, but again, I don't get why I need to be involved in this. I'm a bean counter now, not a fighter." What was she hiding from him? Was she going to take off with the money, books, and incriminating evidence— run to a country without extradition agreements? She never did anything without a reason. There had to be something in this for Isabel.

She threw her hands up. "I want you to get into that *loco* preacher's compound, get the baby and while you're at it, bring back his gold."

Alejandro knew his mouth was hanging open. "You can't be serious."

She frowned. "As a heart attack."

"You and I both know the legends of the hidden Jesuit gold aren't true. People have torn up churches, tunnels, roads, caves, and mines. There's no treasure in those hills."

"I'm not talking about the Spanish expulsion of the Jesuits. That's ancient history. And, you're right, that's never been found."

"Then what?"

"Angie asked that stinking bag of bones where the gold was. That crazy old man must have it hidden in his church, or commune, or whatever he calls it."

"How do you know she wasn't saying that just to sweeten the pot, you know, to get you behind her rescue mission?"

"Did she look like she was trying to play me?"

Alejandro recalled Angie holding the pitiful wreck in her long pale arms, her beautiful copper hair tumbling across her luminous face. "She's a lawyer, trained to interrogate people. Angie knows how to get what she wants."

She shook her head. "My gut told me otherwise, and it never lies to me. That's why I'm still alive."

"Who's going to mind the store, keep the books?"

She laughed. "My poor husband was so bored after he moved here, he started taking online courses. Just finished some accounting courses toward his MBA. I think he can handle the books while you're gone. And if he screws them up, you can fix them when you get back."

"Okay, okay, but please tell me you don't expect me to go alone."

She stood, stretched, and yawned. "Don't worry, I'll send my best guys with you, plus you'll have my two favorite arm-twisters, Tio and Pepe."

"When do we start planning?"

"Right now." She opened the door and waved at the big brothers standing guard. "Oh. One more thing."

"What's that?"

"Angie's going too."

Heat rushed up his neck and face. *No. Not good. A terrible idea*. He couldn't travel cross-country with that woman. The risk of getting involved with Angie was greater than being shot by a crazed cult member. He flashed on the scene in Raul's office, her wild red hair, flushed face, and exposed breasts demanding his undivided attention. Out in the wilds, trekking through rough and cold wilderness, the temptation to abandon his "No sex with women on the job" rule would be strong. No, rephrase that: *Ir-re-sistable*. How could he keep his distance from a smart, sassy, sexy woman—

especially one who made his blood buzz when she laughed? There was more to lose here than his life. He could lose his *heart*.

Alejandro shook his head. He had to stop this runaway train. He couldn't allow this to happen. Bad enough he'd have to abandon his undercover ATFE assignment of monitoring the books, keeping an eye on Izzy, and passing information along to his handler. But taking a civilian along on a potentially suicidal rescue mission? That was an *unacceptable* risk. He couldn't have Angie's death on his conscience, too. Esteban was already living there night and day, haunting his memories and dreams.

"We don't even know where we're going, or what we'll encounter. Copper Canyon is a vast area, we could be searching for months. She stays put. She can wait here until we come back with the baby."

Isabel whirled on him, eyes narrowed, fists on hips. "If it were my kid, I'd make damn sure I was with the rescue team, too."

"Be reasonable. We have *zero* intelligence on a cold, rough area of the country, dangerous for experienced hikers and hunters, much less for a tenderfoot gringo. If this operation goes sour, we could bring down the wrath of the US government and Homeland Security. I doubt you want them all up in your business."

Isabel glared at him. "Do you have a death wish? You're doing this my way—or you know the drill." She ran her red-tipped index finger across her throat. "And, at this rate, the way you're going, I may just take care of you myself."

The red-haired Amazon in question filled the

doorway. "Tenderfoot gringo? Seriously, did you just say that?"

Now two women—strike that—two *mothers*— were really pissed and snarling at him. Angie stomped into the office and came toe to toe with him. "I'm betting the only tenderfoot in this room is you, my flabby friend."

Flabby? His hand flew to his abdomen. *Was he gaining weight?*

The redhead continued, "I'm betting I can out run, out climb, and out kick your ass in the great outdoors." She put her hand out. "Do we have a bet?"

Alejandro shrugged and extended a palm.

She surprised him with a bone-crushing grip.

"Yes, fine, we have a bet." He jerked his hand away, but she wouldn't let go. What was she, part wrestler, part pit bull?

"All right, enough. I give up." He shook his aching digits. "Let me do some research. Then we can start planning our search for the treasures of the Sierra Madre."

****

Angie stormed back to the guest room suite and slammed her fist against the rough stucco wall. Tiny flecks of white paint fluttered to the floor and speckled her scraped knuckles. *How dare he mock her?* Damn straight she was going to search for her treasure, her son, hidden, God only knew where, in Copper Canyon. The cult follower had given her that scrap of information just moments before he died in her arms.

She had a right to be there when they found her son and her sicko father. Angie closed her eyes and imagined the old man on his knees, bloodied, beaten and begging for his life. His lips would move but no sound would come out—only faint grunts because her hands would be around his neck—crushing his larynx with her thumbs, silencing his sadistic voice forever. Zeke Edmonds was hers and hers *alone* to destroy. No one was taking that away from her, not even a beguiling, intriguing, ridiculously handsome cartel underboss.

Thug. Pig. Disgusting dealer of drugs, disease, and death. Where did he get off acting so high and mighty, ordering her to stay back? Since when did she take orders from criminals? The room was too damn hot. She was too damn hot. No. Alejandro was too damn hot. She needed to take a run, blow off this steam, or she'd tear the silk drapes and smash the gold framed mirrors in the suddenly too small room. Where were her athletic clothes? She found them in her duffle bag, along with her shorts and tee shirt, miraculously clean despite the multiple aggressive searches, first at the border, then at the mercy of Raul's filthy paws. Raul. *Where the hell was he?* And what had Isabel done to him? One could only hope that he'd been at the receiving end of some form of medieval torture that left the man crippled and impotent.

Running clothes on at last, she flew out a side door into the pool area and smack into that damn man, Alejandro. Half-naked. Despite her verbal jabs about flab, his six-pack abs and sexy scar made her fingers itch to touch his skin. He wore a tiny, tight Speedo that left absolutely nothing—*nothing*—to the imagination. Had he no sense of modesty? Were there no laws about indecent exposure or just plain lewdness in this freaking country? Or unconcealed weapons of Miss and Mrs.

Destruction? The man was, without a doubt, a humongous danger to anyone with a vagina.

At last she tore her gaze away from the man's groin and up to his smirking face. She hadn't even worked up a sweat, and she was already breathing hard. *What the hell was wrong with her? Did she have altitude sickness?*

"Are you following me?"

"No." He frowned and gave her a slow once over. "Are *you* following me?"

"Don't be ridiculous." She tossed her head, and her ponytail smacked her in the face. For God's sake, even her hair was attacking her now. She grabbed her eye.

He touched her wrist. "Need first aid?"

"No." She swatted him away. "I need you to leave me alone." She turned to get away from him, from his smarmy good looks, and his teeny-weenie swimsuit.

"Hey."

She turned. "What is it? I really need to get some exercise." She jogged in place, then stopped when she saw his eyes moving up and down in sync with her bouncing breasts. She folded her arms over her chest and glared at him. "You have my full attention." She struggled to keep her eyes on his face and not below the belt. She pretended he had a giant python in his pants. That helped. Sort of.

"Look, I didn't mean to upset you before. I had your best interests in mind. If your father's cult is in the mountains or valleys of the Sierra Madre, we're going to be traveling over rocky terrain, some of it at high altitudes and steep grades."

"And?" This was not news to her.

"Goats have no problem making their way around

there. Well, goats and the Tarahumara."

"Pardon me?" *What the hell was he saying?*

"Indigenous people, here way before the Spanish arrived. Subsistence farmers, goat and sheep herders, tireless runners. As in they can run thirty to fifty miles a day without breaking a sweat."

"Cut to the chase. What does this have to do with me?"

"You're not a goat. Or a native of the area. I'm worried about your stamina. The days are hot, the nights cold and windy. It's a desert in areas, wooded in others, and generally uninhabited except for a few thousand hardy Indians, Mexicans, mixed bloods, and Mennonites."

"Skip the travelogue. Here's what I hear you saying. You think I'm going to slow you down and be a burden. Is that right?"

He had the grace to look sheepish.

"Okay, Mr. Hot Shit. Put on some clothes." *Please put on some freaking clothes and cover up that snake.* "And your running shoes. I challenge you to a race."

He put his hand up. "That's really not necessary."

"I insist. And, how about a little friendly wager to make it fun?"

"Sure." He grinned. "What's the prize?"

"Loser gets to ask Isabel where we can find Raul's body parts."

His face fell. "That's not a good idea."

"What are you? Chicken?" She flapped her arms and clucked.

He laughed. "No, I'm more of a rooster. But that was an impressive imitation."

"I grew up on a chicken farm. I also do roosters

and lawnmowers, but that's only when I've been drinking, and I don't do that anymore. Aw. C'mon, let's go for a little race."

He tossed her a puzzled look. "Give me five minutes. I'm going to whip your ass."

In her dreams. She enjoyed the view of his nice tight buns as he walked into the changing room. Her feet itched to take her in the same direction. *Stop, woman.* A two-year dry spell didn't give her permission to hop into a bathhouse with the first cabana boy she met. She ordered herself to do some stretching exercises. Mid-lunge, Alejandro appeared. In khaki shorts, a white T-shirt and sneakers, he still looked too freaking hot. The shorts did a terrible job of hiding his pet python. She swore the damn thing looked larger released from its Speedo captivity.

She cleared her throat and licked her dry lips. "You know the area, you go ahead of me." A reasonable suggestion. Plus, she'd get to see that nice tight ass in motion.

"There's a trail around Isabel's property, a few hills, some rocks—"

"Shut up and run."

He started with an easy jog, red dust kicking up behind him on the well-traveled running path. A few scrub pines and boulders dotted the landscape. A hawk circled over head, diving down, then up again, riding the air currents. She welcomed the strike of her foot on the hard ground, the pounding of her heart, and the mesmerizing rhythm putting her into a semi-hypnotic trance. Running brought back memories of the only times she felt free and easy as a child, back when a young woman named Janice had joined the cult.

Angie had been ten years old when her mother drove up to the house in the muddy pickup truck and announced that she had found "this poor young thing" outside a grocery store, panhandling and crying. Nineteen years old, abandoned by a boyfriend she'd followed to the Eastern Shore, Janice had no family, no job, and no prospects. Her father's initial wrath at the arrival of the intruder subsided as soon as he saw the young woman. With her corn silk hair, big blue eyes, and freckles, Janice looked as if she belonged in heaven, not on earth. The following year was the best one of Angie's young life. Janice told her stories about life outside the farm and the cult, about how women could be equal to men, and how there were some very bad people in the cities. Away from her parents disapproving eyes and ears, Janice taught Angie forbidden rock and roll songs, how to braid her hair, and how to run for the sheer joy of it. Then Janice disappeared.

Angie had cried for weeks. Her mother told her the girl had gone back to the Devil's playground, and that Janice didn't deserve her tears. That only made her cry harder. She wondered if she'd done something wrong and driven Janice away. Tightlipped, her father thrashed Angie with a leather belt, shouting, "I'll give you something to cry about."

Angie glanced up at the clear blue sky and saw dozens of turkey vultures circling overhead, diving and weaving in an erratic elliptical pattern. She ran harder, passing Alejandro, pushing herself past her pain, past the stitches in her side. Alejandro called after her to slow down, but his warnings only served to spur her on faster, toward whatever dead creature was being picked apart on the other side of a tin-roofed shed. Had Guillermo Goat met an untimely demise? She loved animals, and that creature had the personality of a pet dog. Her breath rasped in her ears, and as she rounded the shed, the stench of rotten meat hit her. A swarm of huge vultures gathered around a mound of dirt and fought over bits of flesh and bones. She screamed and stomped her feet at the hideous creatures, crying and shrieking at them at the top of her lungs. In that moment she was eleven years old again, struggling to drive buzzards off the body of her beloved Janice.

Chapter Six

Miriam gazed around the village square of El Paradisio and wondered how anyone could have named this flyspeck on a map Paradise. Beady-eyed chickens and roosters scratched in the dirt near a trading post. A band of brown-skinned children with stick-thin legs ran barefooted through the square, shrieking and chasing each other in what appeared to be a game of tag. A young girl watched them from the sidelines, her black hair wild, a brown-eyed baby in a sling on her back. The girl's assessing gaze slid over Miriam, sizing up this outsider, another *chabochi* in their village. Yes, this was a poor village by anyone's standards. But were they *desperate*?

She tore her gaze away from the little urchin. "Sister Anne, where will we find the nun in charge of the orphanage?"

Anne pointed to the dust cloud left behind by the roving band of children.

A woman in a head covering and dress the same color as the sand in the village square materialized on the steps of the church. Sun reflected from the mission's stained glass windows and bathed the nun in a rainbow of colors. A feather of doubt tickled at the back of Miriam's mind. Was this a sign from above that the Lord was protecting this Papist? She shook her head and the multihued vision disappeared, leaving only an elderly woman in a traditional nun's habit in its stead.

The nun called out, *"Hola! Es usted perdido?"*

Sister Anne translated. "She wants to know if we're lost."

Miriam chuckled. "Tell her no. We think we can help her and her graduates find their way to a better life."

"That's a little pushy, don't you think?"

"If they really are Sisters of Poverty and Mercy, shouldn't they be looking for opportunities for their flock?"

Sister Anne nodded, "You're right. Without us, these girls would lead such dismal lives. With Father, they can play a great and glorious role. Their children will be the select leaders of the future world order."

"Exactly. Let's go choose the future Mothers of the Twenty-Four."

Sister Teresa, a short compact woman with olive colored skin and gray hair peeking out from beneath her wimple, led them down the narrow hallway, chattering in Spanish as she walked. Sister Anne translated as they went along, indicating points of interest like a tour guide.

"Our boarding school and orphanage have been in continuous operation since the early nineteen-forties. We had a fire in the late fifties, but thank God, we were able to rebuild and re-dedicate ourselves to taking care of our girls."

Sister Teresa opened one of the doors. "Girls sleep two to a room, and we have a total of a hundred beds, not all occupied. Some leave the school and go back to their villages before graduation because they miss their families." The stocky nun shrugged and looked upward. "God only knows what the plan is. I took a vow of obedience. It's His will, not mine that is done."

Sister Teresa waved the two women into hard wooden chairs in a tiny, book lined office. Everywhere Miriam looked, a crucifix with a tortured Christ stared back at her. She tore her eyes away from the graven images and shuddered. *Idol worshippers.*

Sister Anne asked, "What do the girls do when they graduate?"

Sister Teresa pushed her wire-rimmed glasses back up her nose. "Some go to Chihuahua and find work as nannies or maids. Most get married, go back to their caves and cabins, and have lots of babies, just like their mothers and grandmothers."

Miriam sensed an opportunity. "How does that make you feel?"

The nun gave her a sharp look. "It's not my job to judge. The Provincial Mother reminds me that I must honor their customs, while teaching them reading, writing, math, and Catholicism. I don't want them to lose their culture, but I hate to see my girls go back to subsistence farming and goat herding. They deserve a better life."

Now they were getting somewhere, Miriam thought. "What if we could help your girls to have a better life?"

"You have jobs?"

"Oh, yes, very good ones." She gave the nun a winning smile. "Your girls would be valued. Not goat-herders, but child care workers for a sacred trust."

Sister Teresa leaned forward. "Tell me more."

"Like here, they'd have their own quarters. Your

orphans would be protected from bad influences."

"Not all of the girls are orphans. In fact, most of them have families who love them very much. Would they be able go home for monthly visits?"

Miriam put her hand on her heart. "You have my word on it."

"How many nannies do you need?"

"Oh, we're thinking at least a dozen."

"Twelve girls? There are so many children?"

"Yes, we have many little ones to care for."

"Let me think on this. Ask the *ejido* for their opinions."

She didn't like the sounds of that. "I'm sorry. Who is that?"

"A government approved council of elders," Sister Anne translated. "They control the town."

"Do we need to be there?" Miriam racked her brains for a strategy to overcome this unexpected obstacle. She could have used the Chosen One's powers to persuade them.

"No," the nun shook her head so hard, her wimple slipped back on her head. "They don't like *chabochis,* outsiders. It took ten years for them to trust me. You're in luck, the monthly meeting of the *ejiditarios* is tomorrow. I'll take your proposal to them." She stood, signaling the end of their meeting. "Do you have a place to stay tonight?"

Miriam shook her head.

"Please be my guests."

Returning empty-handed to Edmondstown was not acceptable. Not to mention the long trek back. It was a momentary bump in the path, that was all. In twenty-four hours, Father's plan would be set in motion. "Yes,

yes, please. That would be perfect."

"Excellent. You can stay in the dormitory, meet my girls. You're going to *love* them."

Miriam smiled. "Oh, yes, I'm sure we will."

****

Still shaking, Zeke stood in the middle of his spacious white living room and pointed a long finger at Aaron. "You did this to me. You're the only one who knows the nooks and crannies in this place well enough to have an accomplice hidden, ready to swap places with that woman."

Sister Ellen frowned and cast a furtive glance at the engineer.

"Guilt is all over your face, Ellen. Don't think I don't see it."

Aaron stepped in front of the trembling woman. "Ellen is one of your most loyal followers." He lowered his voice to a whisper. "Her foundation paid for our windmills, the majority of our construction costs—and sends monthly payments to our friends here in the government to keep nosy police and politicians away. Think, man. Why would she play a trick on you?"

Zeke peeked around Aaron. Tears ran down Ellen's cheeks, and her eyes were red and puffy.

Where had that witch come from?

"Let her go, Father."

Shoulders slumped, he nodded. "Go back to your quarters."

"I'm so sorry I didn't please you." Tearful, she grabbed his hand and kissed it.

He yanked his hand away. "Just go."

She scurried away, leaving Aaron and Zeke alone.

"I'm telling you the woman was a stinking, filthy,

maggot-ridden *witch*, not Ellen." *Why wouldn't Aaron believe him?*

Aaron furrowed his brow. "Have you had any headaches since you arrived in Edmondstown?"

"Not as bad as the ones I have when the Lord speaks to me during my spells, but yes, some."

"Sleep disturbances or feel like you have the flu?"

Zeke nodded. "Hard to sleep, strange dreams when I do."

"Sounds like altitude sickness. You should see the doctor, get some medications."

"But the visions—were so real. She *reeked* of methane and sulfur, like some creature from hell."

"You're overworked, overextended, Father."

"You know how I feel about drugs." His head throbbed, reminding him of the Phenobarbital hangovers he used to get when the quacks treated his so called seizures. They just wanted to stop him from communicating with God.

"I understand. It's just to get you through a rough patch. Please. We need you to be strong for us. We need you to be healthy."

"Fine." Exhaustion seeped into his muscles, and he had an overwhelming urge to go to sleep—if only he could. "Send him in."

Aaron stepped out into the corridor and returned with Warren and his little black bag. "I'll leave you to take care of Father." Aaron saluted his leader. "Feel better."

"You have something non-addictive?" Zeke asked the physician.

"Have a seat, Father. Let me take a look at you." Warren lifted Zeke's eyelids, shone a light in, asked how many fingers he saw, and told him to raise his arms and smile. "Not a stroke."

A stroke? He hadn't considered that possibility. He needed a cure for whatever ailed him. "Hold on. No need for drugs." He leaped to his feet. The room swirled, and he grabbed a chair back to steady himself. Should he wake the child? Yes, yes, the Chosen One was needed right now. Zeke took the still sleeping baby into the living room.

"Watch this, Warren."

The physician frowned.

A skeptic, was he? Well, Zeke would show him. "Wake up, little one." He jiggled Jake and tapped him on his feet. *Damn kid.* "Come on, now. I *need* you."

Jake jerked awake, took one look at his grandfather's face, and screamed.

"Jake, it's Grandpa, you know me."

The baby shrieked like a banshee, his voice echoing off the hard stone walls. Zeke's head throbbed and pounded.

"There, there, Grandpa didn't mean to startle you." He stood with the infant on his hip and rocked back and forth on his feet the way he'd seen Miriam do it. What was wrong with the kid?

Warren cleared his throat. "Father, let me take the child, put him back to bed."

"No, I have it under control. He's going to cure this headache, this altitude sickness, whatever it is and he's going to do it right now."

The sobbing child arched his back and clawed at the air.

Zeke could not believe the lungs on the brat. "Calm down, kid. You're fine. Knock it off."

Warm liquid trickled down Zeke's arm at the same time the unmistakable odor of feces filled his nostrils. The insolent brat had *purposely* pooped and peed on him. Pain stabbed his eyes, and his vision blurred. The child was just like Angie. He began to shake the brat. "Why you little—"

Warren snatched the child out of Zeke's hands. "Father, please, calm down, you're only making things worse. It's the altitude sickness making you unbalanced. Let me give you a shot, please. You'll sleep and feel better. I swear."

What was wrong with the kid? He'd cure everyone except his grandfather? The little ingrate. Zeke rubbed his temples.

"The Chosen One may be suffering from altitude sickness, too," the doctor suggested.

The Chosen One was a *healer*. He'd cured Rose. Miriam had told him he'd healed her broken leg on the plane. When he'd abducted the child, the idiot day care worker had told him the child had never been out sick, not even one day. Why would he be now? Was the altitude messing up the child's abilities, too? Zeke needed the baby's gift to maintain his powerbase.

"Give me the shot and call for Sister Rose." The prick of the needle was nothing compared to the sting of the boy's rejection.

Had Angie, the child's Jezebel of a mother, planted the seed of the serpent's tooth in Jake while in her belly? Zeke needed the child—but there were *limits*, after all, on how much a man of his importance would take. *Limits.*

Chapter Seven

Alejandro pulled Angie upwind from the grisly find, away from the irate vultures. Still screaming and sobbing, the woman trembled in his arms and repeated, "No, no, no." He clutched her to his chest and tried to get through her hysteria with soothing words. "It's okay, they can't hurt you. See the vultures are leaving now, they're afraid of *you*." Truth be told, he was afraid of her, too. What the hell happened to her? One minute she was sassy, taunting him to go faster, making him crazy with desire and thinking about taking her to bed. The next minute she blew past him, straight to the shed and the flock of feeding buzzards. He found a spot of shade and set her down on a boulder.

He wished he had water to offer her. A horse trough sat by the shed, empty and coated with red dust. He spoke in a low voice, the one he used to interview skittish confidential informants. "Wanna talk?"

"Wh-what?" Tears still streamed down her stricken face. Sure, the gruesome scene had looked like something out of a Hitchcock movie, but her reaction was way out of proportion. Buzzards ate dead things. What was the big deal? She seemed to be looking over his shoulder, as if she was looking at someone behind him.

He placed his palms on her cheeks and forced her

gaze to his. "I need you here with me. Tell me what's going on." If she didn't snap out of it soon, she was off the mission. No way could he take an unstable person, male or female, out into that godforsaken wilderness. Lives depended on good planning and calm ops. "Angie, can you hear me?"

Her green eyes focused on his, and she took a deep shuddering breath. "Is th-that the body of the cult member?"

Startled, he dropped his hands. *Isabel wasn't stupid. She didn't crap where she ate.*

"No, the guys took his body far away from here and buried him, God only knows where."

"Raul?"

He shook his head. "No. It's a dead pig. Struck by lightning. Then the coyotes got to it. Looks like the ranch hands did a lousy job of disposing of its remains."

"A pig? You're sure?"

"Yeah, it happened last week. Tio and Pepe told me there were guts everywhere." He stopped when he saw her face blanch. "A mess."

"Not human?"

He put three fingers up in the air. "Scout's honor."

She shook her head, and her ponytail flicked at her cheeks. "You must think I'm an idiot."

What could he say? That he was worried about her compromising their attempts to find the cult compound and save her son? He offered an olive branch, a fib. "Hey, if I had thought that was a person, I would have had the same reaction."

Her eyes narrowed. "You're lying."

Perceptive, wasn't she? He shrugged. "If it was

someone I knew, I'd be upset, too."

She cocked her head. "Upset, but not hysterical." She sighed and covered her face. "Now you're convinced I'm a hazard to the rescue mission. You're going to go back to Isabel and get me locked down in Casa Ramirez."

"What are you, a mind reader?"

Her voice came out muffled from behind her hands. "A litigator. I read people's faces, body language, the little tells. You don't want me at your poker game."

Alejandro squatted down to eye level and touched her shoulder. She looked into his eyes, and his chest felt tight, as if someone had reached inside and squeezed his heart. Why did she have to be so beautiful and vulnerable? Pity and the desire to protect this driven woman pierced his macho armor. Didn't he have his own agenda, his own need for justice and revenge? "I won't pull you off the mission—if you'll tell me something."

Her brow furrowed. "What?"

He really needed to know if she'd flip out again. The only way to predict that was based on previous behavior. Today's meltdown was not an auspicious indicator. "Isabel didn't give me much information. She likes to keep things close to the vest. I need to know who you are, and what happened just now."

Angie passed a shaking hand over her face and took a deep breath. The words tumbled out, as if they had needed someone to unplug the emotional stopper that held them back. "I'll give you the short version. Born on a chicken farm to two died-in-the-wool religious fanatics. My father is a self-ordained minister on a mission from God. He thinks. I think he's Satan in human form. Over the years, however, not only has he buffaloed my mother—poor woman—but also a couple of thousand followers."

Angie's shoulders stiffened, and she drew herself up a little taller with each sentence, her resilience and strength returning to her bit by bit.

"My mother was raised Amish. Believes women are the weaker vessel. She does whatever he tells her to do. I was home-schooled. And I was a real farm girl. Lots of physical labor. No brothers or sisters to share the work with me. Not much fun, I can tell you that. The chickens were my classmates. I was only allowed to play with the children of other cult members. Brainwashing one-oh-one. Isolate and brainwash. Repeat the same crap day after day until everyone chants in unison. Until—" She closed her eyes and tilted her head back. "Oh. God. This is so hard."

He took her small cold hand in his larger warm one. "Tell me. Please."

"I was ten. My mother found a teenager, a runaway." At first Angie's tale about her good times with the lovely Janice cheered Alejandro. At least the poor child had had some glimmer of what the outside world was like, a role model of someone who wasn't totally programmed by the cult. But when she reached the part about Janice's disappearance, Alejandro knew the ending of the story would be bad. Angie had been eleven, Esteban's age, when she found her friend's body. He stood, stretched his legs, and paced. "Did you go to the authorities?"

She shot him a look filled with disbelief. "You're kidding, right? I'm positive my father killed Janice. If I

87

ever tried to tell anyone, I knew I'd be next. Being the daughter of the cult leader didn't protect me from his wrath. In fact, I was the focus of his public paddling sessions, to prove his family wasn't exempt from the rules."

He stopped and faced her. This woman had been beaten in front of the cult by her father to prove he was in charge. How had she made it out, become the incredible woman who sat in front of him today? "How'd you get away, become a lawyer?"

"Ha. All part of my father's great and glorious plan to infiltrate the US government, get rid of non-believers, and rule the country. He failed to factor in a few things, like me having a real brain and graduating at the top of my class in law school—then getting a plum clerkship." She gave him a wry smile and shook her finger at him. "I failed to factor in a few things we won't go into right now."

She was holding back. Something important. For some strange reason, he had a sense that it related to him. But how could that be? He'd only known the woman a week—barely. His logical brain wanted to push her, but his gut told him she'd only clam up if he did. "And the baby?"

Her eyes filled with tears, and she gave him a crooked smile. "Best thing that ever happened to me was getting pregnant with Jake. Worst thing that ever happened was I went home to the farm for a 'quiet dinner' late in my third trimester and wound up being held captive by my father and mother until I delivered the baby. I almost died." She shivered and rubbed her arms. "I came to with my father and mother shouting Jake was the 'Chosen One' as prophesized by a book that never made it into the Bible, the Book of Enoch."

That explained the dead cult follower's obsession with the child—and its mother. "As in the Messiah?" He put quotes around the word in the air.

"You got it. I'm his mother. I'm assure you, Jake is just a normal, healthy little boy. He plays with his toys and friends and loves animals. When we used to go to the park, he had to pet every dog we saw. They ran to greet him." She shook her head. "One man told me he planned to put his arthritic eight-year-old Labrador down. Couldn't bear to see him in so much pain. He claimed that after Jake petted his dog, the Labrador was cured of his arthritis. Told *everyone* in the park my son had healed his dog. I had to stop taking Jake to the park. People were lining up to bring their sick dogs and cats to him." She shook her head. "People *want* to believe. They *crave* miracles."

She flicked a tear off her cheek.

"Unlike my father, I'm not delusional. He has some serious auditory hallucinations, along with some nasty seizures. Direct pipeline to God, he says. Untreated temporal lobe seizures, my medical friends say. Anyhow, crazy man decided I was Jezebel, undeserving of the honor of being Jake's mother. His plan was to take my newborn away from me and prepare Jake to rule the world." She paused and looked around as if seeing the tree and boulder for the first time.

Hands and teeth clenched, Alejandro struggled to keep his own suppressed emotions in check. Everything she said touched on his still raw nerves of grief and loss. Angie's father had been driven by religious delusions. Isabel's father had been driven by the need for power and control. Was there any difference between the cult leader and the cartel boss when it came down to what they did to the people around them? Alejandro decided the hypocrisy of the cult leader was worse than that of the cartel boss. At least the thug was upfront about his criminal intents and didn't suck people in using God as his front man. Part of him wanted her to stop telling the story, to stop scraping at his raw wounds. But the logical side of his brain knew he had to press her for more. "And?"

"I escaped, left Jake on his married father's doorstep—and got caught by one of my father's corrupt cops. My father tied me up, beat and tortured me to try to get Jake's whereabouts. I never broke. Still have the scars."

She turned her arms over, exposing a myriad of criss-crossed paper-thin white lines. *Razor cuts.* How had he not noticed them before?

"Anyhow, my father did some exciting things, *finally* got arrested and jailed. I was hired by a great lawyer, had a good relationship with Jake's father and his wife's family, took up martial arts and rock-wall climbing. Life was good. And you know the rest of the story. Went to the daycare to pick Jake up. He was gone. My lunatic father and mother struck again. I want my happily ever after. I want my kid back. Or I'm gonna die trying. So, why should I trust you to help me get my kid back? What's *your* story?"

****

Angie stared at the man in front of her and for a split second, Alejandro looked like a deer caught in headlights. A shadow passed over his face, and he reverted to the swaggering asshole he was when they began their run. *What was he hiding?*

He glanced up at the sky. "If we don't get going, we'll be caught in a deluge. Besides, we should get back before Isabel sends out a search party."

Hmm. A double 'Let's get going' message. He really didn't want to tell her anything. She shivered as the clouds darkened the sky and the wind shifted, dragging the smell of the dead pig to her nostrils. "Yuck. You're right. Time to go."

His shoulders relaxed. Good. She'd cross-examine him on the way back. She picked her way across the rocky terrain, careful not to move too fast. "What brought you to Mexico?"

Alejandro averted his head, scanned the sky, and avoided her gaze. At last, he recited what sounded like a well rehearsed story about a dishonorable discharge from the Green Berets, multiple arrests for embezzlement, fraud and money-laundering. Plus being a poster child for Interpol.

Angie had heard much worse from her Baltimore clients. Why would Isabel trust this guy enough to bring him into her inner circle? What did the badass boss see in him, aside from his ridiculous good looks and *other* attributes. She shook off those dangerous memories of him in that tiny bathing suit. "How'd you meet Isabel?"

"Hanging around *El Hombre Loco*. I met Tio and Pepe and asked them if there might be any work for an accountant in the area."

"An accountant? You really asked if they needed an accountant? Not a bookkeeper, embezzler, or money launderer?"

He laughed. "Well, maybe I mentioned I was good with shell corporations and cooking the books."

That was more like it. "So just like that," she snapped her fingers, "Isabel hired you and gave you the keys to the cartel kingdom."

His fingers twitched and his face flushed. Ahh. Now she was getting somewhere. "Well? I told you my story." *Minus a few details.* "I'm waiting. I need to know if I can trust you to help me save my son. *Quid pro quo.*"

They came to the top of a little ridge. Below them, Isabel's sprawling home and turquoise pool beckoned. Just a few more minutes, that's all she needed.

"Raul had similar questions. His interviewing technique, as you know, lacks finesse. He broke my eardrum in the process. He was about to kill me when Isabel stormed into that same room you were in. If it hadn't been for her impeccable timing, I'm pretty certain I would have been one of those headless corpses in the desert." He clenched and unclenched his fists. "Tio told me I 'passed the test,' that the *federales* had been trying to infiltrate her cartel for years."

She stared at his face, looking for any inconsistencies between his verbal and body language. This part of the story was true. His emotions came to the surface when he talked about the rat-faced cop, Raul. She shuddered, recalling the creep's vile breath and filthy hands.

"So now you're part of the tribe." *And what a clan to be part of.* A tight network of arms dealers, drug traffickers, and murderers bound by greed and gang loyalty.

He threw her a sharp look and a grim smile came to his lips. "You might say that. But, being a member of *this* family doesn't mean you're any more protected than you were in yours. I'm always watching my back, worried that my usefulness will expire when I least expect it."

The truth, at last. The other bullshit had been window-dressing.

Alejandro turned toward the path back to the house, away from this private moment. She had to extract a pledge from him now. She couldn't go back without it.

"Stop." She grabbed his hard-muscled upper arm and his head whipped around. "If we're going to be partners in this rescue, we have to be able to trust each other, despite our differences."

He furrowed his brow, pondered the question for a moment. "Yeah."

"Our goals have to be the same, or we won't save Jake. Do you agree?"

The rising wind ruffled his thick, dark hair. She wanted to run her fingers through that hair, tousle it herself while straddling the huge python in his pants. *Stop thinking about—sex. With him.*

He nodded assent.

"I need you to promise me one thing." He raised an eyebrow, and her heart fluttered. *Nerves. That was all. Putting her on edge. Making her think crazy, lust-filled thoughts.* She was about to ask for something totally out of bounds, something that she craved, but would never have requested under normal circumstances.

"What's that?"

She took a deep breath. "After we rescue Jake, I want you to kill my father. Kill them *all*."

****

Alejandro stared at the redheaded woman as if he'd

never seen her before. Did she have a multiple personality disorder? One minute she's sobbing over her dead friend, the next she's asking the unthinkable. "What did you just say?"

She put her fists on her hips and lifted her chin. "You heard me. I want you to kill my father. Kill them *all*."

"What makes you think I could kill someone?" *Think man.* Don't let this spiral out of control. "I'm an accountant, remember?"

"Ha. And I'm a lawyer. You think I don't know you, your type? You may not do the actual dirty work, but you have those two gorillas who would break someone in two if you asked them."

He relaxed. She didn't know he was under cover. "Point taken. But you don't want to pursue this." Tio and Pepe and the rest of the blood-thirsty lot would be more than happy to comply with her request. But the price was too high. "A thousand followers, whose only sin was to believe your father's delusions. You want me to have those innocent people killed, too?"

"Not one of them stood up for me when I was beaten in front of the congregation as a child. And his henchmen dragged me back to the farm to be beaten and tortured. There are no innocents in that cult. Mindless robots."

"Come on, be reasonable. That can't be the whole commune. You told me yourself there were a lot of elderly folks he duped, stole their money, and sold them the promised land. You want me to kill old ladies?" He hoped she'd understand the absurdity of her demand. This was a rescue effort, not an all out war.

She poked him on the chest. Hard. "You, of all

people should understand a blood vendetta. Whether my father lives or dies, if any of them is left alive, they will come after my son. I can't risk Jake's life for these crazy people."

At the moment, the only lunatic he saw was the one in front of him. Not only could he *not* kill unarmed citizens, he couldn't even think about bringing this up with his handler. The guy would go off like a rocket-launcher. And rightfully so. Alejandro had to get control of the situation right now.

"At the moment, I have no intention of killing anyone. The boss lady told me to take Tio, Pepe, and her best men, rescue your son Jake, and return with him. Period. Slaughter not included." His technical skills did not need to be displayed, and his cover did not need to blown.

Face flushed, eyes wild, hair falling out of her pony tail, the woman looked like a very sexy Greek fury ready to pursue and avenge unpunished crimes. "Do you think it's right that I have to live in fear for the rest of my life? That I might have to change my identity, move to another country, leave my friends and job behind? When is it time for *me* to get justice?"

"I hear you. I understand you." He wanted to grab her, pull her into a passionate embrace, and kiss away her hurt. Instead, he put his hands up in supplication. "I empathize with your urge to kill your father. He has made your life a living hell. And, if he killed that young woman who was your friend, no doubt in my mind, he deserves to die. But I won't endorse your idea of slaughtering them all. We do that and the *federales* will be crawling all over this place. The costs outweigh the benefits; it's just bad for business."

"Bad for business? That's how you classify protecting my son's life and his future?"

He passed his hand over his face. *God, woman, let it go.* "I need to talk to Isabel about this. She's the boss, what she says goes. You want to make a case for killing them, you go to her. But I'm betting she'll put you on the first plane back to the States."

Angie's face blanched, and she whispered. "I have to be here."

"Then be reasonable. We *will* rescue your boy. But you have *got* to do what you're told to do, okay?"

She nodded.

Thunder clapped and lightning ripped across the sky, bathing Angie in a surreal purple light. "Now we really have to make a run for it. We have no cover and the lightning strikes out here are deadly—just ask that pig."

Chapter Eight

On the evening of Miriam and Sister Anne's second day in El Paradisio, the little nun's beaming countenance told them they'd been victorious in their quest for the Mothers of the Twenty-Four. Yes, all was in place, as predicted. And she, Miriam, would lead the virgins to their place in history. Father would be so pleased. Miriam sighed in anticipation of his praise.

Flushed and out of breath from her trek up the hill from the town square, the stocky nun led the way to her office.

"We've been so anxious since you left, praying for the Lord to guide the *ejiditarios*."

Sister Anne translated for Sister Teresa.

"You must have believed when you prayed. They were very worried when I first introduced the idea. Thought you were yet another *evangelista* group set on converting the girls, taking away their customs."

"We're not missionaries. We're not recruiting members. We need child care." *We need those virgins to fulfill the prophesy, to create the children.*

Sister Teresa held up her hand. "I told them that. And I told them the girls would be allowed to visit their families every month and attend the week-long Easter celebration."

Miriam sat back in the chair, her spine pushed

against the hard wood. This wouldn't do. She had to be calm, but firm. "A week? I'm not sure we can let them go that long."

The nun shook her head. "That was the only way the *ejiditarios* would agree."

"We've been chatting with the girls," Sister Anne interjected. "Several said they wanted to come with us whether the *ejiditarios* approved or not. They're eighteen, adults really."

Sister Teresa's lips thinned. "Impudent girls. The *ejiditarios* have these foolish girls' best interests at heart. Nothing of this magnitude is decided without their input."

"My apologies. We were just trying to tell the girls about our community."

The nun appeared mollified.

"Does the Easter break have to be that long?"

"The Tarahumara have made the holiday their own. The centerpiece of the weeklong preparations is a procession and a pageant. Hundreds of tourists come to see it. The girls wouldn't miss it."

A weeklong *party*. That's what this "religious holiday" meant to these girls. Miriam nodded. "I see, of course." Once they had them in the community, they weren't going *anywhere*, much less to some idolatrous revelry.

"Good," Sister Teresa said. "I'm glad you understand. Now, about payment for the girls' work. How will that be done?"

"As members of the community, we have no personal possessions and no money is needed." She waited as Sister Anne translated.

The nun frowned. "You said you had jobs. That

means pay."

"I just wanted you to understand, we have very little cash on hand. A foundation underwrites our expenses. They make our payments to outsiders. The money will be sent to you, Sister Teresa. That way you can be sure we are paying the girls."

The nun's expression went from annoyance to pleasure. *Money always had that effect.* From what Miriam had seen, the cash would come in handy.

Sister Teresa licked her lips. "How much money are we talking about?"

"What do you think would be fair wages that you would hold for the girls?"

The nun looked her straight in the eye. "Thirteen-thousand pesos each, upfront."

Miriam's breath came out in a whoosh, and Sister Anne gave an audible gasp. It seemed not all bandits wore masks. Sometimes they wore habits.

Two could play this game. "We don't have that much money on us. I have five-thousand pesos, nothing more. But I can tell our foundation they should pay you as soon as possible. To whom should they make out the check?" *The one you'll never receive.*

The nun scribbled on a piece of paper and handed it to Miriam. She carefully placed it her pocket and patted it. "My safe place." She smiled. *So safe, it won't ever be found again.* "Now, let's talk about the girls. Which ones do you think would make the best mothers—I mean nannies?"

A list of eligible girls appeared in Sister Teresa's hand. As the nun read the first name, a cheer went up in the hallway. She smiled and shook her head. "The girls have been eavesdropping again, I see. You are going to have your hands full."

No, Miriam thought. Father will have his hands full. A disturbing thought snuck into her mind. What if Father casts me aside and takes one of these young women as his wife? What will happen to me then? Will he send me away, make me live in the women's quarters? She flushed at the prospect of being humiliated that way, tossed aside like garbage. No. Father needed her to take care of the Chosen One. He had to know that the child was bonded to Miriam. *Silly woman.* Married over thirty years, there'd only been one occasion when a younger woman had come between them. That little harlot.

Miriam had opened her home to Janice. How did the girl repay her kindness? By trying to steal her husband. The girl was smitten with Father. Who wouldn't be? But she had no right to act on her vile impulses. That day when Miriam came across them in the woods, she found Father struggling to get away from the girl. But the whore wouldn't let go, just kept pulling him down on top of her, screaming like a cat in heat. Miriam had to save her husband and her marriage. She did what she had to do. If necessary, she'd do it all over again. Nothing, and no one, would ever come between Miriam and Father.

****

Six days after his unsettling conversation with Angie, Alejandro made his weekly Saturday night trip to the cartel boys' favorite brothel, accompanied by Tio and Pepe.

El Harén or The Harem, boasted an array of women from around the world. Festooned in swags of hot pink, orange, purple, and red gauzy materials, the parlor was designed to look as if the gentlemen had entered a Middle Eastern bazaar infused with layers of the local tastes in décor. Sponge painted in splashes of similar colors, the walls of the house of ill repute displayed a vast array of velvet paintings. Elvis, John Wayne, Michael Jackson, and George Bush stared across the room at clowns, Aztecs, bullfighters and lions, as if daring someone to question their presence. The first time he went there, it was all Alejandro could do not to burst out laughing. Where were the eunuchs, he wondered. Were they behind the door painted with the lady or the tiger?

Senora Roja, a woman well past her fifth decade bearing bottle-red hair that practically glowed in the dark, greeted the well-muscled body guards with hugs and squeals. "Where have you been? I've missed you!"

She threw herself on Pepe. He pawed at her bottom and pulled her skirt up. "Ready for me now?"

Senora Roja squealed and smacked Pepe's hands away. "I'm old enough to be your mother. However, I had this lovely Thai flower flown in special for you boys," Roja gushed.

The slender black-haired girl, dressed only in a short royal blue silk robe, swayed in her high-heels and stared at the floor. Senora Roja lifted the girl's chin. "Siri's a country girl. Very shy, never been with a man before. But she'll warm up."

A smile glued to his face, Alejandro bit back a string of curses. The girl couldn't have been more than fourteen, fifteen tops. Her dilated pupils and glassy eyes told him how the madam was keeping her charge under control. Seething beneath his calm exterior, he wished he could close the place down, release these captives and arrest the madam right *now*. Roja must have paid a small fortune for that girl, not to mention the costs of legal fees, documents, and transportation. Somewhere in Thailand, a farmer sold his daughter to a broker looking for fresh meat, the younger the better.

Then, to get the girl out of the country, police, politicians, and lawyers had to have been paid off, each getting a cut of the deal to send this child into slavery. The madam would work the little thing to death to pay for her investment—if she didn't overdose her with heroin first. Had it not been for the need to keep his cover, he'd have tried to pull the plug on this place long ago. Ever since he'd started coming to the brothel with his *compadres*, he'd been mindful of the constant parade of foreign women, almost none of whom spoke Spanish. In all certainty, their documents and passports were locked in Senora Roja's bank safety deposit box, effectively rendering the women unable to travel, even if they could escape.

Roja licked her bright red lips. "She looks tasty. This one comes with a virgin premium, but you're big men. You can afford this little one, easily."

Bile rose in his throat, and he nearly gagged. Alejandro knew that, like most madams, Roja had been a working girl herself before opening her own bordello. Prostitution was the only occupation she knew. Nevertheless, *why* did she have to get involved in trafficking girls, kids really, from other countries? Weren't there enough adult women around who would do this of their own accord? He knew the answer to that question. Demand. Customers wanted younger, more exotic flesh, not older, local women. If the madam didn't keep up with the competition, she'd be out of business. The girls weren't people to her; they were commodities to be sold like supermarket goods. He took a deep breath. *Stay calm. Think, man. You're stuck. The girl's trapped. What can you do?*

He glanced at the Thai girl. A rivulet of sweat trickled from her pale brow, running down the side of her neck. He knew what he had to do. Alejandro stepped over, took the girl by the chin, tilted her head this way, then that, and dropped his hand as if stung.

"Has this girl been tested for HIV?"

The madam frowned and shook her head. "I told you she's a virgin."

"Even virgins can have HIV. What about TB? Was she tested for that?"

Roja glared at him and put her fists on her ample hips. "Why are you asking all these questions?"

"Are you blind? She's pale and sweating profusely." He shook his head. "I like sex with a sweet young thing just as much as the next guy, but I'm not willing to get sick and *die* for it."

He glanced at his pals, Tio and Pepe. Both men wore expressions of disgust. Tio backed into an armchair in his haste to get away from the "little flower." Good, Alejandro thought, he'd contaminated their party plans and planted the seeds of fear. For the moment, that was all he could do.

Senora Roja narrowed her eyes at him, grabbed the girl by the arm and pushed her toward the back corridor. "I suppose you want your *usual* girl?"

Alejandro nodded.

"She's been waiting for you." The madam tapped on the door with the lady painted on it, and a tall, reserved looking blonde in red thong underwear, crimson patent-leather six inch heels, and nothing else strolled in. She avoided eye contact with the two other men, staring straight at Alejandro.

"Hola, Ally-handro."

"Natasha, you finally learned how to say my name right, I'm impressed." A collective gasp of lust from the strong-arms sucked all the air out of the room. When they could breathe again, Tio and Pepe could only babble "Jesús, Maria, José."

As she grabbed his hand and sashayed out of the parlor, Tio and Pepe blew kisses and catcalls after them.

Ever mindful of surveillance cameras, Alejandro looped his arm around her waist, nuzzled her neck, and whispered, "Got anything for me?"

She threw her head back, laughed and gave an Academy Award winning performance for anyone watching on closed circuit TV. "Naughty boy. You get spanking right now."

Natasha took his hand and led him down a dark hallway lit by flickering candles and scented with musky incense. She dragged him past velvet paintings of naked women with huge breasts and men with impossible sized erections. He suppressed a guffaw and restrained himself from commenting that these depictions were *truly* not to scale.

She led him into a private room, closed the door, and locked it. He turned the radio on full blast. Norteño music filled the room, the bass and drums making him feel as if he was inside the boom box. Now they could talk. Grateful not to have to maintain the mask of his swaggering macho persona, he gave a huge sigh of relief and dropped onto the edge of the bed.

"I get names, countries of other girls, make note." Natasha unscrewed the base of the lamp and extracted a piece of paper. "So many."

Alejandro glanced at the long list. The countries represented a virtual United Nations of sex workers. A couple of the girls were from the USA. Good. Human trafficking was a huge transnational business and a big priority for the US State Department. Even more reason for them to get involved. Someone, somewhere had to be looking for those girls. "Are they all still here?"

She shook her head. "Weekdays, they put us on bus, take us to big marijuana farms for workers. Farm boss likes me. He keeps some girls up there for his, how you say? Employee bonus." A lone tear streaked down her cheek, and she wrapped her arms across her chest. "Some never come back. I ask Roja where my friend Martina go, she tell me mind my business."

"I'm working on getting you out of here. I swear." He tucked the paper into his boot. Twenty-two year old Natasha's little girl had been taken away from her by the Russian mob. They shipped Natasha to Senora Roja to work off the two million dollar ransom. If she didn't pay up, they told her they'd kill the four year old. "I have good news for you. We found your daughter. She's okay."

The cloak of sadness that had shrouded Natasha gave way to tears of joy. She threw herself on Alejandro, kissing his eyes, cheeks, ear, and neck. "*Spasiba, gracias*, thank you."

"As soon as the authorities in Moldova extract her, they'll take her to your mother in Minsk." He wished he could be there when Natasha's daughter was rescued, but he had his own mission to take care of right here in

Mexico.

"Soon, yes?"

"Three, maybe four weeks. She's not the only kid those thugs have. I've been told it's practically a daycare center of hostages."

"Martina, she had baby boy taken from her." Natasha shook her head. "She heard men talk about selling him for adoption." She gave a little sob. "Could have been me. My baby."

Alejandro wished he could tell the blonde the rest. His handler thought he was crazy. Told him to step away from the trafficking issue, "don't rock the boat." But Alejandro *knew* there were deals that could be made for political asylum in the US. All Natasha had to do was convince a US immigration judge that the Russian mob would kill her mother, daughter, and herself if she went back to Minsk. The Russian mobsters were known for their take no prisoners approach. Girls were killed for lesser infractions than running away. The gangsters were everywhere in Eastern Europe, even in so-called safe areas. With the total post-cold war meltdown in the former Soviet Union, all a good immigration lawyer had to do was hold up a newspaper. Then the family could immigrate to the US for political asylum. He just had to get her across the border, into a safe house. But, before any of that could happen, he'd have to extract her from the brothel. *After* he finished his assignment.

"I know." Alejandro clutched her hand and gave her a kiss on the forehead. "I have to go away for a while. Not sure exactly when I'm leaving. I'll be taking Tio and Pepe with me. Not sure when I'll be back, either."

"You pay Roja to hold Saturday nights for you, yes?"

"Yes."

"She like you." She massaged his scalp, soothing and relaxing his jangled nerves. "Tell her you want me rested up for when you come back. Otherwise, she make me work your time."

"Ah, well that wouldn't do, would it?" A former beauty queen and fashion model, Natasha was one of the high-end girls in Roja's stable with an hourly price beyond the normal John's means. He wondered who the madam had waiting in the wings. Someone with spending money. That meant a politician, *narcoterrorista*, or a rich tourist.

"I'll have a few words with her before I go tonight, give her a down payment, tell her I'm coming into some money soon, and there's going to be big bonus in it for her if she keeps you all for me. And that I won't be happy if I come back and find you gone."

"You good man, Ally-handro, even though Roja say you a narco, and I should be afraid of you." She hugged him. "Too bad you no want wife and little girl. I be very good to you."

"Oh, babe, I'm sorry. I'm just not the marrying kind." Seriously, she was killing him. Damsels in distress had a way of pushing his buttons. Look at that beautiful, crazy redhead, Angie. That one drove him crazy. Made him think dangerous thoughts about rescuing her baby and settling down.

By all counts, he should have gone back to Isabel last week after the incident with the dead pig and told her to pack the woman up and send her home. But, no, he couldn't do that because her kid was up there in the freaking mountains, waiting for his Mom to come get him. And, he had no right to keep a mother away from her child. The bond was a sacred one. He couldn't bring his murdered nephew, Esteban, back, but if he had to lie, cheat, steal, even kill a few people, he'd help Angie *and* Natasha get their kids back.

"Why you look so sad?" Natasha cocked her head and frowned.

"Thinking about all the lost kids in the world. Your daughter will be safe with her grandmother soon, I promise." He'd gotten close with the blonde, as close as an undercover agent dared, but he couldn't tell her everything. As it was, he'd spun a story, telling her he had some underworld friends who owed him some big favors. Once she got into the US, she'd be hooked up with a good immigration lawyer. *But* she had to keep it secret or her little girl might disappear. That way he ensured her silence and kept his cover as a Lieutenant-in-training to the biggest Latina badass in Chihuahua intact.

She tipped her head back. "So, big bad man, what you want do tonight?"

He eyed her and smiled. "The usual."

"Okay." She reached into the drawer of the nightstand.

He unbuttoned his shirt, and leaned back on the pillows. "Don't forget, we have to tell Tio and Pepe all about what we did tonight."

"Oh, yes." She giggled and counted off on her fingers. "First we do blindfold, tie up, spank, then very long blow job, and finish big doggie style."

"Exactly." He looked at the cards in his hand. "Go fish."

Chapter Nine

Angie pressed the off button on her cell phone and paced the friendly confines of her guest room like a caged tiger. She needed something to do, to keep busy, to burn off the frustration. Too dark to go for another run and too early to go to bed. Isabel had given her American guest full access to the house, yet Angie had been reluctant to do much more than go to the kitchen. There the omnipresent staff leaped to wait on her, offering coffee, cinnamon drenched baked goods, and entire meals on demand. She wasn't hungry for food, but famished for company. If only she could wave a magic wand and make the nightmare go away. In the weeks after her arrival, as they gathered intelligence on her father's location and obtained satellite maps, the weather had grown unseasonably wet and cold, interfering with rescue plans. High winds, rains, and snowstorms in the upper altitudes of the Sierra Madre made any travel, much less a clandestine rescue, next to impossible. As she recalled the conversation with Dan, a wave of homesickness swept over her. She slammed her fist into her hand. She should be home, dammit. Home with Jake's father and wife, Dan and Sarah, celebrating her son's first Chanukah.

Unbelievably, Sarah still hadn't delivered her baby. No, they didn't know the sex of the child, didn't want to know, wanted to be surprised. Well, the biggest surprise so far was that Baby Rosen hadn't made an entrance into the real world, apparently enjoying the comforts of a womb with no view. Angie spent half the phone call reassuring Dan that Jake was safe with Miriam. Having seen the care her mother had lavished on her grandson the first time he'd been kidnapped, Angie was confident that no harm would befall the child. Yes, Miriam was bullied by Zeke, but no way would she ever harm her grandson. Angie needed to hold onto that sliver of trust while they waited for the weather to break. She glanced out her window. Lights blazed in the main part of the house. She pulled on a waterproof jacket, threw the door open, trudged through the bitter wind and snowflakes, drawn to the lights like a moth to a flame.

Stainless steel appliances gleamed in the large kitchen, and multicolored lights strewn over the walls and windows blinked a Morse code of holiday cheer. A pot simmered on the range. The aroma of roast beef teased her nose and made her mouth water. A silver platter brimming with hors d'oeuvres sat on the center island, and wine glasses sparkled on another nearby tray. *Feliz Navidad* played somewhere in the house, and she caught herself singing along with the chorus. Was Isabel having a Christmas party? She should leave before it became awkward. She turned to go back the way she came and came face to face with her buxom hostess.

"*Hola, chica.* I was just about to send Alejandro over to your room to invite you to join us." Isabel winked. "Or perhaps you could have your own party alone with him?"

Angie's face burned. "I had no idea you had company. I'll leave."

"No, please. I want you to stay. It's just my family—and the families of my employees. Please don't go." Isabel arched an eyebrow. "I was *teasing*."

Angie hesitated. Should she go back to her safe little room and watch *telenovellas*, Mexican soap operas that she could barely understand? Maybe cry herself to sleep again? Or should she accept Isabel's invitation, try to pretend she wasn't socializing with the crème de la crème of drug lords?

That was a no brainer. "Okay." She peeled off her coat. "Thank you. But just so you know, I don't drink. I'm allergic to alcohol."

Isabel waved her hand as if shooing a fly. "I promise you I won't shove a drink down your throat."

Angie nodded. "And I don't do drugs."

The Latina badass stiffened, her face a mask of righteous indignation. "For your information, there are *no* illegal drugs in my house or on my property. I have kids and no one's going to expose them to that shit."

"It's my turn to apologize." Angie placed her hand on her chest. "Forgive me, I have issues—"

"Stop. You forgave me. I forgive you. All is forgiven." Isabel linked her arm through Angie's. "Now let's go have some fun."

A fire roared in the enormous fieldstone fireplace in the great room. Conversational groupings of furniture encouraged little clusters of women and men to sit, sip beer or wine, snack on appetizers and chat. Red and white poinsettias crowded corners of the room, competing with strings of bright lights for attention. In the corner, a huge Christmas tree, decorated with multicolored lights and bright colored glass ornaments glittered with pictures of the Mexican Loteria and Day of the Dead figures. An exquisite brown-haired angel in a blue dress smiled at the homey scene below.

A Christmas star shaped piñata dangled overhead, dominating the room. *Weren't piñatas for children's parties?* Angie scanned the room and listened for little ones' voices over the music. There must have been at least thirty or more people in the room, but no kids. Were they back in the children's wing?

Isabel interrupted her thoughts. "When we lived in Baltimore, we always had the biggest tree on the block. When we moved here, I tried to tell Sean and the kids, that in Mexico people don't have huge trees in their living room for the holidays." Isabel grinned. "As you can see, I was out voted. Let me find you a soft drink."

A miniature nativity scene nestled between hundreds of gaily-wrapped packages at the foot of the giant pine. There were so many different decorations, Angie didn't know where to look next. A string of bubble-lights caught her eye. When she'd lived in Baltimore during law school, her roommate, Patti, had been a Christmas maniac, mad for antique holiday decorations. Angie had tolerated the woman's obsession with the holiday because she liked her friend and enjoyed watching her enthuse over her finds. "Treasures, look at my treasures," she would exclaim to Angie. The last she'd heard, Patti was working for a law firm in North Carolina.

"Peso for your thoughts."

Startled, Angie glanced up and felt a warmth unrelated to the fireplace. Alejandro stood in front of her, dressed in a navy blazer and a white shirt open at his very nice, very lickable, kissable throat. A citrus scent wafted toward her, mixed with his own clean scent. He held a drink out to her. "You asked for a soda?"

She took the glass from his hand, their pinky fingers momentarily brushing. A tingle raced from the tip of her little finger to her nipples, skipped the middle ground, and arrowed straight into her core. Knees nearly buckling from the direct hit below the belt, she struggled to recover the use of her tongue. "So," she whispered in an unintentionally low, husky voice, "Isabel has you tending bar now?"

He bowed his head and whispered, his breath tickling the hot spot between her ear and her shoulder. "And other duties as assigned."

She wondered if that included bedding the brunette? A lightning flash of jealousy struck her, leaving her shaken. She sipped her drink, taking her time so she could recover from the jolt of emotion that should never have been there. *Say something smart, witty, seasonal.*

"Does your family back in the US know what you do for a living?"

His lips thinned, and he looked as if he was in pain.

Shit. Shit. Shit. What was she thinking? That was bitchy—not witty!

"I'm so sorry." She put her free hand on his well-muscled arm. The image of him that day in the jail, shirtless, flashed into her mind and she felt her face flame—*again*.

"I didn't mean to bring up bad feelings. I'm an idiot." Why did she say the wrong things to him all the time? Why did her brain short circuit every time she

113

tried to have a conversation with Alejandro? Yes, the man had a criminal past, one he tried to hide behind his charming smile. She, of all people, knew what it meant to have that albatross around your neck. He had to have a family that mourned his choices, people who wished he was home for the holidays. He probably missed them, too. Why did she have to go and poke at his wounds? He must think she was an absolute bitch. This time her cheeks heated with shame, and with no small amount of reluctance, she dropped her hand from his strong arm and looked around for some place to leave her drink. "I should go."

He put his hand up. "Please. If you walk out on the play, the children's feelings will be hurt."

"What are you talking about?" She glanced around wondering if she had missed a tiny tot hiding among the poinsettias. "I haven't heard or seen any kids since I came in the house."

"Wait. You'll see." His expression grew sad. "For the record, my family has no idea what I do for a living. I wish with all my heart that I could be spending the holidays with them."

Sorrow clutched at her chest, and her eyes filled with hot tears. He had a family somewhere, that loved him, missed him, and wished he was with them. She bit her lower lip. Even a drug lord didn't deserve to be kicked in the *cojones* at the holidays.

"I'm sorry for behaving badly." She shook her head and flicked away an errant tear. "I *hate* the holidays, more than ever because my son is with the man who made me despise them. For me, this time of year isn't full of good memories. Christmas just meant longer sermons from my father. No 'graven images', no 'idols', no 'abominations in the eyes of the Lord'. The beatings were longer, too."

A vision of her father's face twisted with rage, a large leather strap raised in his hand, her mother on the sidelines, urging her father to "beat the little whore" rose up in her mind while Christmas carols played in the background in real time. She shook her head to dispel images and hateful voices. "Little wonder I have no faith in anything or anyone but me, myself, and I."

Alejandro opened his mouth to say something. A chorus of cheers erupted from the partygoers. He grinned. "It's time. Come with me." He grasped her elbow and steered her through the jostling crowd outside into the courtyard.

Dressed all in white and bearing feathered wings and halo, a cherubic little Sherry led a procession of children and adults around the pool. Behind her, Ramon, dressed in a brown robe led a live burro. Sherry's twin, Ruby, looking solemn and dressed in a blue robe, carried a baby doll. Other children, presumably belonging to Isabel's employees, wore angel's costumes or shepherd's outfits and carried staffs. Behind the small platoon of kids, a cluster of adults carried candles. Even Guillermo Goat pranced along in the parade.

Angie had no idea what she was witnessing. "What the—?"

Alejandro put his index finger to his lips. "Shh. Wait."

Sherry stood in front of the open door and called out, *"Posadas?"*

A group of adults, including Isabel, yelled, *"No, no posadas."*

The children circled the pool another time and returned to the open door. *"Posadas?"*

The adults responded, *"No, no posadas."*

On the third attempt, the little angel looked as if she might cry. *"Posadas por favor?* Please?"

"Si, si, posadas! Come in Joseph, Mary, and Baby Jesús. Come in shepherds and angels." Isabel called. "But the burro and Guillermo must stay outside."

The children flew into the house and ran in circles around the room, each child seeking his or her parents, a chorus of little voices asking, "How did I do?" "Wasn't I wonderful?" "Did you ever see a better shepherd?" Trays of steaming hot tamales, cookies, and bowls of punch appeared in the hands of smiling servants. The holiday music started up again, and the children swarmed the tree, searched for their names on the gifts, and called out to each other in glee.

"I think we'd better stay out of their way," Angie laughed, "or we'll be trampled to death by the little angels."

Bumped by the kids, Alejandro led her to a corner of the room, away from the tree and the piñata. Along the way, he snagged two tamales and handed her one. "So, did you enjoy *Las Posadas?*"

Her mouth full, she had to swallow before she could answer. "Is that the Mexican version of 'no room at the inn'?"

"Exactly. Las Posadas begins on the sixteenth of December. It's re-played each evening for nine nights, with Christmas eve being the biggest one in most towns. But with our security issues," he tilted his head toward the boss lady, "she likes to keep it to one night. It's Isabel's version of the company Christmas party."

"And the gifts are from her?"

"Yes. Each one lovingly selected by a personal shopper, sent here to be checked for bombs and wrapped by her personal security staff, including me." He wiped his moustache with a tiny cocktail napkin, but missed a crumb. Her hand automatically flew up to his face and brushed it away from his lips. He captured her hand mid-swipe. "Do that again and I might get the wrong idea."

A trail of flames blazed from his fingers up her arm, to her breasts. Her nipples pebbled and a moment passed, then another. His gaze became a magnetic tractor beam, pulling her toward him. She leaned in and inhaled his scent, his maleness, his strength. He bent down, and his breath sent frissons of excitement across her neck and down her back. Tension coiled in her belly and shot jolts of excitement to her core. Angie closed her eyes and swore she could feel her feminine folds swell, like a pair of heavy butterfly wings, waiting to wrap around him in a warm, wet welcome.

He whispered, "Isabel is watching us."

Angie leaped back. Her heart raced, and her breath came in short gasps, as if she'd run a fifty-yard dash. She had to put some distance between her quivering thighs and his strong hands—fingers she instinctively knew could caress her aching center and bring her to a blinding orgasm with a deft touch. She shook her head to disperse the sex pheromones driving her body wild. *Two. Long. Dry. Years.* She kicked herself mentally. She couldn't believe she was this close to screwing up her life again. Not happening. Never again.

"Time for me to go. Thanks for showing me a good time." She turned on her heel and pushed her way through the cheerful crowd, past the smirking Isabel, and out the front door. Angie wished the frosty air would cool her down, get her head clear, and reduce the fever she spiked whenever she came near *that man*.

****

Alejandro watched Angie's fine ass fly out of the room and sighed. *Damn.* One more minute and he'd been about to lose his mind and suggest they go someplace private, away from the prying eyes, to have wild, crazy sex that he knew without a doubt that woman was capable of. His groin ached when he got anywhere near her. If he wasn't on his guard every single moment, he could lose a lot more than his cool. What was his little head thinking? Rule number one: no sex with the women on the job. Both his big head and his little head knew better. *Hands off the hot mama.* He shifted his belt to rearrange his uncooperative little head and listened to the children counting the number of times Sherry swatted the piñata.

"*Uno, dos, tres...*"

Isabel sidled up to him and sipped her red wine. "Nice of you to spend time with Angie. I think she's lonely."

Not now. Please. "She's your friend. I'm just looking out for her. It's all business."

"Didn't look like business to me. If you guys had been alone, you'd have been doing the deed right there on the floor." She fanned herself. "You guys made me hot just watching you. It was like the best movie scene, *ever*. Made me want to jump Sean's bones right here. The air around you two was crackling. I swear I saw sparks flying when she touched your face."

He bit his lower lip. "It won't happen again. I

118

promise."

His boss punched his shoulder. "Are you out of your freaking mind? It's a sign you guys are meant to be together. It's like that for me and Sean. That kind of connection only happens once in a lifetime. I know you're ambitious, want to climb the ladder of success with my company, but life can't be all work and no play. You need to let go of that uptight accountant act once in awhile, have fun. Angie needs it too, in case you hadn't noticed. If she was wrapped any tighter, she'd be a guitar string. She needs a good tuning. For heaven's sake, go for the girl. Don't throw away a chance for happiness, Alejandro."

Love advice from the Queen of the Cartel? What was next? Spiritual counseling? He shuddered at the thought. "I'm not the marrying type."

Isabel shook her head. "Let me tell you a story." She motioned to Alejandro to take a seat and grabbed a bottle of wine out of a server's hands. "*Gracias.*"

He had a feeling he was in for a long evening. He glanced at the front door and wished he could run after the red haired woman.

"Once upon a time, I was on the faculty of Baltimore Metropolitan University. I became good friends with Sarah Rosen who was married to Dan Rosen. Sarah didn't know that well *before* they were married, while she and Dan were on the outs and ex-boyfriend and girlfriend, he had a fling with Angie."

Isabel smiled. "I can see from the stunned look on your face that you never took Angie for a one night stand kind of a gal."

"You got that right. She's so straight, her face has angles." Was this the source of her antipathy toward him. Did she think he was *married*? She'd asked about his family. He would have been happy to let her know he was single. That much was true.

"Angie didn't know Dan had been engaged and had just had broken up with Sarah. And Dan didn't know his little fling with the redhead would produce a child who would literally show up on his doorstep—and that his new wife would take the child in."

His head spun with the layers upon layers. "This sounds like a *telenovela*."

She nodded and laughed, a deep throaty guffaw. "It *is* like soap opera. There's more."

Alejandro stroked his beard and watched the children swinging the baseball bat at the piñata.

"She told me her father tortured her to find out where the baby was. And she escaped."

Isabel nodded. "Yes, she ran to the home of the only man she trusted. Dan Rosen. Sarah rushed her to the hospital, nursed her back to health, protected her from police accusations, and even protected Angie from being killed by her own father, the crazy cult leader, Reverend Edmonds. In short, Sarah became Angie's guardian angel, if you'll forgive the pun."

"Where are you in this story?"

Isabel waved her hand and the wine slopped in the glass. "I had my own issues to deal with. A sleazy husband in the 'construction business', if you get my drift. A missing nanny. A mysterious explosion. When my husband disappeared, I worried my kids might be next—or me. Sean insisted on coming with me to my parents' house." She glanced over at the broad-shouldered man giving Ruby a lift to hit the piñata. "What can I say? The kids love him."

"What am I missing here? How do Sarah and Angie fit in?" The dots were not connecting. He had sources, could find out on his own, but he wanted to hear her version.

"My *darling* ex-husband sent Sarah a DVD, claiming I was a murderer." She gave Alejandro an incredulous look. "Can you believe it? That thug was an enforcer for my father, someone who could torture people without leaving marks. How could anyone believe that *I* could kill *him*?"

Alejandro worked to keep his emotions in check and his mask in place. *Oh, he could believe it, all right.* She had worked over that cult follower with her steel tipped boots. She'd *bragged* about it.

He tsked. "Ridiculous."

"Exactly. Sarah still has the DVD. I have it from a very good lawyer that letters from the grave are inadmissible in court." She shrugged. "But, what can I say, I like Sarah, I don't hold that DVD against her. She asked me to help Angie. And I said yes. Sarah's like the sister I never had. Practically family." He could have sworn he saw tears fill her eyes.

He decided to take a risk with her good mood. "Speaking of family, where are your parents tonight? Seems like they'd want to see their grandchildren in the Christmas pageant."

Alejandro locked gazes with Isabel. Despite the blazing fire, a chill settled over him. Her emerald green eyes were as cold as any hired killer's he'd ever seen. In that split second, he knew without a doubt that if she had wanted to kill her parents, she *could* have done it. The real question was, did she kill them—and why?

Smart, sexy, and beautiful, *Professora* Ramirez

wanted for *nothing*. In some parts of Chihuahua, the people revered her as a female Solomon, arriving in impoverished villages with great fanfare, giving food and money to the poor, holding court for the little people, ensuring rough justice was dealt to thieves and bad teenagers. To top it all off, she ran rehabilitation centers for alcoholics and drug addicts, of all things. She was, for all intents and purposes, Queen Isabel of Chihuahua. Why *bother* killing her parents?

Her nostrils flared and her eyes narrowed. "They're on a trip around the world, too busy having fun to bother with a little thing like grandkids." Isabel threw the rest of the wine down her throat. "My parents are selfish people. Nothing like Sarah or Angie. Jake belongs with his mother. Not stuck in some crazy, abusive cult. God only knows what they'll do to him." A tear slid down her cheek, and she dashed it away with her fingertips.

"Kill her father. Kill them *all* if you have to. Bring back that child." She stood. "And while you're at it, don't forget the gold."

Chapter Ten

Rigid with anger, Miriam tapped her thigh with the Disciplinarian and strode down the corridor toward the women's quarters and the Crèche. What was wrong with these people? They had their orders, said they knew what they were supposed to do. So, why was she cleaning up their messes? Why did she have to do *everything* herself?

She strode past a cluster of female congregants, their clucking silenced by her presence. Good. That was as it should be. She marched up to Sister Anne.

"What's going on?"

Sister Anne stood in front of the locked door of the Crèche and wrung her hands. "They want to go home." Her red-rimmed eyes filled with tears. "They want to know why they're being kept prisoners."

"They were selected to serve Father and the Chosen One. There is no greater glory on this earth. Who's the ring-leader of this insurrection?"

The other woman trembled under Miriam's gaze. "Mina."

Guillermina. Of course. No good could ever come from naming a girl after a man. "She's been trouble from the start."

Sister Anne nodded. "Brother John isn't much help. He's afraid of them, just keeps telling them to calm down. And they yell more."

Miriam lifted her chin. "We'll see about that. Open the door."

Wide-eyed, Sister Anne pulled back the deadbolts with shaking hands and followed Miriam into the dimly lit chamber. A din of high-pitched voices assaulted her ears. Enough was enough. She gripped the Disciplinarian until her hand hurt. She had to get control. Right now. She kicked the door shut. "Shut up."

Sister Anne translated in Spanish, her voice a pale imitation of Miriam's.

The jabbering ceased, and the unruly youngsters tightened their cluster. Twelve pairs of wary brown eyes stared at Miriam. She scrutinized the room for the useless eunuch.

"Where's Brother John?"

A muffled voice moaned, "Over here."

Brother John dragged himself out from under a bed. Bloody scratch marks stood out on his pallid skin, and the beginning of bruises mingled with his blue tattoo.

"It was horrible. They attacked me *en masse*. I had to hide." He rolled his eyes and shuddered. "They were going to *kill* me."

"Grow a spine. The Lord helps them who help themselves. Watch and learn."

Miriam scanned the group of girls for the root of evil and spotted her in the back of the crowd.

"Mina." She locked gazes with the girl and crooked her finger. "Come here."

Mina lifted chin and shook her head.

Miriam wasn't without compassion. She'd been

young and foolish once, too. She'd give Mina the chance to repent. She waved her over and repeated the command.

Mina flipped her the bird.

Miriam gasped, and her pulse kicked up a notch. "Where did she learn that disgusting gesture?"

Sister Anne mumbled something about movies and tourists.

"It was a *rhetorical* question, you idiot." Her last thread of patience snapped, and Miriam's pulse thundered in her ears.

Mina would pay a heavy price for her defiance. Dressed in white flannel nightgowns, the girls parted like foam on the Red Sea when she pushed her way through them. She dug her fingers into the soft part of Mina's upper arm and laughed at the look of surprise on the brat's face.

"I'm a lot stronger than I look." She dragged the whimpering adolescent to the door and pushed her face into the wood.

"This is for your insolence." Air whistled through the holes of the wooden paddle, and the girl shrieked when the Disciplinarian struck the back of her thighs. "Do I have your attention now?" Miriam slammed the paddle down a second time, this time on the young woman's round rump.

Mina screamed and cried out in Spanish.

Sister Anne shouted, "She's begging for mercy, please stop."

"Mercy? All she had to do was come forward when I gave her the opportunity. She chose the hard way. She's going to learn who's in charge here."

The air whistled, and the crack of the

Disciplinarian rang out again and again. The girls behind her wailed. She slammed Mina's back with a staccato series of strikes until, at last, the little bitch slid to the floor in a sobbing heap.

Miriam turned and faced the weeping horde. "Anyone else want to cause trouble?"

Sister Anne translated through sobs, tears streaming down her face.

The teenagers cowered and shook their heads. "Nononononononono."

She waved the Disciplinarian at the huddled girls. "The next one of you who gives Brother John a hard time will be beaten even harder than Mina."

Sister Anne could barely get the words out.

Good. Now maybe she'd get some respect.

"Sister Anne, bring me that little one in front."

The other woman stepped over to the group of shuddering, whimpering girls and led a wide-eyed teenager over to Miriam. "What's her name?"

"Chita."

"Lovely name for a girl." Miriam took her small brown hand into her large work worn one. "Come Chita, it's time for you to meet Father."

****

Zeke Edmonds slid into the warm water, rested his head back on the edge of the clawed bathtub, and closed his weary eyes. If only he could rest, maybe the visions and visitations from the Lord would be less frequent. Once he'd welcomed his spells, embraced his visions. But that was before they'd taken over more and more of his life. He loved the Lord, but—

The smell of sulphur filled his nostrils..

Oh, no. Not again. He pressed his fingers to his

temple, closed his eyes, and took a few deep cleansing breaths. The odor disappeared. *Was it possible? Had he staved off another attack?*

The red fog filled his vision and his ears buzzed with white noise. At last the Lord spoke unto Zeke as clearly as if He stood next to him, his voice a roar of rage.

"Why have you not done as I've commanded? Where are the Mothers of the Twenty-Four? Why haven't you begun spreading your seed as I commanded?"

"I have limits to my abilities. I need to rest."

"You will rest when I tell you to rest. End times are coming soon and you haven't prepared the way for the progeny who will follow the Chosen One. I am displeased. If you fail to follow my commands, another will rise up among your congregation and take your place."

"Who, Lord? Who is this traitor?"

"Do as you're told and all will be well. Fail me and you will lose everything you've worked for."

Just as quickly as the Lord had descended, he was gone. Zeke looked around the room, half-afraid the traitor would be standing at the side of the tub with a gun in his hand. He'd been warned. He gripped the side of the tub, dragged his bone-tired body to the bedroom, and collapsed on his bed.

****

"Father? Are you not well? Father?"

Zeke blinked his eyes and looked up into Miriam's worried face. "What?"

"I've been trying to wake you for five minutes." Her brow furrowed. "Should I send for the doctor?"

"I had another vision. The Lord was displeased. If I don't start on Progeny soon, He said he'd—"

"What?"

"Replace me."

Miriam stumbled back as if struck. "Replace you? That's impossible. You're the Prophet, the Leader."

"There is someone among us who would rise up and take my place."

His wife's eyes and lips narrowed. "A Judas in our midst."

He nodded. "We must be vigilant, Miriam, or the Chosen One will be taken away from us, and we'll lose all we've worked for."

Fury twisted her face. "He belongs to us. I will *never* let anyone take the child away from me."

"Oh, woman of valor, I'm so blessed to have you at my side."

Tears filled her blue eyes. "No one will ever love you the way I do. I would do anything for you." Her voice grew gutteral. "I'd kill to protect you and the Chosen One."

Zeke recalled the time when she'd come upon him and Janice. She'd screamed at the girl to get off her husband. Shovel in hand, Miriam's vengeance had been swift, and she'd shown no mercy. He'd been terrified she'd kill him next. Instead, she pulled him to his feet and hugged him. They'd buried the body together.

"I know, Miriam. I know."

She brushed a tear off her cheek and gave him a wobbly smile. "I have a surprise for you. I've selected one of the Mothers of the Twenty-Four for your bed tonight." She began to turn.

"Wait." He called her back. "Where is she now?"

"I left her playing with the Chosen One so she could see the importance of her role in the world to come. I think you'll be very happy with her. Now close your eyes." She left the room.

"Are you ready, Father?"

He grinned. "Very ready."

"Okay, you can open your eyes now."

A troll with a wart-covered nose, huge yellow teeth, one bulging black eye, and three pairs of tits stood before him, reeking of dead fish. He gagged and leaped up on the bed. "Woman, what kind of trickery is this?"

Miriam frowned and glanced at the cyclopean troll, then back at him. "I thought you'd like this young woman."

He backed into the bed frame and grasped the wooden pole. "Can't you see? It's a monster."

"Father, you're upsetting her."

He shouted, "Stupid woman, get that—that *thing* out of here, now."

"Calm down."

Zeke jumped down to the floor and circled the monster, keeping an arm's length away from it and his wife.

"Miriam," he called. "Where did you find this hobgoblin?"

"What's wrong? Are you ill?"

The Lord warned him. Told him "another would rise." A plot to discredit him. That's what it was. First Ellen. Then Chita. The only logical explanation was someone was drugging him. But with what? LSD? No. Peyote. Aaron had told him some of the natives used it in their religious rituals.

Aaron. The ever present, hard-working man at his side. The engineer who planned and built all of Edmondsville. It *had* to be Aaron. Was he collecting evidence against Zeke to discredit him? A hidden camera. Why hadn't he thought of that before? Where was it? He ran his fingers across the rough walls, searching for holes, nooks, crannies, anyplace a tiny lens could rest. Nothing.

"What's going on?"

Somewhere in this room a technological termite was eating its way through the foundation of his life. He looked up and saw a hole in the ceiling. That had to be it. He pointed upward.

"They're watching us."

Miriam pushed the troll out of the room. "What are you talking about?"

He whispered in her ear. "The Lord warned me, told me we had a traitor in our midst. Someone is putting peyote in my water."

Her eyes widened, and she sucked her breath through her teeth.

"I think it's Aaron."

"Judas."

He led her out of the room, into the dimly lit hallway. "Trust no one."

Miriam's gaze searched his face. "What should I do now?"

"Take the girl back to the Crèche."

His wife nodded. "Yes, Father."

She entered the baby's room and emerged holding a lovely young woman's hand. Aaron would pay for his treachery. But first Zeke had to expose him to all of Edmondsville as a traitor.

Chapter Eleven

Angie shaded her eyes against the red glare of the late afternoon sun, chambered a round in the 300 Win mag, raised the Remington 700, and adjusted the butt on her shoulder. She was happy to see that it had a muzzlebreak to lessen the recoil. *Big bullet. Big kick.* It would not be fun. She peered through the scope and focused on the line of beer cans in the distance. Finger resting alongside the trigger guard, she sighted the weapon, readjusted her position, and felt the tickle of Tio's breath on the back of her neck. Someone had garlic for lunch. And *something* was bumping against her butt and it *wasn't* a banana. *Blech.* Enough of this crap. She stepped back and stomped on his foot.

The big man yelped in surprise.

"I'm *so* sorry," she said. "I didn't know your foot was there." *And that his hands were hovering over her hips. And that his groin was bumping up against her ass. Horny bastard.*

He licked his lips. "Sure you don't want help, you know, setting up your stance?"

So subtle. He'd been drooling over her ever since she'd climbed onto the ATV. The moron really shouldn't mess with a woman holding a weapon, much less a high powered rifle that could hit a target at a thousand yards. Bullets trumped muscle every time.

"Tio, did I ever tell you I grew up on a chicken farm on the eastern shore of Maryland? Smack dab in the middle of God and gun country. My father began my shooting lessons when I was five. Used eggs for target practice. I could barely lift the rifle. He forced me to lay down in the chicken shit and learn how to hit a dozen eggs in a row. My job was to keep guard over the chickens, watch out for foxes. Said it was good training." She glanced up at her overeager instructor. "Little did he know I'd be using it to plan his demise twenty-six years later."

Tio shook his bald head and took three steps back. "Man, that's screwed up."

She laughed. "Not as screwed up as he is, I assure you." Good. Now maybe he'd leave her alone. Angie bent her head back to the task. Beer can in the scope. *Check.* Feet shoulder width apart. *Check.* Deep breath. *Check.* Gentle squeeze of the trigger. *Check.* Beer can transformed into shrapnel. *Priceless.*

"Holy shit, woman," Tio whooped. "You can back me up anytime. Wait till I tell Pepe. He won't believe it."

She lowered the weapon and grinned. "Your turn."

He shook his head and guffawed. "No way. I'm just gonna look bad after you."

"Handguns, then?" She slid the pistol out of its carrying case and snapped the magazine filled with .40 caliber Winchesters into the butt of the semiautomatic. She admired the simplicity and dependability of the high capacity Glock. "Well, hello there, gorgeous gun of my dreams. Where have you been all my life?"

Tio cocked his head to one side. "You know, if I didn't know any better, I'd be worried you were an undercover *federale*."

"Ha. As if any undercover agent would get past Isabel and you guys." She shook her head. "He or she would be dead meat."

"Well, *chica,* you sure know your way around guns. Never would've taken you for a gun lover."

"Looks can be deceiving. I was raised by a lunatic. My father believes you have to be prepared for End Days. Lawlessness. Chaos. The fall of governments." She waggled her eyebrows. "Every cult leader's wet dream."

Tio blushed. "You're bad."

"To the bone." Angie turned, aimed, and fired the semi-automatic. Beer cans, rocks, and dust flew in every direction. "Whoo-hoo! Got any rocket-launchers? I think I'm ready to take down a fortress."

"Sorry, those bad boys are back at the ranch." He glanced at the horizon. "Sun's going down. Time to get back." Tio began packing the ammo into duffle bags.

She lifted her handgun and popped the magazine out. "Don't we need to clean these?"

"Yeah, but not now. Once the light goes, it's pitch black out here. We don't want to run into a pack of coyotes, either." He placed the rifle and the pistol in their carrying cases and handed them to Angie. "These are yours."

Reluctance to accept expensive gifts from a criminal dampened the thrill of excitement of having the weapons to destroy her father in her hands. "Oh, I don't think I can accept—"

"Boss Lady won't take no for an answer."

God only knew what the Latina would want in return. Angie had the feeling Isabel was like the

Godfather, only worse.

Tio started for the ATVs. "Alejandro told her you should have your own weapons. You keep them, *chica*. They're your new best friends."

She zipped up her windbreaker and slid the desert camouflage headgear over her head. She was going to have helmet hair, for sure. "Tell me about Alejandro. Where'd he come from? How long has he worked for Isabel?"

"I don't know where he's from. I saw his rap sheet and wanted poster on Interpol. That was good enough for me."

The professional world turned upside down in the cartels. Here a good criminal background check meant the opposite of what it meant in the civilian world. A rap sheet was indispensable. But an Interpol wanted poster meant the criminal ranked among the crème de la crooks.

"Been with us about a year." He gave her a sly glance. "You interested? I can, you know, be your go between, sort of like a matchmaker. Set things up for you."

"This is strictly business." She frowned at the man.

He smirked. "Whatever you say."

"I need to know if I can trust this guy. I'm putting my son's life in his hands."

"He saved you from Raul, didn't he?" Tio piled the bags in the back of the ATV.

"Yes. But this is a huge operation. How do I know he can pull off a search and rescue mission like this? It's not as if he trained for it or has been a cop."

Tio climbed onto his ATV. The giant made the vehicle look like a child's riding toy. Angie had a sudden flash of Jake in his red and yellow toy car, scooting around the house. A pang of longing for her boy left her weak-kneed.

"Pepe and me, we got strength." He flexed his biceps. "But muscle without brains won't do it. Don't ever tell Isabel I said this, but Alejandro is the real brains. Before he came, the books were a mess. We didn't know who had paid for what, and Isabel was pissed off all the time. She went through six accountants in a year."

Angie could only imagine what being terminated by Isabel really meant. Even if she didn't kill them, what would an ex-cartel CPA put on his resume? *Worked for narcoterrorista for two months. Excellent book-keeper. Superb analytical, critical thinking, and money laundering skills. Looking to move to not-for-profit sector and out of organized crime. Seeking asylum in any country that does not have an extradition treaty with Mexico. References unavailable on request.*

"Once that guy started working for the family, things got calmer, smoother."

"Good record-keeping is one thing. Having the skills and ability to stage a complicated raid like this is another."

Tio waved his hands and made a big show of looking around. "You see anyone else jumping up to do this?"

She sighed. "No."

"Then let the man do his job. Besides which, he's the only *hombre* who ever withstood Raul's interrogation and lived to tell the story."

"That thug beat up Alejandro?"

"While he was handcuffed to a metal chair."

135

She recalled her near rape and shuddered at the thought of being at the creep's mercy. "Whatever happened to Raul?"

Tio gave her a wicked grin. "Let's just say he's on a *permanent* vacation."

Seemed like a lot of people went on vacation around here. Isabel's parents were away on some kind of round-the-world tour. Now Raul. *Wait. Back up a moment.* She'd missed the subtext. He wasn't on a *real* vacation. Hadn't the bodies of half a dozen men been found in a resort town a short time ago? Had that been the fate of the crooked cop, too? Her stomach rolled. She hated Raul, but even he didn't deserve to be tortured to death. Angie swallowed hard. "Was Alejandro involved in planning Raul's 'vacation?'"

"I already told you too much. Forget about it." He snapped his helmet into place, pressed the starter, and twisted the throttle.

The giant lawnmower sound of the ATV made talking impossible. She turned the conversation over in her mind. She couldn't stop thinking about what he said. As a defense lawyer, she thought she'd seen it all. People told her she had good instincts, could sniff out bad characters. This revelation blindsided her. She would have never taken the handsome, soft-spoken man who made her pulse spike and her celibacy vow weaken for a killer. Was Alejandro a money launderer *and* a murderer? Was he capable of that level of ruthlessness? She needed to know this man could save her child. If Alejandro was responsible for Raul's death, he was the right man for the mission—but the wrong man for her heart.

****

Alejandro assessed the mountain of tents, lanterns, cook sets, stoves, metal bowls, dishes and cutlery, sleeping bags, duffle bags, backpacks, water bottles, repair and first aid kits, hiking poles, binoculars, whistles, and other assorted camping supplies and equipment piled up in a bay of Isabel's six-car garage. If they added any more crap to the heap they'd never make it out of the compound, much less to the other side of Tarahumara country. In addition to the fact that not one of the thugs on the mission had ever been involved in a search to *save* a life, Alejandro had never been in charge of task force equipment and supplies. He'd always been a member of the ATFE Special Response Team going in on the raids, doing the actual work.

He had a newfound respect for all the work done by the ATFE support staff. He had to get into Edmondsville without being discovered, extract baby Jake, and call in the chopper to lift both mother and child out of harm's way. That assumed all went as planned and everyone survived. He had to have contingency plans for the contingency plans. If he went down, he had to have a second in command. He shuddered at the thought of choosing between Tio and Pepe. Each of them could kill, but which one could save a life? He'd think about it tomorrow. They needed to rehearse the operation, but first he had to come up with a tactical transport plan for getting everyone and everything across the desert, canyons, and mountains.

If they staged the mission and ferried materials by helicopter to safe houses ahead of time, they could stash the needed supplies and weapons along the way. In a large city, people would ignore a helicopter buzzing overhead. An urban population would assume it was a traffic chopper or medical evacuation. But in the remote regions where they needed to go, helicopters were either adventure tours for rich gringos or *federales* making an annual show of hunting for *narcoterroristas*. Either way, another chopper flying around the Sierra Madre would put them in the public eye. Big news. Too big. That type of activity would draw attention to the rescue team. The cult leaders would get wind of their pursuers and flee, taking baby Jake even deeper into the canyons and caves.

On the other hand, if they took the Hummers over the unimproved roads to the highway, then the capital city, they could take scenic Copper Canyon route on the Chihuahua al Pacifico Railroad. If they had a week to spare, that is. The train took thirteen-hours at the best, a week or longer at the worst if rockslides or storms slowed it down. According to one of Isabel's informants, the cult leader's wife had last been sighted three months ago in a tiny village ten miles from the train depot. Local hotels ran a transportation service from the station to the village, which would be a big help with transporting everything. But what the hell kind of rescue mission drives up in a tour bus? Might as well bring a megaphone and shout, "Hola, we're here! We've come to pick up the baby."

If it hadn't been for the crappy weather over the last three months, they would have tried to rescue the kid sooner. Now that the enemy was dug in, an overland approach, while long and arduous, would be the stealthiest. The dearth of paved roads from Isabel's compound to the cult fortress necessitated the use of heavy duty all terrain vehicles, ATVs. Using camouflage and lightly traveled routes, the team could cut across canyons and creeks. If they stayed in the canyons, the weather would be tolerable this time of year. The higher altitudes would be frosty, perhaps even snowy in February. He had to plan for every possibility. He shook his head. When Isabel had assigned him to this mission, she'd told him he was in command. What she didn't tell him was that he was, in essence, chief, cook, and bottle washer in charge of a muscle bound mob of morons. The only exception was Angie.

Angie. His pulse kicked up a notch just thinking of her name. The woman drove him crazy. Not just because she was a red hot mama, but because she was so damn determined to take charge of this mission. The redheaded Amazon had marched into his office and demanded to see all the intelligence he had: weather, aerial maps, railroad schedules, and informant reports. Isabel had shown up in the middle of one of their loud discussions, taken her aside, and told her to let Alejandro be in charge. Isabel's ringing endorsement had ended with, "He's smarter than any other employee I have." Since Tio, Pepe, and the rest of her musclemen had the collective IQ of a swarm of gnats, the compliment fell flat. If *only* he had his ATFE Special Response Team buddies at his side. He'd take one of them for four of Isabel's guys.

He tried to organize the equipment by categories, but everything just kept sliding into a mess on the concrete floor. They'd need some kind of storage system, trailers for the hunting quads. He made a note to add tarps to the shopping list. On second thought, he'd have Angie research which ones would do the best job. Every morning for the past month, Angie had shown up in his office with a cup of coffee in one hand and a computer printout in the other.

She questioned everything from the time it was taking to mount the attack, to the type of footwear she needed, to the reliability of the GPS equipment in the mountains. Since Angie wasn't allowed out of the compound for fear of being spotted by her father's spies, she printed out long shopping lists and sent Tio out for weekly purchases for the expedition. She could have given instructions to National Geographic explorers.

Between barking orders at Tio and relentless nitpicking questions directed at Alejandro, she kept up a running commentary about her son. "He's over a year old now, probably walking and talking. He'll need new clothes, warm bunny suits for extraction from the high country. I wonder what my mother is feeding him. Do you think they have cow's milk, Alejandro? Or do you think they have him on a diet of *pinole* and goat milk? He was always such a healthy baby. I hope he's well. I wonder how big he is now. Will he know me when he sees me?" The most heartbreaking of all of her questions, the one that arrowed straight past his undercover armor was, "Do you think he'll recognize me? What if Jake forgot me? He was just about to turn a year old when they stole him. He's fifteen months old now. What if I'm just a nebulous face in his mind?"

Alejandro tried to respond, to tell her the child would be fine, all would be well. But he knew no matter how often he tried to reassure her, her anxiety would never go away until Jake was in her arms. Her fears were like pebbles dropped down into his well of memories, each one sending ripples through his repressed emotions. He longed to hold her, rock her like a child and stroke her hair. In unguarded moments, his thoughts roamed from stroking her hair to kissing her lips, caressing her breasts, and making her moan with pleasure. At times, his biceps ached from the tension of gripping his pants to keep his arms from shooting up, from surrounding her in protective custody. He knew if he touched her, he wouldn't hold back, couldn't resist bringing his lips down to hers and smothering her tears, and every luscious inch of her body with his kisses.

Each day he wished Isabel's observations would come true, that the sparks between them would burst into flames of molten desire. And every day, he cursed himself and his little head for even thinking about breaking his cardinal rule: No sex with women on the job. Today was no different. If he didn't stop thinking about that woman and how crazy she made him, he'd have an erection and no one to share it with. After mentally giving himself a good ass-kicking, he placed his clipboard and checklist on a workbench, turned to go back to his office, walked halfway across the enormous garage and stopped.

Angie stood in the doorway to the house, one hand on the frame of the doorway, the other covering her mouth. Her face was flushed and tendrils of hair escaped from her ponytail, giving her the look of a Renaissance painting. Her damp tee shirt clung to her high breasts and hard nipples, small waist, and womanly curves. He dragged his eyes back to her face and her gaze snagged his. His breathing became rapid and shallow, as if he'd just run five miles across rugged terrain. Every muscle in his body tensed, waiting, wanting, willing her to come to him. *If she takes one step closer, if she comes into the garage, it's a sign she wants me.* If there was such a thing as telepathy, he yearned to employ it now. The words surfaced in his brain and threatened to escape from his parted lips. *Come in, come closer, please. Let me hold you. Let me comfort you. Let my hands roam over your luscious body, my lips brush your long lovely neck. Let me make love to you. One step closer, please. One step closer to my hands and aching groin.*

Her hand fell away from her mouth. "How's it coming?"

"Overwhelming. I could use your help getting it organized." He paused. *Why not just ask her? Where was the harm in that?* "Would you like to come and see my inventory?"

Angie cocked her head to one side and raised an eyebrow. "Is that a variation of 'Would you like to see my etchings?'"

Busted. His face felt warm under her penetrating gaze. "Um. Not exactly. There are no paintings in this pile. And I know you want to stay on top of everyone. I mean everything." *Shit. Did he really just say that?*

Angie strolled over to the mountain of equipment and reached for the clipboard in his hand. "Let me take a look."

She came in. She wanted to be closer to him. This was it, the sign he'd been waiting for.

He sidled up behind her, pretending to look at the clipboard. *Breathe, man, just breathe normally.* A tendril of her hair lifted and fell with his breath. The healthy scent of sweat from her run addled his brain. He could barely read the words on the paper. He wanted to slide his arms around her waist and nuzzle her neck, nipping at the spot between her neck and shoulder.

"So much to do." She sighed and her large breasts rose and fell beneath the thin cotton T-shirt, calling to him to caress them, stroke them, make her nipples hard beneath his fingertips.

He inched forward, and ran his finger down the list, his forearm grazing hers. He could almost feel the crackle of electricity between them. "We're really close, I swear. Look at all the things I've checked off on the list."

She nodded, then turned without warning and handed the clipboard back to him. "You're the expert. I have to trust you to do the right thing."

Angie stepped out of his reach, and circled the mound of equipment. "How will you get all this stuff loaded up? Do you have trailers? "

He held the clipboard over his groin and his growing problem. Tongue thick, brain muzzy, he could only nod and beg with his eyes.

Please, please, please come to bed with me.

"Are all the ATVs good to go?"

He found his voice at last. "Batteries and tires are all good. Extra fuel was loaded on the trailers. Everything was checked by me. I hate surprises."

She stretched her arms upward, and her shirt rose—exposing a tempting belly button. An inny. He loved innies. He could nuzzle and play with chocolate sauce and whipped cream in the saucer of her belly for hours. He wondered if her skin felt like silk or satin? Did she wear a lace bra and panties? Or was she more practical? Cotton or some other natural fiber, perhaps? Or did she eschew underwear altogether and go commando? He had a sudden burning desire to know all those things and many more, like what her kisses tasted like and what her soft inner thighs felt like under his fingertips. He took two steps closer. *Okay, he'd go to her, he could do that.*

Just as he was within reach of her, a garage door opened, and Hummer headlights blinded him. The driver honked the horn, and Alejandro jumped out of the way. Hip hop music rocked the car, then ceased as the vehicle shut down and extinguished the lights. He waved at the driver and turned back to speak to Angie—but she was gone.

Chapter Twelve

Zeke Edmonds sat on his throne and looked down at the concerned faces of his congregants. Armed followers ringed the sides of the room and stood guard at the exits. The crowd grew anxious.

Showtime.

He stood and raised his hands on high. "I call upon you to bow in prayer."

A thousand people knelt and touched their foreheads to the stone floor.

"We are so blessed to be here in this lovely land, in our fortress high above the rivers, canyons, and those who will not survive End Days."

He stared at his second in command's back, wishing his eyes were laser beams that could pierce the man's skin and make him shriek in pain.

"While I was falsely imprisoned, Brother Aaron led our flock here and established our very own modern village, with running water, solar panels, windmills, electricity, and food. During my absence, Brother Aaron made alliances with the police and politicians. Thanks to Brother Aaron, we are ready, oh Lord, ready for End Days."

He scanned the whitewashed cavern, looking for telltale hand signals, note passing, or whispers.

"But, the Lord has shared visions that tear at my

heart. I bring bad news."

Murmurs followed his declaration.

"Arise, so I can look you in the eyes."

Waves of whispers rolled across the group and echoed on the hard walls.

Yes, be afraid, be very afraid.

Worry creased each face.

He choked back a sob. "I don't know where to begin." He paused, took a deep, shuddering breath. "My heart is so heavy." He raised his hands up to the ceiling. "Lord, I beseech Thee, take this cup away from me. Don't forsake me." Zeke fell to the floor. Back arched, he flailed his arms and legs.

Miriam shouted over the growing rumble of voices, "Father is having another celestial vision. Do not disturb him."

With concern almost palpable, the crowd fell silent and waited.

No longer thrashing about, Zeke lay on his side and peeked between his lashes. Brother Aaron stood right in the front row, his brow furrowed. Was the engineer worried for Father—or was he afraid of being exposed?

"Lord, no," Zeke moaned.

Miriam knelt beside him, the baby on her hip. "What is it Father?" She shouted. Then she whispered, "Speak up. They can't hear you in the cheap seats."

"The cut is too deep, the pain too much," he shouted. He threw in a conglomerate of Hebrew, Latin, and Greek to ratchet up the tension.

The level of whispers rose again. Speaking in tongues was *always* a crowd pleaser. He had them right where he wanted them.

"No more pain, Lord, no more pain." Zeke

shuddered, went rigid, then completely still—his eyes wide open.

Miriam wailed, "No, Father, don't leave us. We need you here, now." She placed the baby's hands on his face. "Oh, Chosen One, use your powers. Save your grandfather." Jake shrieked and smacked Father in the nose.

Real tears sprang to Zeke's eyes. *Shit. That hurt.* He took a deep breath, fluttered his lashes and asked, "Miriam, is that you?"

"Yes, Father." She stood and lifted the baby over her head. "The Chosen One saved him!"

The crowd roared its approval and chanted, "Father, Father, Father!"

Zeke dragged himself up to his knees, crawled over to the throne, and pulled himself up to the seat. "I've had a vision."

Every woman and man in the crowd wept openly—except Brother Aaron. Eyes flat, his face a mask, the man looked like a statue.

Zeke placed his right hand over his heart. "I've been betrayed."

"Who, who, who?"

He shook his head. "It pains me, because it is so unfair. I asked the Lord to take me, rescue our lamb from Satan. I have to punish the traitor so others will remember right from wrong."

Miriam shrilled, "Who amongst you has betrayed Father?"

Jake cried and shrieked, adding his outrage.

"Come forward now," Zeke coaxed in a soft voice. "You who have betrayed me. Repent and all will be forgiven."

Miriam raised the Disciplinarian with her free hand. "Let physical pain be your friend. Come forward and take your punishment."

Brother Aaron glanced around the room and took two steps forward. "Father, let's talk. In *private*."

"So you *admit* you betrayed me?"

"I'm your strongest supporter. We need to talk about your horrifying visions—"

Induced by the peyote you fed me. "Guards," Zeke shouted. "Seize him."

People melted away from the sinner.

"I've done nothing wrong, I've—"

"Gag him. I'm tired of listening to his lies."

A guard stuffed a rag into Brother Aaron's mouth and another bound his hands.

"Take him to the chamber of solitude where he will fast and reflect on his sins."

The guards fell into a phalanx around the big man and marched him out of the chamber.

"Who else is involved? If you don't tell me, I *will* find out. The Lord speaks to me directly." One by one, he stared deep into his congregants' eyes. They dared not speak. Fear of being next kept them in check.

"Father, let's go back to our chambers." His wife took his hand in hers. "You need to rest."

He nodded. "I'd be lost without you."

Miriam's eyes welled with tears. "Thank you, Father."

Zeke allowed her to lead him down the steps. The silent crowd parted to let the couple and the baby pass. Just as they were about to exit the chamber, shouts erupted.

Zeke stopped, turned, and stared at the little man

standing in the entryway on the other side of the room. His bowl hair cut, bright orange shirt, white loincloth, and *huaraches* sandals left no doubt as to his origins. Instead of the usual shy, smiling expression of the Tarahumara, this man's brown eyes blazed and his face twisted with anger. He stared straight at Zeke.

"Dónde está mi hija? Dónde está mi Mina? Where is my daughter? Where is my Mina?"

****

Miriam struggled to suppress outward signs of her rage. She had to put on a concerned face. Play dumb. She had a better command of Spanish than she liked to let on. First and foremost, her duty was to protect the Chosen One and her husband from this savage.

"Father," she said in a low voice, "I think it would be best if you took the baby and a few of the men and returned to our chambers."

Zeke tore his gaze away from the furious little man. He lifted Jake out of Miriam's arms and signaled to a cluster of unarmed, but burly men. "Come with me please." The four men closed ranks around their leader and the child and hustled them out the rear exit.

Now that her husband and the baby were safe, she could focus.

"Sister Anne," she called. "Could you assist me, please?"

The sea of congregants stepped aside to allow the mousy woman to scurry to Miriam's side. All eyes were upon her now, not Zeke. *She* was in charge, the star of this particular show.

Miriam dragged Sister Anne over to the short brown man. "Offer him some food and water."

Sister Anne translated as fast as she could.

The man's shook his head so hard, his hair twirled in a dark nimbus.

"Ask him who he is and what he wants."

"He says his name is Juan, and he wants his daughter, Mina."

This guy was a one note Johnny. Whiny, too. Just like his bitch daughter.

"Tell him we sent the money to the nun. Sister Teresa has all the money for the girls." A bold faced lie. Why not put the blame on the nun's shoulders? Let him go back to her and demand the *dinero*. They can squabble over the pittance she handed over that day to purchase the adolescents.

He stomped his sandaled foot when Sister Anne conveyed the message.

"He says it's not about the money," the other woman whispered. "He was told he'd get to see his daughter every month. It's been three months."

Miriam cocked her head and gave the man a puzzled look. "Tell him we never agreed to let the girls go home for visits."

Sister Anne shot her a sharp look. They locked gazes for several long moments. At last, Sister Anne looked away and translated.

Mina's father shook his fist at Miriam. Two male congregants stepped to her side. She waved them away. "It's a simple misunderstanding. Tell him we told Sister Teresa the parents could come *here* to visit the girls. The nun turned things around."

A puzzled look crossed Sister Anne's face. Miriam stared at her until the woman did as she was told.

"He wants to see Mina. Now. His wife died. His daughter is all he has."

Miriam nodded and put on a sad face. "Oh, how *tragic*. Of course he misses her." She turned and faced the sea of worried faces. "He's going to see his daughter now. Everything is fine."

An audible sigh of relief filled the large chamber. The crowd at last left Miriam alone with the visitor and her underling.

She felt as if her cheeks would break from her phony smile. "Sister Anne, could you please lead the way."

"Yes, yes." The other woman scurried ahead and the little man followed her.

Miriam waited a moment, and then grabbed the Disciplinarian off its hook. She tapped the wooden paddle on her palm and contemplated the situation at hand.

Brother Aaron had paid politicians and police to look the other way. But he hadn't thought to bribe the Tarahumara. Letting the man go could endanger Edmondsville and Father's plans. Despite their peace loving reputation, Mina's father had a temper. If he went back, complained to the *ejiditarios*, found sympathy—well who knew?

She caught up to the native and her mousy underling in the dimly lit corridor. "Sister Anne, could you run ahead and let Brother John know we're coming to the Crèche? They might need to tidy up a bit."

The other woman broke into a trot, leaving Miriam alone with Mina's father.

"Juan, we need to talk."

He turned and stared at her, his brow furrowed.

"Yes, I speak Spanish. And I think you understand some English, so we both hid a little something from each other, didn't we?"

Juan gave her a sly smile. "*Si.*"

The Disciplinarian felt solid and right in her hand as she tapped her thigh. She continued in his language.

"Your daughter is very important to us."

His eyes lit up, and his chest puffed. Pride oozed out of every pore.

"Mina will make a wonderful mother."

His head began to nod. Then the proud papa stopped and gave her a puzzled look.

"She's been given the gift of a lifetime. As one of the Mothers of the Twenty-Four, she will ensure the right people will serve the Chosen One when he comes of age."

"*No comprendo.*"

"End Days are coming, my little brown friend. Soon the Apocalypse will be upon us. The seas will churn blood, the earth will split, and nuclear fires will roar through all the cities."

"Evangelista." He shook his head, turned his back to her, and began to walk in the direction where Sister Anne had gone.

"Don't dismiss me, you ignorant savage." She grabbed his shoulder and swung him around to face her. "I'm giving you time to repent, to save yourself and your daughter. Leave us now, go back to your village. Allow your daughter to fulfill her sacred destiny."

He stared up at her and spat in her face.

Fury boiled in her chest, and her vision tunneled to see only the man's back as he headed toward the Crèche.

"Don't you *dare* walk away from me when I'm speaking to *you.*"

He flipped her the bird over his shoulder and kept walking.

She ran after him, yanked at his thick black hair, and threw him down to the stone floor. Foot on his chest, she pinned the struggling heathen to the ground, gripped the handle of the Disciplinarian, raised it on high, and brought it down.

Chapter Thirteen

Angie arose before dawn and pulled on thermal underwear, two pairs of thermal socks, a one piece insulated suit, work boots, and heavy gloves. Rivulets of sweat ran down her back, and her thermal underwear was giving her a wedgie. *Ugh.* She tried to adjust her clothing, then gave up. Even though the weather forecast had been for a sunny, dry, and pleasant twenty-degrees Celsius or sixty-eight degrees Fahrenheit, she knew once she started driving the ATV, the wind would cool her down. Right now, time was of the essence. She *had* to get out of the compound.

Most of the household would be asleep at this hour, and the sentries would be taking a coffee break in the guardhouse soon. Much like the ancient kings, isolation and lack of bold enemies had lulled the cartel watchdogs into predictable routines and complacency. Ninety days, three months of observations, note taking and clock-watching was about to pay off. Ever since she'd arrived in early December, her repeated requests to rescue Jake *now* had been put off by Isabel and Alejandro. She'd suppressed her shrieking maternal instincts, gone along with the program, and waited.

Rather than curl up in a ball in her room, she'd trained every single day, never missing a five mile run, a shooting session, or an opportunity to practice her climbing skills. Despite her approach-avoidance reaction to the drug lord and his vile business, she'd forced herself to work alongside Alejandro so she could learn everything they knew, memorizing each piece of intelligence as it came in.

She slipped into the kitchen, set down the duffle bag packed with her rifle, handgun and ammo, and filled a thermos with coffee. The Multipurpose Utility Vehicle, or MUV, already packed with a repair and first aid kit, cases of water, protein bars, extra fuel, and every piece of long trip survival gear she could filch without drawing attention, awaited in a dark corner of Isabel's mammoth garage. She'd memorized the owner's manual and picked what few brains Tio had about maintenance and spare parts needed for the expedition. She'd asked for driving lessons and over time, she'd been allowed to take the machine out without her hulking buddy. She'd explored every square mile of Isabel's compound, ranging further with each trip, pushing her boundaries and practicing driving through streams and the roughest terrain she could find, but always returning before sundown. Three months of practice driving, three months of planning, three months of waiting were at last over.

Her biggest fear was that someone would attempt to stop her from leaving. If she could get an hour's head start, she was certain she could evade Tio and Pepe.

Alejandro was another matter.

Alejandro.

Dammit. Why did her heart race when she thought of him? She should be immune to the man and his charms. She needed him to save her son, that was all. Nothing more. Besides which, they'd been working side-by-side for three months and not once had he ever made one move on her. A damn good thing, because she'd either have to take flight, fight, or sleep with him, and she was afraid she knew already which part of her brain—and body—would win.

This morning, her focus had to be on her son and getting him away from her lunatic father. Victory would be even sweeter if she could save her poor mother at the same time. Perhaps once Miriam saw Angie and realized help was there, she'd at last stand up to, and escape from, her abusive husband.

Maglite in her mouth, she let herself into the cavernous space and felt her way to the darkened corner where her chariot awaited. Getting it outside without making a lot of noise was key. She tossed the backpack onto the passenger seat of the two by two, strapped down one of the tarps she'd ordered for the expedition, and approached the smallest of the garage doors. She pressed the opener, held her breath, and strained to hear footsteps. She waited five minutes, then began steering and pushing the vehicle out the door.

Freaking thing didn't seem that heavy before, she thought. If it weren't for the fact that it sounded like a giant lawnmower and would wake the dead, she'd jump in and drive like a bat out of hell. Instead, she continued with the slow roll across the floor, its rubber tires squeaking like enormous mice. At last, she cleared the door and made it to the blessed downward slope of the concrete driveway. Just as it appeared the vehicle would escape from her clutches, she leaped in and veered it away from a pile of jagged rocks. According to Tio, the tires were the most aggressive ones in the industry, but if they hit something the wrong way, even they could be flattened. That was all she needed. She'd be finished before she even started. The wind whipped her ponytail into her eyes, reminding her to put on her helmet. Now or never. She turned the key in the ignition, and the MUV roared to life. She clutched the steering wheel with one hand, shifted into all wheel drive, punched the latitude and longitude of her father's compound into the GPS, and floored it.

****

Angie admired the rosy fingers of dawn as they turned the sky red. What was that saying? Red sky at morning, sailors' delight, red sky at night, sailors take warning? Or was it the other way around? Good thing she wasn't on a ship.

Butt numb from the hour-long ride across rocky terrain, she needed to get off, take a pee, and stretch her legs. Up ahead, a dry arroyo cut into rock walls offered a temporary hiding place. She found a gentle path down to the riverbed and stopped the machine under an overhang. Angie unclipped the protective netting, climbed out and looked for a private spot. Designed for a man on a hunting trip, the camouflage one-piece suit afforded great protection against the wind, but sucked when it came to bathroom breaks for a woman. Boots off, she hopped on one foot then another and finally got down to her thermal underwear. Mercifully, that was in two pieces, not one. She squatted, used a tissue to blot herself, and debated her next steps.

Tio had told her the MUV had a top speed of forty miles per hour, but the darkness and terrain had slowed her down. The GPS told her she'd traveled only twenty miles, not nearly as far as she wanted to be. Now that it was light, she was ready to put the pedal to the metal.

She pulled up her pants and looked at the one-piece suit. Here in the valley, the sun was already warming the air and clouds barely moved across the sky. Did she really need that thing? She crammed the suit under the tarp. If she got cold, she could always stop and put it on again. Boots on, time to roll. She dug a protein bar out of the backpack and slugged down some hot coffee. Beneath the tarp, a waterproof one-piece suit awaited Jake. Without his height or weight, she'd been forced to guess and ordered a size larger just in case. Eyes closed, she imagined holding him in her arms again, her tears of joy falling on his face. His smile and coos would be her reward.

Was he talking? Or had Miriam learned how to communicate with Jake with sign language? His vocabulary had been limited to "Mama," "Dada," and "Doggy." If he was speaking now, was it in English or Spanish? She sighed, tossed the remains of the coffee onto the parched ground, wiped the dust off her visor, and turned the key. She had sixty-six miles to go before she ran into the side of the mountain where her father's fortress perched. Time to eat some more dirt.

****

Isabel stood in the middle of the kitchen and shrieked at the top of her lungs. "What the hell do you mean, she's gone?"

Nerves tight as a piano string, Alejandro bounced on the balls of his feet and repeated, "The MUV is missing and so is Angie."

The boss lady whirled on Tio. "How'd she get past the guards?"

The big man shrugged. "No one heard anything, no one saw anything."

"So she's a ghost? Is that what you're telling me? She can walk through walls, disappear without a trace?" Isabel put her fists on her hips. "I want a complete investigation. *Now*. What if she's an undercover *federale*? I should have never taken that bitch in."

Alejandro restrained an audible groan. His handler had been driving him nuts, asking about Angie, and her real intentions. Was she working for the cartel? Now Isabel was questioning the poor woman's loyalty. This was ridiculous—and dangerous. He had to stop this freight train. He cleared his throat. "*Professora*, could I say something, please?"

She glared at him. "Well?"

"She's been begging us to rescue her son ever since she arrived. I explained to her that we had to hold off until the weather got better, that it was unpredictable until March."

Her red nails drummed on the granite counter. "And?"

"Guess she got tired of waiting. The MUV is gone, along with an *entire* cargo bed full of long trip supplies and equipment. Plus, weapons and ammo. Plus, baby clothes."

Isabel's eyes widened. "*Madre Dios.* She's going after him alone."

Tio shook his big bald head. "That is one crazy *chica*."

"Not crazy," Alejandro said. "Desperate."

Isabel covered her face with her hands and took a deep shuddering breath.

Was the Latina badass actually crying? Alejandro waited.

The boss lady dropped her hands. Her cheeks

shone with tears, and her voice was thick. "Organize the men, go after her. She'll get herself killed."

Tio turned to leave the kitchen but Alejandro touched his shoulder. "Wait." The big man stopped. "If we send in the army, she'll rabbit, or get herself hurt. I know her better than anyone else." He would probably live to regret his next words. "Let me go after her. Alone."

Tio guffawed. "*Hombre*, you better watch out. That redhead is nothin' but trouble. Trust me."

Alejandro stared at his big buddy. "What are you saying?"

"I think she's playing for the other team, man." He rolled his eyes. "I put my best moves on her. Bitch acted like I had a snake in my pants."

Isabel snorted. "A woman doesn't want to screw you, so you assume she's a lesbian?"

Tio pouted. "Most ladies can't get enough of me."

"*Madre Dios*, you *are* an idiot." Isabel turned back to Alejandro. "Do whatever you have to, take whatever you need, just go find her. If she gets hurt or worse, Sarah will never forgive me."

Once again, Alejandro wondered what Sarah had on Isabel. She said it was a damning DVD, but was there something more? Enough about Isabel. He had to prepare for his tracking expedition across a rugged, unforgiving terrain. He hoped he caught up to Angie before someone or something else did.

****

Gray, anvil shaped clouds swept across the sky, and the wind, formerly non-existent, whipped the sand into a frenzy. Clouds of red dust surrounded Angie's MUV, forcing her to reduce her speed to a crawl. The

GPS, coated in a layer of grime, told her she'd travelled only ten miles. Unbelievable. She had waited three long months for the weather to be perfect. February was much warmer than January, and the forecast was for sunny skies for the entire week. Where was the sun? And was that thunder?

A crack of lightning ripped across the sky, making the hair on the back of her neck stand up. That was close—too close. Aside from the occasional pine tree, the vehicle was the tallest thing on the surface of the canyon. Open to the elements, she'd be soaked in minutes when the sky opened up. She had to find shelter. Now.

The dust ebbed. A structure appeared, then disappeared. She shook her head and wiped her visor. The windscreen was covered with crap. She stopped the MUV, got out and peered ahead. A small cottage nestled in the distance in a field far below her. After wiping the windshield, Angie hopped back into the driver's seat and headed toward the house. If she could reach it before the rain started, she'd be fine.

Lightning crackled around her and struck a nearby pine. Flames shot up from the tree.

She swore and pressed the vehicle onward. The wind howled and rain began pelting her, soaking through her thermal underwear.

Angie shivered and prayed the person who owned the home would let her in. Would it be too much to ask for a fire to warm her up?

Rain pelted the sun-hardened ground. Where once had been parched terrain, water now rippled across it, carrying along gravel, mud and debris. She struggled to keep control of the vehicle, but the cargo behind her slipped and slid, fighting her every twist and turn. She might as well have been driving on black ice in Baltimore. The rain became a wall, obscuring her vision and bombarding her with cold hard pellets. Was that hail? In Mexico? The weather gods mocked her. If she could keep control of the MUV a little longer, she was positive she'd make it to the cabin. Just then the sky lit up again and her world went black.

****

Alejandro grabbed the list of supplies and equipment he'd been stockpiling for the rescue expedition and conducted a quick inventory. A shit load of stuff was missing.

Damn it.

Angie must have been planning this stunt for weeks, maybe even months. He should have seen it coming, should have known she'd try something like this. She'd been too friendly. Every morning she'd shown up in his office, coffee cup in hand and asked what the game plan was for the day. Not only had he given her every detail of his preparations, he'd also shown her maps, GPS coordinates, and all the potential problems with each approach. He had looked forward to each morning of working alongside her just so he could hear her husky voice, smell her scent, and feel her feathery "accidental" touches on his hands, shoulders, and neck.

He'd been conned.

He should have known she was planning something. The day she'd asked about destroying her father's compound should have been a red flag to him. Lulled by her beauty, mesmerized by her quick mind and rare laughter, he'd given her every answer. Were there clues he missed in her questions?

He closed his eyes and tried to recall each detail of that morning. She'd leaned over his shoulder, the strands of her long red hair brushing the back of his neck. The scent of her shampoo mixed with an undercurrent of her own essence had given him an instant hard on. He slid his chair further under the desk to hide his growing erection and struggled to maintain control of his voice when her warm breath caressed his ear.

"Give me something *bigger*."

Had she known he was about to burst out of his pants? Had she seen his hands shake when he moved the mouse to zoom the satellite map? Attempting to take deep slow breaths, he'd pointed to the monitor and shown her the outlines of the wind mills and solar panels that powered Edmondsville.

With her cheek close to his face, he felt her heat pulsing against his brow. She whispered, "Why can't we blow these up, throw them into panic and confusion?"

"That's part of the plan." He cleared his throat, his voice thick. "We'll do that *after* we have Jake."

"What will we use?"

"C4."

Alejandro covered his face with his hands. Two bricks of C4 and a bunch of detonators were missing. She could blow herself up before she even had the chance to use it against her father.

Dogging his every step, asking a million questions, Angie had been all over him for the last three months. She never wrote anything down.

Now he realized she didn't need paper and pen. As

an attorney, she'd probably memorized an entire library for law school. This whole expedition was locked into her brain. And she'd taken enough supplies to last a month in the wilderness. If the C4 or her father's goons didn't kill her, he'd kill Angie himself—if he found her.

Anxious to get going, he grabbed meals ready to eat, MREs and bottles of liquid protein off the metal shelves and ran scenarios through his mind. It wasn't as if he could have her tracked by her cell phone. Coverage in many areas of Mexico was spotty on a good day. In the remote Copper Canyon areas, she was completely off the grid.

He spotted the untouched satellite phone charging on the workbench and decided to add that to the bag, but his hands were full of bottles of concentrated protein drinks. He jammed them into his pockets any which way he could for the time being. Alejandro packed the mobile phone into its carry case and prayed the thirty-six hour standby and four-hour talk times were true. He had no idea where or when he'd find her. Again, if he found her.

The thought stopped him cold. Don't go there. Don't even think about the possibility that she might be captured by her father. Or blown up. Or kidnapped and sold into a Mexican brothel. The thought of the beautiful, proud redhead enslaved like poor Natasha and forced to parade around naked in front of filthy pigs—

Someone grabbed his shoulder.

Alejandro whirled and punched the intruder on the jaw.

The giant staggered back and shouted, "Stop. It's me, your buddy, Tio."

"Shit." Alejandro shook his hand. "I think I broke my hand on your face."

"You're jumpy as a crack head." The big man gazed at him with a puzzled expression. "What's the matter, bro?"

"I'm worried about Angie. She took C4 and detonators with her." Alejandro shook his head. "Pissed I missed all the signs. I should have known, should have prevented this."

"*No Manches!* Don't say that, man. You a mind reader?"

"No, but—"

"But, nothing." The big bald guy lowered his voice. "I know you've got a thing for her. It's cool. I can live with it. Maybe you can get in her pants. I sure couldn't."

"It's not like that." Even as the words fell out of his mouth, Alejandro knew he was lying, and worse yet, sounded like an idiot.

Tio's eyes widened. "Holy shit. You're really sweet on her."

"Maybe." His lowered his eyes, and his voice choked up. "Yeah. A little."

"*Compadre*, that's screwed up. You can't go getting involved like that. It's no good in our business."

Alejandro shrugged. "I know." *It's bad for the undercover ATFE business, too.*

"What will you do if that *cabrón*, her asshole father, has her?"

Alejandro raised an eyebrow. "What would *you* do?"

"I'd bury him up to his neck in the desert and let the buzzards eat his head for breakfast, lunch, and dinner."

"I'll keep that in mind. Right now, I've got to finish packing. Since you're here, you can help. Whatever guns you'd take on this trip, that's what I want."

Tio's eyes lit up. "How much room you got?"

"Not enough for a rocket launcher. I need to travel light." He pointed at his ride. "I'm taking an ATV and whatever I can strap down behind me."

"Then you need the same as Angie—a Remington and a Glock."

"*Bueno.*" Alejandro turned toward the duffle bag and stopped. "And, I'm really sorry I punched you in the face."

"You surprised me, that's all." Tio rubbed his jaw and gave Alejandro an odd look. "Funny. You don't hit like an accountant."

"It was a reflex. I was all wound up, worrying about Angie."

"Yeah, sure. One thing."

"What?"

"You *ever* hit me like that again, friend or not, I'll kill you."

Time froze and Alejandro locked gazes with the big man. Tio wasn't joking. Fuck. He was *supposed* to be a computer nerd, a dishonorably discharged Green Beret and technogeek, with minimal military or martial arts training. All his training with guns, he had told Tio and Pepe, had come from working alongside drug dealers in the US. The big men had laughed and tousled his hair like a kid and treated him like a mascot.

Dammit to hell. Had he just blown his cover with that stupid knee jerk reaction? The Glock tucked into his waistband burned the flesh of his back like a red-hot poker, and sweat trickled between his balls. Could he get to the gun before the big man reached his shoulder holster? He held his breath. *Don't flinch, don't give him any reason to shoot you.*

Tio pointed at Alejandro and burst out laughing. "I really had you going, bro."

Alejandro blew out a huge breath and gave a shaky laugh. "Ha. Yeah, you sure did."

Still laughing, the giant ambled toward the house. "Wait till I tell the guys I made you piss your pants."

Alejandro looked down at his crotch. It was soaked. He reached into his pocket and pulled out an empty plastic bottle. Somehow, the top of a protein drink had come off—and saved his life.

Chapter Fourteen

A thick quilt of silence enveloped Angie. Alert and pain free, she opened her eyes and watched the earth fall away beneath her. A charred pine tree smoked near the overturned MUV. Rose quartz gray clouds whipped themselves into a frenzy and pelted the vehicle and a white clad figure with rain drops the size of golf balls.

Her body. Her corpse. Oh shit. *Dead again.*

Not only had she failed to reach the cabin, she'd managed to kill herself in the process.

What would become of Jake? Would Alejandro still try to rescue him? Or would Isabel call off the mission? Dammit. She'd *really* screwed up this time.

Or had she? Maybe she was just having a terrible dream. Or hallucinating. After all, hadn't she been raised on a steady diet of hellfire and brimstone, laced with a side order of toxic threats?

Get it together, woman. Every time she had a physical injury, it seemed her mind flipped out to the dark side of crazy. Hadn't the same thing happened when Jake was born?

She'd done the research. Pregnancy hormones mixed with hypoxia from loss of blood had caused massive delusions, not an out of body experience. Neurons firing randomly, creating images so vivid, she thought they were real. Just like her father with his freaking temporal lobe seizures and "visions" of God.

That's all it was. In a bit, she'd come to, be a bit battered, but ready for action. She pinched herself.

Felt nothing.

Pinched again and watched her fingers pass through her wrist and reappear on the other side.

Deep breaths. Don't get all freaked out. You'll wake up, you always wake up.

She might as well relax and play along with the hallucination.

Okay, let's see where this one went. Demons or angels? Which would her addled neurochemistry conjure up this time?

She strained her eyes, searching for the long, dark corridor in the vast sea of white clouds. Come on. She couldn't hang out here all day. She had to get back to work, back to her mission, back to saving her son's life. She spotted a dark swirl up ahead and began walking toward it. The spinning hole in the white clouds grew into a tunnel. Now they were getting somewhere.

Where was the angel? It was her hallucination. She was in control of it. He had to be around here somewhere. She'd find him and strike a deal. Her life for Jake's. Send her back long enough to rescue her son, get him to safety. Then she'd die. Maybe that would jolt her back to reality.

At the end of the black tunnel, a blinding light shone. About time he showed up. It felt as if she'd been waiting for hours. A large figure emerged between the darkness and the light. She watched as his huge white wings unfurled before her. And more wings. And more wings. And still more wings, so many wings she lost count. Against her better judgment, she felt her jaw go slack. This was not the same hallucination she'd had before.

This creature burned like a pillar of fire, yet was not consumed. Sparks flew off this delusional being and thunderclouds whirled around him. And he was gigantic, taller than any tree she'd ever seen. She felt like an ant must feel around humans. Something was very wrong.

Rather than being elated by his presence, she was terrified. This could *not* be good. Who was he? Did she smell sulfur? Had she fallen into hell instead of heaven? Was this fiery being Satan? Or was it one of his demonic minions?

Feet frozen in place, her heart competed with her lungs to escape from her constricted chest. She wished she were dead. No. Yes. Well, perhaps technically she *was* dead. Was there something worse than death and was it coming for her now?

Blazed into his chest was the Tetragammaton, Yod, He, Waw and He, or YHWH, four letters in Hebrew that indicated God's divine name. She racked her brains, trying to recall her father's endless sermons and exhortations on demons and angelic beings. Why hadn't she paid better attention? She should *know* this hallucination by name.

The creature roared. "Why have you rejected my gift? I sent you one who would save you, yet you abandoned him."

Her heart dropped from her throat to where her stomach had once been. She struggled to cling to her attachment to reality, to the thoughts that tethered her to earth. And lost the battle.

She was beyond dead. She was in deep shit.

But what did she have to lose? Ears ringing, eyes filled with tears, she shouted into the tempest of his wrath, "I didn't reject my son or abandon him. I know he's special. Jake was *stolen* from me. If you're truly an angel, you'd *know* that."

"How dare you speak to me in that way?"

The flaming pillar grew before her eyes. She shielded her face from the blaze.

"How dare you say I rejected my child?" She stomped her foot. "And get down here. I will not negotiate with someone I can't see eye to eye."

Thunder rumbled.

"You wish to stare at my face?" He popped down to her size and stepped next to her. The flames died down around him, and he flicked a few final embers off his wings. Up close, he was younger than she thought. And he was laughing.

His name flashed into her mind and she fell to her knees.

"Metatron."

"Exchange not Yahweh for me. Arise that we may speak."

She stood and faced the Lord's messenger. "Forgive me. I've had a bad day. I didn't recognize you." She knew she sounded like a dolt. It was her world, her creation, her hallucination.

But, on the off chance he was real, what did one say to God's envoy? To the being who spoke through another predicting the great flood and the end of the world? The one who saved Isaac from his father's knife? To the angel who sat with Moses as he lay dying?

He laughed again. "You have many questions."

She stared at him. Had he read her mind?

"Yes, I can hear your thoughts and see what's in your heart." He took her oh so pale hand in his large dark one. "Walk with me."

****

Alejandro pushed his ATV up the hill as fast as he dared on the slick surface. If he got hurt, it wouldn't help Angie. The storm had lashed him for the last twenty miles, and his hands cramped from the effort of staying upright and on track. Thunder rumbled, but this time it was further away. He crested the hill, looked down and spotted the wrecked MUV. His heart lurched.

From this angle, he couldn't tell if she was inside. Was she safe? Had she made it to the cabin at the bottom of the hill? He couldn't bear the thought of losing another person he cared about. He bit his bottom lip and took a deep breath. *God, if you really exist, please let her be okay.* He cranked the throttle and pushed onward until he came alongside the other vehicle.

Thrown onto the roll bar and captured by the safety net, Angie lay on her side, motionless. Drenched and splattered with mud, her white thermal underwear afforded her no protection, but at least she still had her helmet on.

Alejandro removed his headgear, leaped off the ATV, and raced to her side. He'd have to care for her here. It wasn't as if he could call 9-1-1 or summon a Medivac.

"Angie, it's Alejandro. Can you hear me?"

No response.

"I have to pull you out of the vehicle so I can help you. Say something, anything, please. Can you move a finger?"

No response.

Limp-limbed, her shoulders weighed heavy in his hands. He pulled her out of the vehicle and lay her alongside the MUV. Failing to find a pulse in her wrist, he placed his middle finger under her jaw and held his breath.

Nothing, no, dear Lord, that couldn't be. He took another deep breath and pressed against her cold skin. There it was. Weak, thready, the beat was erratic—but it was there. The helmet had to come off so he could do an assessment. Taking great care not to jostle her neck, he folded his waterproof jacket and slid it under her neck. Then he removed the damaged, but not shattered headgear.

He sucked in his breath. Bloody abrasions stood out against her pale cheeks, and blue bruises bloomed on her forehead. Without a hospital or CT scanner, he'd have to rely on his powers of observation and his first aid training. No penetrating head trauma. No shards of plastic stuck out of her skin. He pried her eyes open and to his immense relief, the pupils in her beautiful green eyes reacted to light.

She exhaled and moaned. "Mmmph."

His heart leaped in his throat. Incomprehensible speech was better than none.

"Angie, speak to me baby."

She sighed, moaned, and went silent. He hated the next step, but he had to do it. Alejandro rolled up her sleeve and pinched her tender inner arm. She blinked and twitched. Good, she was in there somewhere; he just needed to help her find her way back.

First, he had to move her inside the cabin, get her

warm before hypothermia could finish off what the accident had started. The only thing that seemed to be a possibility for a transport board was her one-piece insulated suit. He slid it under her one limb at time, dragged her to the cabin, and stopped at the steps. Supporting her head and neck, he reached under her legs, lifted, and kicked the door open to the empty cabin.

****

She floated alongside Metatron. This was even weirder than her last so-called angelic encounter. A pillar of fire, three dozen wings, thunderstorms and whirlwinds. Last time the trauma of childbirth had been responsible for her hallucinations. But this one was a doozy. She must *really* have head trauma.

"I'm not a dream. Or a vision from your injuries." His voice rumbled and resonated in her chest.

"I told you, my son was kidnapped. Why can't you let me die *after* I rescue him?"

Sparks flew from his head. "Don't be like Lilith. She thought she could do everything herself, too."

"What is it I should be doing? Tell me. I'll do *anything* to save my son." Why wasn't he listening to her?

"Have you heard the story of the man who heard a flood was coming? The water rose, and police came to take him to safety. He refused to go, said he was waiting for a sign from the Lord. The water covered the lands and as he sat on his roof, a boat came by and offered to take him away. He refused again, saying he was waiting for a sign. A helicopter came next. Yet he still refused, waiting for a sign from the Lord."

"And?"

"He drowned. When the man appeared before the Lord, he chastised the Divine One for not sending him a sign. Yahweh said, 'I sent you warnings, police, a boat and a helicopter. Those *were* my signs, you stubborn fool.'"

She stopped and stared at God's messenger. A white feather fluttered down from his uppermost wing. It landed on her arm and stung her skin.

"Ouch." She jerked away.

Metatron gave her an indulgent look. "I am here for one reason and one reason only. To help you and your son, who is *very* special. Your son has powers handed down from generations of healers in his father's family. YAHWEH has added to and amplified these powers. He truly is the Chosen One as prophesized. Not in the Book of Enoch, but elsewhere, in yet to be discovered scrolls."

"My father is going to be so pissed when he finds out he was wrong."

Metatron roared with laughter. "That one has many things wrong." His expression became somber. "He misleads many on a dangerous path. I have more important matters to discuss with you. I bring you a message from the Divine One."

This is a hallucination. Don't get emotional.

Still, she blinked away tears. Jake. First and foremost, she had to save her baby.

"Please tell me my son will be rescued."

He dropped her hand. "Sometimes you need a deputy angel, sometimes you need a warrior, and sometimes you need both."

Thunder rumbled in the distance and lightning sparked off his head. Thirty-six wings flapped in unison, created a windstorm, and pushed her away. She reached out to grab his hand and missed. Angie fell to her knees and began to slide backward down a slippery slope. Even though it was a dream, a delusion, panic filled her chest.

"No, don't go," she shrieked. "I want you on my side."

"YAHWEH breathed life into you. His blessings abound in and around you. Your son is a healer, your children will sing the Lord's praises. You have all the strength and help you need."

Metatron disappeared, but his booming voice remained.

"See with your heart and not your head."

The sharp grade became a silent cyclone, its force sucking Angie down to earth and pulling her back into her body. Utter panic overtook her. She had to go back, had to make a deal with an angel, had to save her son. The silence was torn asunder by the force of a booming voice, oh dear God, was it Metatron? Was he real? Had he come back?

"Angie?"

She blinked and looked into the dark eyes of her deputy angel.

****

"There you are." Relief streamed through his muscles and tingled his fingers and toes. Tears sprang to his eyes. "You scared the crap out of me."

Angie blinked rapidly, then licked her lips. "How long?"

"I'm guessing you've been out about four to six hours. You had a good head start on me." He stroked her hair and gazed at her long lashes, upturned nose, and sprinkling of freckles. Where had the bruises and abrasions gone?

"Can you move your fingers?"

She withdrew her hands from the blanket and waved at him. She stopped, glanced down, and her eyebrows shot up. "Um. You're in bed with me."

Elbow crooked, he placed his cheek on his hand. "You had hypothermia. I started a fire, but it wasn't warming you fast enough."

"Am I naked?"

"Your clothes were drenched."

"Are you naked?"

He'd been so worried about her while she was unconscious, all thoughts of sex had flown out of his mind. With Angie awake and alert, however, his little head had woken up and was attempting to burst out of his boxer shorts.

"Not completely."

"That's too bad."

Alejandro pulled back and stared at her. What was the punch line? Was she about to knee him in the balls? "Pardon?"

She smiled, pulled his head down, and whispered, "Make love to me."

Alejandro rolled out of the bed and backed up to the roaring fire. "Bad idea."

Her gaze fell on his groin. "You're pointing at me. I think that means you want me." She dropped the blanket, exposing her large breasts. They were even more luscious than he'd imagined. Rose colored nipples pointed back at him. "Come back to bed. I want to show you my appreciation for saving my life."

His big head fought with his little one. "You've

had a traumatic experience. You probably have a head injury. I think you need to get your rest."

"I've never felt better."

Keeping the blanket wrapped around her waist, she stood and walked in front of him. The fire reflected flecks of blue in her green eyes and sparked copper highlights in her hair. A white aura surrounded her.

He rubbed his eyes, convinced it was a trick of the lighting. What happened to her bruises, abrasions, and scratches? It was as if she'd been healed while he dozed beside her. She licked her full red lips and dropped the blanket.

Months of training had given her rock hard abs and muscular legs. Nestled between her ivory thighs was a triangle of red hair that commanded his attention.

"I've been celibate for two long years. I almost died, had the weirdest freaking dreams I've ever had in my life, and I feel as if I'm more alive than I've been in years. I want you to lick and suck my tits and make love to me until I pass out. Then start over again when I wake up." She reached down and rubbed his crotch. I want you, no I *need* you to make love to me. Now."

Angie grabbed his buttocks and pulled him to her, pushing her groin against his. She rubbed her hard nipples on his chest and whispered, "Doesn't this feel good?"

He could hardly breathe, much less speak.

She ran her hand inside his boxers and seized his throbbing cock. Running her fingers first around the moist head, then up and down the shaft, her nimble hand turned his brains to pudding. A miasma of desire enveloped him. His attention zeroed in on the feeling of her hands on him, her floral scent mixed with a musky female smell, and the sound of his heart pounding. He wanted her more than he'd ever wanted a woman before in his life. She had nearly died and the only thing she wanted now was for him to make love to her. How could he refuse?

He grabbed her shoulders, pulled her close, and slanted his mouth over hers. She tasted like honey and milk. How was that possible? He brushed aside the thought and ran his hands across her back, pulling her even closer, pressing her nipples into his chest, as if he could burn their image onto his flesh like a tattoo. He wanted to touch her soft skin and bury himself inside her until he blacked out from exhaustion. Years of training kicked in. He stopped kissing her and pulled away.

"I don't want to take advantage of you."

She pulled him back, curving her long luscious body against his. Their bodies fit together, jigsaw puzzle pieces carved to perfection. "Sure I'm not taking advantage of you?"

Dizzy with lust, he abandoned logic and returned her ardor. He turned her around, putting her back to the fire, and knelt at her feet. Spreading her legs slightly apart, he nuzzled her silky triangle with quick licks and nips.

She giggled. "Your beard tickles."

Alejandro growled, pulled her wet center to his face and ran his tongue along her folds, grazing her bud as if by accident, teasing her. Moaning, she dug her fingers into his hair and pulled his head tighter in an attempt to force him to lap at her button. Just as she was about to come, he stood, lifted her by the waist and set her on the bed. "One moment."

A red condom from *El Harén* flew to the floor when he scrabbled in his wallet.

Her eyes widened and she grinned. "Emergency rations?"

"I never leave home without one."

She straddled his lap, her milk white breasts and hard nipples begging for his kisses. Mind-reading, she pulled his head to her and whispered, her breath teasing his neck and ear.

"Suck them."

Suddenly ravenous, Alejandro fell on one, then the other breast, alternating between them, sucking, holding one nipple in his teeth, pulling the other with his fingers. She clutched his head, ground her molten center against his hardening cock and moaned. He wasn't the only hungry person in the room. Angie was starving for her child and for love.

She pushed him on his back and began kissing his neck, chest, and belly. She worked her way down with nips between kisses. His skin tingled and his little head danced with anticipation. When she arrived at his penis, he heard a gasp.

"Oh. So. Big."

"That a problem?"

"Not at all."

And as the thought of where he would put that throbbing rod entered his head, she ran her sharp nails down the side of his cock and across his balls. "Oh. My. God."

"You like?"

"I *like*." A rose color suffused her pale skin like a canvas. He couldn't believe he was having sex with this smart, sassy, beautiful woman. If only it could be more than a one-night stand. A pipedream. He'd savor the moment, enjoy every second, and keep this experience in his memories to warm him on long cold nights when she was gone from his life. His chest tightened at the thought of losing her. His job, her son, what would become of them? This obsession, no matter how wonderful, would not, could not, ever hold up in the light of day.

He gasped as she put the condom on the head of his penis, and then unrolled it all the way down to base of his thickened shaft with her ever-so-slow-dancing fingers. His cock stood at attention and saluted. She was *killing* him. And he'd die a happy man.

She rolled on top of his belly and hovered over him.

"Wait." He feathered his fingers up her inner thighs and slid a finger across her inner, then outer lips, and she gasped. Angie threw her head back when his finger grazed her rock hard bud. Using slow, gentle strokes, as if he was calming a frightened kitten, he brought her to the brink of orgasm and stopped—again and again. Just as it appeared she was about to come, he pulled her down on his raging hard-on deep within, filling her hot core with his wishes, hopes, and prayers that this wonderful feeling would last forever.

Chapter Fifteen

Angie woke up with a start, rolled over in the cramped bed and stared at the sleeping man beside her. Where was she? How did she get here? What the hell had she done? *Think, woman.*

She'd been on the MUV, trying to get to the cabin to get out of the rain. The tires had skidded and the vehicle had gone into a one-eighty. The next thing she knew, she was reliving her near-death hallucination, complete with strange apparitions, only weirder. The tunnel was the same, but the "angel" was a pillar of flames with a booming, ear-pounding voice.

Unlike the first angel, who was mute, this one had talked up a storm, *literally*. Yet she had no recollection of what he said. The next thing she knew, she was awake, bursting with energy, euphoric, and horny as a cat in heat. After a night of passion that would make a sex addict run for rehab, she had passed out from exhaustion. Now here she was, naked, reeking of sex, in bed with a drug lord.

She eyed Alejandro as he slept. Not *again*. The last time she'd hooked up with a drug dealer, he'd shown her the joys of coke. *Yeah, that had been a great decision, right?* What she needed to do was get the hell away from this man. Fast.

Unsafe at any speed, this guy revved her engines in

all the old ways. If he hadn't been key to getting her son back, she'd be out that door and running away screaming right now. A tendril of black hair curled over his eyes, making him look childlike. How could a cartel thug look so innocent, not to mention desirable? A thin wool blanket covered him from the waist down, exposing a sprinkling of chest hair, cut pecs, hard abs, and that intriguing scar. She wanted him again. Bad. She flopped her head back on the pillow and whispered, "I am so screwed."

Alejandro rumbled beside her. "Any time, babe. Any time."

The hand hewn ceiling beams bore the marks of years of cooking fires and wood smoke. If she squinted, she could make out animal shapes in the swirls. She sighed. "Was it good for you, too?"

He popped up next to her and stared down at her, bewilderment on his face. "*Good*? No, it wasn't 'good,' it was *supernatural*. You were the goddess of love, and I was your supreme worshipper."

"I think I lost my mind last night." Guilt ripped at her heart with its talons, and a tear trickled down the side of her face. She pounded the bed with her fist. "After everything I went through with Jake, I *swore* I would never sleep with another man until I was in a stable relationship."

He flopped back on the pillow beside her.

"Oh. Shit."

"Yeah."

His hand reached for hers, and she pulled away. Angie tried not to think of the touch of his lips on her breasts and the feel of him buried deep inside her, thrusting his way into her heart. *Stop thinking about that part of him.* This was the definition of insanity.

"Now what?"

"I don't know. I was kinda hoping for a repeat of last night. You, me, we were awesome. You inspired me to new heights of imagination. You were incredible."

"Thanks for the five-star review." She suppressed a sob, but it came out like a laugh.

He cleared his throat. "You don't think we should have an encore performance? See if you change your mind?"

"We can't do *this* ever again. I'm sorry. I wasn't thinking about anything or anyone except me and what I wanted last night. I was out of my mind."

And you're a narcoterrorista lord, she thought. But if I say that, you might not be happy. You might decide I'm better off headless, like Raul.

Alejandro sat up and locked gazes with her. "When I found you, you were almost dead. Hypothermic, thready pulse, lots of bruises, abrasions, and blood." He shrugged and held up his palms. "I started a fire, got in bed with you because you were still corpse cold. I dozed off and woke up to you screaming."

"What was I saying?"

"Meta-something, don't go, I need you."

She chewed her lip. "I don't remember that at all."

"Do you remember asking me to make love to you?"

Heat flashed over her entire body, and her traitorous nipples pebbled. Her voice came out low and husky. "Yes."

"Your cuts and bruises disappeared, like magic." Alejandro nuzzled her neck and brushed her belly with a soft caress. "You remember this?"

Her thighs quivered and heat pooled in her core. "We shouldn't." She tried to push his hand away, but he thrust it between her legs and flicked her nub until she arched her back and moaned.

"You were radiant. You looked like your name. My angel, my Angela." He whispered, "I want to make love to you until you can't walk straight." His fingers stroked her slick lips and pinched her tingling nub. "Tell me you don't want that, too."

His erection poked at her thigh, begging for her fingers to grasp it. She dug her nails into the palm of her hand. "I. Don't. Want. You."

"Liar." He kissed her neck, her throat, her collarbone. "Lovely, lovely liar." He raised his head, looked her straight in the eye and said, "Tell me not to make love to you, and I'll never touch you again."

Just as Angie opened her mouth, someone pounded at the door and shouted, "*Ayuda, ayuda, por favor*. For the love of God, help us!"

****

Alejandro leaped to his feet, pulled on his pants and grabbed his Glock. He put his fingers to his lips and motioned to Angie to get away from the door. She gathered up her dry clothes and hopped on one foot then the other to pull on her pants and boots.

He cracked the door open and choked back a laugh. What was a *nun* doing here?

"I know you're not the owner of this cabin," the nun spouted in Spanish. "And the Raramuri," she turned and pointed to the cluster of six native men standing in a silent semi-circle behind her "are horrified that I knocked on the door, think I'll raise ghosts, but we've been sitting out here since sunrise, hoping you'd come out and invite us in." She took a breath. "We don't have time to stand on formalities. There are lives at stake."

"Sister—"

"Teresa. I run the boarding school and orphanage over the ridge."

"How did you find us?"

Sister Teresa frowned. "The Tarahumara have eyes and ears all over this countryside. Besides, you left your expensive toys lying around outside."

He glanced over his shoulder. Angie was dressed. She raised her eyebrows and shrugged, perplexed as he was. "Please come in, Sister Teresa."

"This is all my fault. I made a terrible mistake, and God help me, I have to make things right." The short woman stomped into the cabin, nodded at Angie, and fired her next barrage at Alejandro. "I let the girls go with those women, they said they had good jobs for them, they'd send money to me for safekeeping, and the girls would come home to visit every month. It's been three months, we haven't seen a peso, and more importantly, we haven't seen the girls. Now Mina's father is missing, too. Something is terribly wrong."

"Let's back this up a bit." He put his hand on his chest. "I'm Alejandro Espinosa Santoyo Torres." He pointed at his lovely liar. "This is Angie Edmonds."

The nun's face turned beet red and whirled on Angie. "Edmonds? That crazy preacher and his wife? Are you in on this with them?"

Alejandro jumped between the nun and Angie. "Not on your life. Take a deep breath. Start from the beginning and speak *slowly* so I can translate for

186

Angie." Visibly shaking, Sister Teresa eyed Angie with suspicion, but started over again, beginning with the day Miriam and Sister Anne arrived at the little village and ending with the disappearance of Mina's father, Juan. "He wanted to see his daughter, so he went there two weeks ago. It's twenty miles away from our village, over rugged terrain, but not a problem for a runner like Juan. He could have made the journey there and back in a few days. He never returned. It's not like him. He wouldn't go that long without letting his family know *something*."

"And who are these other people?" Alejandro pointed out the door at the group of dark-skinned men wearing white loincloths, colorful shirts, and denim jackets. Three of the little men sat on the porch in silence and stared at him, while two inspected the overturned MUV. The youngest one in the group bounced on the seat of the ATV and made *vroom-vroom* noises.

"Those are representatives of the *ejiditarios.* The girls who went to work in Edmondsville weren't *all* orphans. The Tarahumara take care of their own. They're here with me to ask for your help."

"Did you go to the *federales*?"

The nun gave a mirthless laugh. "Pah. The government is no friend of these people. It's been robbing the Tarahumara for centuries, stealing their land, lumber and minerals. The *federales* wish these natives would give up their old ways of life and disappear."

Alejandro shook his head. "What makes you think I can do anything for you?"

Sister Teresa tapped her foot, put her fists on her

hip, and addressed him as if he were a slow student. "You're a *narcotraficante, si*?"

"Why do you say that?"

The nun held up three fingers and counted off. "*Uno*, you are not from around here. *Dos*, you are not *federales*. *Tres*, with those expensive ATVs, that leaves a *capo* from a cartel."

He bit his lower lip. "I work for Isabel Ramirez."

"Senora Ramirez is in charge of Chihuahua, not the government, not the police. Your boss has men, guns, power. If her gang can't get our girls back, no one can."

Angie grabbed his arm. "Ask her what the girls were hired to do."

Alejandro translated, and the nun looked surprised. "Why nannies, of course, they said they had a lot of little children to care for."

Angie shook her head. "There aren't any children. The followers all take a vow of celibacy. The only one allowed to—" her eyes grew wide, and her face became so pale her freckles stood out in three dimension. "My mother took the girls to have sex with my father and get them pregnant." She turned her back to the little nun and whispered to Alejandro. "They're the Mothers of the Twenty-Four."

****

Angie reeled in shock as she processed Sister Teresa's story. Her *mother* did this, not her father. Sister Anne was a puppet, a mindless drone for her parents. A mousy woman with no spine and an overwhelming need to please her preacher. She would have moved heaven and earth to find just the right group of girls for the Mothers of the Twenty-Four. She could just imagine Anne's simpering expression as she told Angie's mother about the "perfect candidates." But the lackey wouldn't have had the ability to con this nun into willingly handing the girls over. That required finesse and cunning. That task needed someone who could tell a convincing story using pious words and demeanor. Her mother could play any role her father chose for her. The woman had called the daycare center and pretended to be Angie, hadn't she?

There was no doubt in Angie's mind that her mother had lied to the nun about jobs, promised her money and recruited those girls. Why not play recruiter? Her stomach turned. No, her mother hadn't recruited those innocent teenagers. Her mother had *enslaved* them. What else had her mother done for Angie's father? How deep would her depravity reach so she could please her husband? Or was she in it for her *own* motives now? And what did that mean for the "Chosen One?" Stop. He was her grandchild. She *loved* Jake. She would *never* harm him. Or would she?

"Angie?" Alejandro grabbed her shoulders and looked into her face. "You okay? Talk to me."

The nun stepped outside to speak to the waiting Tarahumara.

"I feel sick to my stomach."

"You haven't eaten. I have some food in my pack."

She accepted the food bar and chugged the bottle of protein liquid. "Ack. This is vile."

"Sorry. It was the best I could find on short notice." He gave her a meaningful stare.

She ignored his pointed reference to her ill-timed rescue attempt. "They're moving faster than I thought they would."

"Meaning?"

"When I was pregnant and held captive on the farm, he and Brother Aaron spent hours after dinner each night planning every detail of their new fortress. My bedroom was right over the dining room. My father built the place himself, so there was no insulation between the first and second story. I found a knot in the floorboard, pried it out, and eavesdropped on their plans."

"And?"

"Aaron and a thousand followers were to sell all of their belongings and convert everything to gold. In their apocalyptic reasoning, they figured that even if all the governments fell and currency was toilet paper, gold would still have value."

Alejandro' eyebrows shot up. "So your question to that follower wasn't a red herring to gain Isabel's cooperation?"

She shook her head. "Instead of gold bullion, they had a jewelry maker, one of their congregation, manufacture thin sheets of gold for people to *wear* out of the country. It was the easiest way to get it across the border."

"The gold could be hidden on anyone in the compound."

"No way would my father allow people to keep their gold. He would have collected it as soon as they entered the compound."

"And buried it?"

"No. My father's thinks he's so clever, it would amuse him to hide it in the open where he could keep an eye on it. He'd snicker to himself about how no one else knew it was right under their noses."

"What's this have to do with the missing girls?"

"Aaron was supposed to build Edmondsville, bring the followers, and prepare for the arrival of the Chosen One. My father said it would take two years of isolation and lack of contacts from the external world for the community to be 'cohesive'. Then they'd find the Mothers of the Twenty-Four and bring them into the fold. With a thousand brainwashed cult followers making certain they didn't escape, the women would have no choice but to surrender themselves and their babies. "

"He really *is* as bad as Jim Jones."

"Worse." She threw the empty bottle into her duffle. "Did you find my weapons and bring them in?"

"Yes. Why?"

"We're going to need those and lots more. Now that he has the Mothers of the Twenty-Four, the stakes are even higher. An ex-sheriff has trained a group of followers to be my father's bodyguards. My guess is they have orders to kill if anyone tries to escape from Edmondsville."

"This is getting way too complicated. I'm calling Isabel." He plucked the satellite phone out of its carrying case. "Wonder how your father's goons would hold out against a group of former Mexican Army elite forces?"

"Who are you talking about?"

"Tio and Pepe. They may look big and dumb, but they were in the military. Taught all of Isabel's guys. They're disciplined, tough, good in urban or desert warfare—but not familiar with caves and cliffs. This terrain isn't part of their training."

Angie chewed on her lower lip and glanced out the open door. With her stiff bearing and grim expression,

Sister Teresa looked like a general addressing her troops.

The short, sinewy Tarahumara stared at her with frowns creasing their dark faces. From everything she'd read and heard, they were a peaceful people who just wanted to be left alone and keep their ancient ways of life.

Nevertheless, with Sister Teresa and God on their side, this group was riled up enough to try to get the Crime Queen of Chihuahua involved. An idea began to coalesce in the back of her brain. Would Alejandro go along with it?

"When you call your boss, ask her if she'd like to have God on her side."

Finger poised to hit the send button, Alejandro stared at Angie. "She's the *least* religious person I know."

"Let me rephrase the question. How would she like to have some cave dwelling allies who know the nooks and crannies better than anyone else?"

He followed her gaze out the door. "Holy shit."

"That nun came to you because she knew you had clout. She called you a *capo*. It's not as if she's harboring any illusions about who you are or what you do for a living. She knows you're one of the bosses in Isabel's organization. Sister Teresa may be working for God's agenda, but she's nobody's fool. She wanted help from the most powerful person in Chihuahua. "

Alejandro nodded. "Queen Isabel."

"For her, like me, the ends justified the means. Sister Teresa is willing to make a deal with the devil to get those girls back. What would you say if we asked those men to join forces with us and become our scouts? They know the terrain better than anyone else and can move around without stirring up too much interest, unlike us with our 'expensive toys.'"

Alejandro grinned and hit the send button. "I'd say we're about to help them serve up a nice cold dish of Tarahumara revenge."

Chapter Sixteen

Miriam walked toward the Crèche, glanced up and down the hallway, and peeked into the cleft where she'd hidden the stupid native. Once she'd taken care of him with the Disciplinarian, she hadn't had much time to dispose of his body. Riddled with crevices and fissures, the wall of the cave solved that problem for her. Wedged behind a huge boulder, his small body had fit nicely into the tiny space. With the change of seasons and this sudden humidity and heat wave, the man was getting ripe. She had to move him, before Father found out.

He'd never really forgiven her for beating Janice to death with a shovel. He'd been most emphatic that she was not to kill anyone ever again, *unless* Zeke's life was at stake. Little did Father know, but the very existence of the community had been in danger, and she'd done the right thing. But, just in case he didn't see it that way, she had to get rid of their stinking guest. Where was that dumb cow, Sister Anne, when she needed her?

As if on cue, the very person Miriam was thinking about appeared in the hallway, walking toward her.

"Mother, how are you doing?"

She pulled a sad face. "I made a bit of a mess and now I need help cleaning it up."

The mousy woman stopped and sniffed the air. "Good Lord, what is that foul smell?"

"It's what needs attending to." She took Sister Anne by the arm and pointed to the opening in the wall. "In there."

The other woman took one look and leaped back, ashen faced. "Mina's father. You told me he left that day."

"He left. I didn't say how."

Sister Anne glanced back and forth between the crevice and Miriam. "You killed him."

"I had no choice. He attacked me."

"If it was self-defense," Sister Anne eyed Miriam with suspicion, "Why didn't you tell someone? Why did you conceal his body?"

"What with Brother Aaron betraying him, Father doesn't need to be troubled by this."

"My husband did *not* betray Father."

"I know you still have feelings for the man." She patted the other woman's arm. "But, all marriages—except Father's—were dissolved when you joined our congregation, remember."

The mousy woman glared at Miriam.

"Let's put all that aside for now." She pointed at the corpse. "We need to move him away from the Crèche. It's not hygienic to have him around the girls."

"What do you propose we do with him?"

"You pull him out." She began to walk away. "I'll go get a blanket to wrap him in."

Sister Anne shouted, "Don't you dare leave me alone with him."

Miriam turned and glared at the insolent woman. "One more word out of you and I'll tell Father you helped Aaron drug him with peyote."

The other woman's face drained of color. "You wouldn't dare."

"That's what that Indian said to me, too, just before I killed him."

****

Zeke paced the small room where Brother Aaron sat and glared at the man. Despite multiple beatings, lack of food, and sleep deprivation, the prisoner denied any wrongdoing.

"This is for your own good." Zeke gripped Aaron's shoulder and the man winced. "Save your soul. Repent now, and you can go to your execution with a clear conscience."

Sweat trickled down the side of Aaron's head. "I've done nothing wrong."

"Where'd you get the peyote?"

"I don't know what you're talking about."

"Of course you do, Aaron." He used his most soothing voice. "C'mon. Just between you and me." He jerked his thumb over his shoulder at the armed guards standing outside the door. "They can't hear you. What if I *wanted* to get more of that stuff?"

The other man's brow furrowed. "Then I'd say you were out of luck."

Zeke's patience was wearing thin. He'd treated this man like family. Trusted him with millions of dollars worth of gold. Given him everything he asked for. What did he get in return? Betrayal. He slapped Aaron so hard, the outline of his fingers burned on the man's cheek.

"That's for lying to me."

Tears welled up in his eyes. "I'd *never* do anything

to harm you."

"When did you decide you wanted to be in charge?"

Wide-eyed, Aaron shook his head. "Never."

"Was it while I was in prison?"

"I built this place for you, Father, your leadership. I serve you, only you."

"Or was it when you saw the Mothers of the Twenty-Four?" Zeke whirled on the man. "You swore an oath of loyalty and celibacy. Did you fantasize about those young, ripe women in the prime of their sexual lives?"

Aaron shook his head so hard that sweat flew off and hit Zeke in the face. "I never thought about those girls. They belong to you, to the future of Edmondsville. Besides—"

"What?" He flexed his hands.

"My wife is the only woman I ever wanted."

Sister Anne? That washed out, plain thing with the flat chest and skinny hips?

"You were supposed to give up all things, including marriage, when you joined with me. I'm the only man who is allowed to be married. " A thought struck Zeke. "Was she in on it? Did she poison my food?"

"She's done nothing wrong."

"I bet you two have been conspiring to get rid of me. Guards," Zeke called. "Bring Sister Anne to me."

The big man's face crumpled, and he sobbed. "Leave her alone. She's innocent."

"I'll be the judge of that."

****

The guards arrived to summon Sister Anne scant

minutes after the two women had dropped the native's body into a dry well. Covered with a slab of stone to keep people from falling in, the hole was so deep, that no matter how long they strained their ears, there was no *thunk* to indicate that the body had landed. Replacing the boulder had been torture. She and Sister Anne both had bleeding palms.

Miriam wiped her hands on her skirt, as she explained to the guards that the lid had been askew and she'd been worried someone might fall in and get hurt, so she'd asked Sister Anne to help her put it back.

The taller of the two men took Anne by the elbow. "Father wishes to see you. Now."

Sister Anne pulled back. "What is this about?"

"Not at liberty to tell you. Come with us."

Oh, no. This would never do. Not after what she'd just seen.

"Don't worry, Sister Anne." She patted the woman's arm. "I'll come with you."

Zeke stood outside the half-open door of a small room, a smile on his face. He took one of her hands into both of his. "So good of you to join us, Sister Anne."

Miriam knew that modulated voice and two-handed grip all too well. She'd seen him soothe mourners and disarm critics with his high touch tactics that mimicked compassion and concern. He was up to something.

"Your husband would like to see you," Zeke whispered.

Tears spilled down the simple woman's cheeks. "Aaron asked for me?"

Zeke pushed Anne into the chamber. "Not exactly."

Miriam had to get in there, make sure the idiot didn't jabber about the dead man. She grabbed the handle just as Father tried to pull the door behind him. "Let me come with you."

"I have everything under control."

"I know her well, I can watch her every move. Tell you if she's lying."

"Good point, Mother. Yes, please come in."

The door slammed behind her, and it took a few moments for Miriam's eyes to adjust. Sister Anne knelt at the side of a man tied to a chair. Until the bloodied person spoke through his split lips, she didn't realize it was Brother Aaron.

"She's done nothing wrong."

"I have reason to believe she conspired with you to feed me peyote."

"No," the accused shouted. "I swear I never did any such thing."

Zeke yanked at the woman's gray hair.

Sister Anne cried out, "Oh, Lord, protect us now, *please*. We are innocent. The ones we loved and followed to this forsaken wilderness are murderers."

Zeke raised his hand to strike Sister Anne.

Miriam's heart lodged in her throat The idiot was about to tell Zeke what she'd done.

He wouldn't go easy on her this time, not with all the Mothers of the Twenty-Four waiting for him in the Crèche. She had to *do* something.

"Father." She grabbed his hand mid-swing. "I have a lovely surprise for you."

Rage twisted his face as he turned. If she didn't speak fast, she'd be his next punching bag.

"One of the girls asked for you today. Said she

couldn't wait to spend time with you."

Hand still raised, his expression faded from anger to suspicion. "Really?"

Sister Anne sobbed and clutched her husband's legs, too busy blubbering to blab.

"Yes, it was one of the young ones, Daniella. She has the beautiful teeth."

"Well, why didn't you tell me sooner?" He ran his fingers through his steel gray hair and smirked. "Where is she now?"

"I had some things to take care of today, so she and Sister Rose are babysitting for the Chosen One."

"You mean she's already in our home?"

The old fool. She knew just what to say to control him. Miriam nodded. "Yes, she's very lovable, truly wants to *please* people. I think you'll enjoy her."

"I'm worn out from all this exertion. I think I need to rest a while."

Sister Anne glanced up at Miriam and mouthed the words *thank you.*

Dim-witted cow. She didn't do it to save Anne and her idiot husband. Miriam shook her head and shot a glance at Zeke's back.

Fools. They were all nincompoops and fools. Even Zeke. Early on she had figured out there were no hallucinogenic drugs making her husband see beasts instead of beauties. It was Jake. He had touched each of the women before they were supposed to be bedded by Zeke. The horny old man's vision had been turned inside out. Instead of angels, Zeke saw demons straight from hell. The baby not only healed people, but protected them from harm. She wondered how strong his powers really were. *Could he stop bullets?*

"Hold up, a moment Father." She pointed to Brother Aaron and Sister Anne. "Why don't you untie the traitor and leave his wife with him. Your food can't be poisoned with both of them locked up."

He motioned to the guards. "Give them both what they need—food, water, medicine. Just keep them locked up here until I decide what to do with them."

Miriam took her husband's hand. "Let's go greet the future of Edmondsville."

****

Zeke stood in the living room and shook the small brown-skinned woman's hand. Mother was right. She did have a lovely smile. Big brown eyes. Long dark hair. The modest dress she wore did little to hide the fact that she had large, perky breasts. He could hardly wait for her to join him in the bedroom. His pulse quickened, and his mouth grew dry. First, he had to get rid of the old crones

"Mother, why don't you and Sister Rose take the Chosen One out for a little while. I'm sure the congregants would love to see him."

He watched as Miriam lifted Jake out of the crib and handed the baby to Daniella. The toddler cooed, leaned his forehead against hers, and patted her cheeks.

A sense of déjà vu washed over Zeke. *Why was the child doing that?* The girl wasn't sick, was she? Nonsense. She was as healthy as a horse.

Miriam and Rose left with the baby, and he approached the young woman. He placed his hands on her shoulders and turned her around.

He smiled and she grinned back. Her smile continued to stretch, then twisted like a rubber mask. The smile, once inviting, grew enormous, lewd and leering. Red eyes rimmed with black glared at him and bugged out of her ashen gray face. Her hair writhed with thousands of snakes. A forked tongue licked his face and burned his cheek. Her fetid breath reeked of methane and sulfur.

Stumbling over furniture, breathing heavy, he shouted, "Get back, you demon, Satan's child."

She hopped toward him on cloven hooves, her pointed tail whipping around her, shredding his pants and slicing his legs.

She tore at the waist of his pants and hissed, "Give it to me. Give it to me!"

He screamed, ran into his bedroom, and slammed the door.

Chapter Seventeen

Alejandro spent an hour on the satellite phone with Isabel explaining the situation. The boss lady was not happy. Failed to see how six little Indians could be of any assistance in the rescue efforts. Couldn't appreciate their contribution to the party, until he pointed out the cliff-dwellers' extensive knowledge of the caves. Emboldened by her silence and tacit agreement, he convinced her the cabin's location, well out of sight of Edmondsville and its armed lookouts, would make an excellent staging area for the operation. For good measure, he threw in the fact that it was well away from *her* compound—so no one would ever know where she and her family lived. At last, she agreed to send Tio, Pepe, and the troops. Then, the boss lady said she was coming, too.

Now he stood outside the cabin door and watched the billowing cloud of dust rise up from behind the hilltop. Had the phenomenon not been accompanied by the sounds of giant lawnmowers, he would have thought a tornado approached. In a sense, a tempest *was* on the horizon: Hurricane Isabel.

A dozen ATVs and six MUVs descended upon the little cabin's front yard blowing gas fumes, dust, and gravel in the air. Alejandro covered his eyes with his forearm to deflect the detritus. One by one, the vehicles shut down until he could hear his own voice again. "*Hola!* Welcome to base camp for Operation Jake."

Isabel removed her desert camouflage helmet and shook out her long dark hair. She glanced around, her face a mixture of disgust and amusement.

"This is not what I would call a five-star hotel."

"It's more than adequate for our purposes." He pointed to the nearby stream. "We have water and are completely out of sight." The door squeaked and Angie slid alongside him. "I'm told the cult members don't get out very often, so it's unlikely they'll wander through here anytime soon."

Isabel nodded at Angie, then frowned. "What's with the nun?"

Alejandro glanced down at the little woman who had appeared at his side without a sound. "Sister Teresa? I told you about her."

"There's no need for her to hang around." Isabel flicked her hand. "She can go. Now."

The nun bristled. "I'm not going anywhere."

Alejandro stared at her. "You speak English?"

"*Un poco.*"

He wondered what else the woman had failed to share with them.

Sister Teresa continued in Spanish. "I'm staying right here until the girls are returned to their homes. If it weren't for me, they wouldn't be in Edmondsville, being forced to do God only knows what."

Isabel rolled her eyes. "Tio, Pepe. Set up camp. As soon as you find the vodka, bring it to me. It's going to be a long night."

The nun watched the flurry of activity with wrinkled brow and pursed lips.

"Sister Teresa," Alejandro whispered. "If you really want Senora Isabel's help, you need to wipe that look off your face."

She shook her head. "I've made a deal with the devil."

The tone of her voice irritated him. She came to *him*, not the other way around. "Sister, you, of all people, should know better than to judge a book by its cover."

She shot him a sharp look. "What do you mean by that?"

He waved Angie over. "This woman is here to tell you that her father, a 'very religious man' *is* evil incarnate." He translated and the redhead nodded agreement. "That woman over there" he pointed to Isabel "may have crime in her blood, but she's done more to help poor villagers in Chihuahua than the government has."

"You call growing marijuana helping people?"

"I *heard* you." Isabel strode over to the porch and joined the heated conversation. "What do you give them? Prayers? I give people *jobs*. There's no market for rocks and stones. What *else* would you have them grow?"

The two women, one young, curvaceous and raven-haired, the other old, squat and wimpled, faced one another.

Isabel placed her fists on her hips.

Sister Teresa's face grew red, and she took two steps closer to the cartel boss.

Half-expecting a cat-fight, Alejandro grabbed Angie's elbow and pulled her away from the confrontation.

"Apples, coffee, wine." The nun shouted. "That was my plan all along. It's why the *ejiditarios* agreed to send the girls to go work in Edmondsville. The money they earned was going to go into the agricultural cooperative."

Mouth agape, Isabel glared down at her now weeping opponent.

"What are you talking about?"

"The Tarahumara have plots of land, *ranchos*, with two or more households on them. They work together, help each other out. Mostly they raise corn, beans, subsistence farming." She hiccupped. "There are some areas in the Sierra Madre where the natives have been able to get enough capital to buy apple trees, grapevines for wine, and coffee plants. They aren't millionaires, but they aren't starving to death." Her voice hitched. "Our babies are dying of malnutrition."

Isabel's face softened. "Children shouldn't go to bed hungry." She put her arm around the nun's shoulders. "Let's go sit down and talk."

Alejandro whispered to Angie, "Are you seeing what I'm seeing? Or am I hallucinating?"

"I heard that," Isabel shouted over her shoulder and flipped him the bird.

****

Over the next few hours, desert camouflaged tents popped up all over the pasture like mushrooms. Lanterns and fires glowed as the men heated up their rations. A semblance of peace fell over the troops, and Alejandro hoped the planning and training for this event would at last pay off. Tarahumara scouts were already en route to the cult compound. Once they returned with the number and location of lookouts, they'd be ready to go. But right now, all they could do was wait. Eyes half-closed, he sat in the dark and recalled the other plans his handler and the ATFE higher ups had set into motion.

Although he had argued against the idea, once the attack on Edmondsville was a go, Alejandro had been instructed to call the town tavern, *El Hombre Loco,* and use code to place beer and liquor orders for the fiesta to celebrate on their return. Through a tap on the seedy dive's lines, the US-Mexico joint task force on disrupting drug trafficking organizations would learn the exact latitude, longitude, date, and time of the attack. When Angie had arrived on the scene, the idea of rescuing a kidnapped baby and capturing *narcoterroristas* and crazy cult members in the same fell swoop had been irresistible to his handler.

Think of all the points they could make, his handler had said. The higher-ups would be happy, both governments would win, and it was hoped, end some of the anti-Mexican sentiments inflaming the American media. Alejandro thought it was a recipe for disaster and had told his handler as much, asking him if he was trying to create Armageddon. US-Mexican relations aside, the two ATFE Special Response Teams from opposite sides of the border hadn't been working together long enough to handle an operation of this magnitude.

He pointed out that the last thing the Mexican government should want was their very own version of Jonesville meets Waco meets Ruby Ridge. When his handler started questioning him, asking if he needed to come in from the field, Alejandro had backed down. But he just couldn't get rid of the feeling that something terrible would happen if the new plans were set into motion. He tried to shake the premonition by thinking of other things, like Ramon Mendez, Isabel's father. Where *was* that bastard?

Just the thought of that monster having a good life after slaughtering his little nephew and maiming his surgeon brother made Alejandro's head pound and his ears throb. He shook his head and took deep breaths to lower his heart rate and calm down. The throbbing remained. He looked around. It wasn't his heart that was pounding, it was drums. And they were coming closer.

Tio rushed up to the cabin and pointed to a crowd of people coming down the hillside, their faces illuminated by flickering lights. "Who the hell are they?"

"I have no idea." Alejandro turned to yell for the men to grab their arms, when Sister Teresa materialized at his side.

"Oh. My. God." She breathed. "I told them to stay away."

"Who?"

"The other Tarahumara. I told them we'd handle this."

The drumming came closer accompanied by a din of violins, accordions, and shouting. What were they shouting? No, it was singing. "How did they find us?"

"The sixth man who came with me, the youngest, was supposed to go home and stay there. Keep his mouth shut. He must have told *everyone* in the valley." Sister Teresa sighed and shook her head. "It's a *tesguinada*. A beer drinking party. Julio's been brewing that beer for a week in preparation for planting corn on his *rancho*. They must have decided to bring it here to thank you for agreeing to save their girls. Odd. Usually they have a party *after* someone does them a favor, not before." She glanced up at Alejandro, her brow creased. "They have *tesguino* at everything except funerals. They must think you and your men might not come back alive."

If he followed his handler's orders, the Tarahumara could be right. There *had* to be a way to stop Armageddon. But how? If he didn't make the call, he'd be insubordinate and get demoted, or worse. If he did make the call, all hell would break loose, and the only people left standing would be wearing ATFE Kevlar vests. He had to think of something, or Sister Teresa's prediction could come true.

Illuminated by the flickering campfires, bobbing flashlights, and waving lanterns, the crowd of colorfully dressed villagers appeared in the center of the campsite, looking like a surrealistic painting of a carnival lost in the wilderness. A burro brayed, and then another and another, in what seemed to be a chorus of complaints about the weight of the barrels strapped to their backs.

Alejandro bit his lower lip. His shoulders and belly shook with suppressed mirth.

Sister Teresa glared at him. "It's not funny."

No, it wasn't funny. It was ridiculous. Absurd. Fellini-esque. How would he describe this in his debriefing? How would he tell his real bosses that in the middle of nowhere, in the midst of the most complicated US-Mexico law enforcement operation ever planned, he had hosted an Indian beer drinking party?

****

Angie sat on the front porch of the little cabin, sipped a cup of scorched coffee, and watched the natives pass around gourds of beer. An old woman had approached her earlier in the evening and offered her a drink. She'd frowned, mimed throwing up, and the woman had backed off. Apparently, Angie had found the universal sign for "I'm-gonna-hurl-if-I-drink-that." After that, the singing dancing crowd left her alone. It was just as well, she wasn't feeling very sociable.

Alejandro, on the other hand, was in the thick of things, hanging with his gigantic buddies, Tio and Pepe, swapping war stories. In the old days, she would have been the life of the party, provided the host offered good booze and hard drugs. Now she observed the celebration as if watching a National Geographic special—except this was one she could reach out and touch. Had she been a sociologist or an anthropologist, she would have thought she'd died and gone to heaven. Instead, she kept thinking, I need to sleep. When will this party be over and how can we make these people go home?

Vodka bottle clutched in her hand, Isabel sauntered over to the stoop and plunked down beside Angie. "Welcome to the *other* Mexico, *chica*." She raised the bottle, took a swig, and nodded toward the natives. "Wait till you get home and tell Sarah about your trip. She's gonna split a gut laughing when you tell her about tonight."

In spite of her annoyance at the fiesta in front of her, Angie smiled. "You're right. She sees the humor in the strangest situations."

"It's her way of dealing. She could make me laugh so hard, I spit coffee out at faculty meetings." Isabel shrugged. "I really miss her. She was a good colleague and friend. The kids loved her. They still ask for Auntie Sarah. Want to know when she's going to come visit them."

"I can't believe how nice she's been to me." Angie shook her head. "She's amazingly forgiving. Most women would have never accepted me and Jake, much less welcomed us into the family. She even organized his first birthday party."

"To Sarah," Isabel raised the bottle and clanked Angie's coffee cup. "And her baby—girl? Boy?"

"She wanted to be surprised."

"Well, I hope she's not surprised with twins, or worse yet, triplets." Isabel laughed. "My girls are adorable, but a handful. Ramon is an angel compared to Ruby and Sherry."

"I think Sarah would manage, no matter how many kids she had."

"You're right about that." Isabel gestured to the noisy beer drinking party. "You know, this isn't what you usually see in the evening news in the United States about Mexico. These people were here before the Spanish arrived. The ancient culture of the Tarahumara, how they live, what they have to do to scrape out a living in the Sierra Madre, those aren't newsworthy. Killings in Juarez, blood baths in Sinaloa, and corruption in high places, *those* are the top stories."

The smell of wood smoke filled the cool desert air, and someone played a tune on a violin. "I don't watch much TV. Too busy with my job and my son." Angie chewed on her lower lip. "I never wanted that freaking lunatic anywhere near my kid. Now he has him twenty-four seven. I was hoping Jake would have the childhood

I never had."

"We have that much in common, *chica*. My father was an abusive son of a bitch." Isabel glanced around and said in a husky whisper. "Did your father ever touch you, you know, the *wrong* way?"

Angie's stomach swooped, turned over, and roiled. Bile rose up in her throat. She closed her eyes, took deep cleansing breaths, and tried to erase the jerky images of *him* coming into her room in the middle of the night, putting his hand over her mouth, and telling her to keep her mouth shut if she knew what was good for her. Her hands shook so hard, hot coffee spilled out of the tin cup and scalded her thighs. She welcomed the pain, embraced it, and walked through to the other side.

"Yes."

"Me, too. Disgusting pig used to come into my room every night." A tear trickled down the brunette's cheek. "When he was done, he'd tell me to brush my teeth and go kiss my mother good night. The bitch knew exactly what was going on."

"It's not fair." Angie fought to control her emotions, to keep them in check, to be in charge of her life. "We didn't cause it, we couldn't cure them, and we couldn't control them. They enjoy their power trips over their victims. They're predators."

"*Were* predators."

Angie thought she misheard the other woman. "My father's still alive. At least until I can get my hands on him. Then he's a dead man."

"Done and done. My mother, too." The Latina sipped her vodka. "Pious bitch knew the entire time, knew exactly what he was doing, and turned a blind eye."

The stars began to pinwheel in the clear night sky, and Angie's breath came in short puffs. She pressed her fingers against her eyelids to slow her racing heart.

Stop. Stay calm. Stop the memories. Close the door. Put the sheet rock over it. Nail it in place. Now paint over it with white paint. Seal all the cracks along the edges.

But the wall, once held in place with alcohol and drugs, cracked and shattered under the sledgehammer of truth. No matter how frantically she worked at pushing the barricade back, she couldn't rebuild it. Recollections of her mother's betrayal erupted in the here and now.

She remembered not sleeping the rest of that night, the night of her father's first nocturnal visit. After he left, she sobbed into her pillow, wishing she was dead. He had hurt her so much, she didn't know if she'd be able to walk again. The next morning when her mother came into her room to get her up for the day's work, Angie had told her mother what happened, showed her the bloody sheets, the marks on her arms.

Instead of rising to her daughter's defense, protecting her only child, she had recited bible verses about the woman's role as the "weaker vessel." When Angie protested, her mother scolded her and told her to stop crying. "Go wash your face in cold water. No one wants to hear your ugly lies. Get to work."

Bits and pieces of that time flew back into her memory. She was missing something. Where did she last see her golden-haired friend? When did Janice disappear? Then it hit her like a punch in the gut. Her mother told her that same morning that Janice was gone, and she had to do her work, too. Two months later, she found the girl's body.

"She knew."

Isabel nodded. "Unbelievable isn't it? A mother is supposed to protect her child, lay down her life if needs be. What kind of woman allows her husband to rape her daughter night after night and blames the girl?"

A pathological liar who'd do anything for her husband, even sacrifice her daughter's innocence. Someone who knew that Janice was dead, that she hadn't run away. That she'd been murdered.

"A sociopath."

The brunette nodded and flicked a tear off her cheek. "Exactly."

Using the name of the Lord to justify everything she did, claiming *He* told her to do this, that Father had seen it in a vision. Her mother had built Angie's life on a foundation of lies, taught her daughter that women were chattel, not worthy. Had it not been for Janice, she would have never known that there was another reality. She would have never dared to think for herself, to plot her escape, and fly away on her own wings of truth.

"Twisting words, hiding behind bible verses."

Isabel's head jerked up, and she frowned at Angie. "I was talking about *my* mother. Who were you talking about?"

"*My* mother." Angie exchanged a long stare with the other woman. "Now what?"

The Latina raised an eyebrow. "Are you serious about getting your son back? Are you ready to take control? To do what I did?"

"What's that?"

"If you ever want to have another moment of peace in your life, you have to kill them. Kill them both."

Chapter Eighteen

Something scratched at the bedroom door. Zeke's hair stood on end. His watch said two hours had passed since he barricaded the entry, but what if the evil one had made time jump forward? Right now, that could be her scraping her talons on the door. He closed his eyes, took deep breaths, and prayed for the evil one to go away.

"Father? Are you in there?"

"Miriam, thank the good Lord it's you. I thought it was that monster." He threw the door open and saw the now human appearing girl standing next to wife. He stepped back and clutched his chest. "Get thee behind me, Satan."

His wife frowned. "Who are you talking to?"

"That creature, that demon." He averted his eyes and pointed to his leg. "See what she did to me?"

"Father, all I see is some dirt on your pant leg."

"She sliced my leg wide open." He stared down at his trousers. "There was blood everywhere."

Miriam took his chin in her hand and turned his head until he looked her in the eye. "What's wrong with you?"

"Make her go away," he whimpered. "She's in league with the devil."

"You must be having those *visions* again."

Sharon Buchbinder

Something about the way she said "visions" gave him pause. Was she smirking at him? Yes, her lips were *definitely* quirked and there was a defiant gleam in her eye. She was hiding something from him.

"Send the girl back to the Crèche. I don't want her."

Miriam turned and shooed the girl away in rudimentary Spanish.

"What the hell is the matter with you? I send you the pick of the litter, and you turn into a babbling idiot."

With her erect back, hands on hips and biting criticism, Miriam was not behaving the way she should. She was his wife, the weaker vessel.

"How dare you speak that way to me?" He raised his hand to strike her.

"You put one hand on me, so help me God, I will kill you."

"Who are you? You're not my wife."

"I'm tired of being your punching bag. It's about time you gave *me* some respect." She took two steps closer and color rose in her face. "Who saved you from Janice? I did."

He opened his mouth to protest. Beating his lover to death with a shovel was murder, not a rescue, but he thought better of disagreeing with her. He didn't see any weapons in her hand, but who knew what she might have hidden in her pockets?

"Who got you out of prison? Me, it was *my* plan—from you faking a heart attack, right up to my parking outside the hospital."

She poked him on the shoulder.

"Who called the daycare center so you could go pick up Jake? I did."

216

Realization of the real traitor came to him. Shaking with rage, he shouted, "You. You're the Judas. You fed me peyote. You're the one responsible for my terrible hallucinations. You're the *only* person who could have planted it in my food or water."

Miriam backed away from him.

He had her. "You are guilty, guilty, guilty, it's written on your face."

"You're insane, old man."

"I don't know how, but you did."

"I wasn't even here the first time you hallucinated."

"You could have laced my toothpaste."

"You have no right leading this group."

At last her real agenda was revealed.

"*You* want to be in charge?"

How dare she? She was a *woman*.

"I'm not the one hallucinating and hiding in my bedroom, shaking in my shoes."

He'd seen how his followers looked at her when she held the Chosen One. They *adored* her as if she were the Virgin Mary. He had to think fast. He needed her to take care of Jake, to ensure his power base. The child was key in his plans.

"Miriam, I need you. I can't live without you."

She gave him a stony stare. He had to reach her. The child. She loved the boy.

"Jake needs you."

"Your prophesies about the Chosen One convinced people to give up their homes, their money, their careers—to be here with *him* in End Days." She drew her shoulders back. "He's here and he bonded with *me*. Not with you. He's mine, you understand? *Mine*."

"He's attached to you, it's obvious." He paused. "Jake likes Sister Rose, too."

Her eyes bore a hole in his skull. "She's not his grandmother. Blood binds us."

"You're right. She could never replace you." He nodded and took her hand in his. "No one could. You're the *only* woman I've ever truly loved."

She frowned. "What about Janice?"

"She meant nothing to me."

"And our daughter?"

His stomach plummeted. "I d-d-don't understand."

He stalled for time. Think, man, what did she want him to tell her?

"Angie told me you came into her room every night after Janice left."

"I'm so ashamed. My flesh was weak." He looked his wife right in the eye. "She seduced me."

"I *knew* it." A tear trickled down her cheek. "To think I almost felt sorry for her."

"My love, please, let's forget our quarrel. We need to present a united front."

She sniffed and nodded. "You're right. The others can't see us this way."

He was back in control. "Exactly, they will divide us and conquer."

"You won't hit me?"

"I swear, I'll never touch you in anger again."

Miriam's face softened. "Okay, Father."

Relief washed over him.

"One more thing." She placed her hand on his cheek.

"Yes?"

"Tell the congregation I'm in charge when you're

not available."

"What? That won't—"

"Do it, or I'll tell them all about your new 'visions'."

Just as Zeke opened his mouth to respond, the former Sheriff of Wicomico County rushed into their chambers.

"Father, come quickly," the red-faced man wheezed. "We need you up top, right now."

"What's wrong?"

"Look outs spotted a bunch of Indians out by the solar panels. They must have been searching for them girls. We shot two, killed 'em. But three got away."

****

The sun was setting when Alejandro observed three Tarahumaran men running into camp, their once pristine white loin cloths splattered with mud. He joined the throng of Mexicans and Indians surrounding the runners. As he got closer to the trio, he realized that what he initially thought was mud was dried blood. He spotted Sister Teresa. Tears streamed down her face. "What happened?"

Choking back a sob, the nun translated for the scouts. "They watched Edmondsville from afar, saw five lookouts. Didn't see any weapons. They decided to get closer, actually got into the compound. The next thing they knew, bullets were flying." She took a deep shuddering breath. "Two of the men are dead."

He shook his head. "Sorry, Sister."

She didn't respond. She held a weeping Indian woman and whispered soothing words. A wife? Mother? No matter. There was a hole ripped in the fabric of their society. When one person in their community died, everyone grieved.

Towering over the native people, Isabel strode up to Alejandro and the nun.

"What the hell is going on?"

Alejandro filled her in. "The crazies will be on high alert now. Forget the stealth attack. We might as well go for a full frontal assault."

"Do we have enough men?"

"If we include Angie, we have about four dozen shooters. The Indians saw only five sentinels. But that doesn't mean there aren't more inside the compound."

She nodded. "What about rocket launchers?"

"Aside from the fact that we could harm the missing girls and the baby, Angie told me there are a thousand innocent people up there." He shook his head. "Their only crime was to follow a crazy man. You don't want another Waco."

The brunette looked puzzled.

"Back in the early nineties, a religious zealot named David Koresh had a compound in Waco, Texas. The feds decided he was stockpiling guns and ammo, so they executed a search warrant. Next thing you know, a couple of agents got shot. All hell broke loose. Over seventy-five civilians burned alive in a firestorm, including two pregnant women." He shook his head. "A lot of them were children. It was a holocaust."

"*Madre de dios.*" She squeezed her eyes shut. "The thought makes me sick."

"Me, too." He hadn't been part of the ATFE at the time, but the aftershocks of Waco still resonated through the bureau. A towering example of what not to do, the Branch Davidian "incident" was testimony to the banality of bureaucratic arrogance and evil. Now the agency taught trainees to take every precaution available to protect innocent lives, to avoid epic disasters. The arrogance of some of the higher ups, however, remained.

Red hair pulled back into a ponytail, Angie appeared at his side.

"I heard about the scouts. What are we going to do?"

Dressed in desert camouflage, knee high boots, and smacking a pair of gloves on her palm, she looked as if she was about to jump on an ATV and head for the cult compound.

"We were just discussing that."

His brain spun with a thousand scenarios, none of them optimal. Adding to the complexity of the current state of affairs, he still hadn't come up with a plan to keep the US-Mexico cooperative Special Response Teams away from Edmondsville to avoid a Waco redux. With two hyped up police military teams in the mix, the entire place could erupt into a fireball. He had to do something. But what?

Think, man, think. Time is running out.

"Boss," Tio stomped over to Isabel. "Gotta talk to you and Alejandro. We have a situation."

Alejandro did not like the tone of Tio's voice. With two dead scouts, a looming ATFE strike force, and a thousand cult members milling around, God only knew where, or what else could go wrong.

Tio moved away from the weeping crowd of natives and huddled with Isabel and Alejandro. "Remember the mole we planted with our friends on the west coast?"

The Latina nodded. "Yes. What about him?"

"Just got a call. Our competition has decided to move a huge shipment of product to Tijuana and San Diego."

"Those bastards." She spat on the ground. "They know that's our turf."

His face grave, Tio nodded. "There's more. And it gets worse."

Isabel frowned. "We're distracted over here. They're over there, with no possibility of cutting them off. How could it possibly be worse?"

The big guy shook his bald head. "They have subs."

"A sub? A freaking submarine?" She threw her hands up in the air. "Where the hell did they get one?"

Alejandro took a deep breath. A drug sub. Not enough the Colombians had been using them to run cocaine up the east coast, now Isabel's Mexican competitors had decided to invest in one. The ones the Colombians had built had been crude at first, good only for one man, one run. But their later efforts had been quite ingenious.

"One sub? How many men does it hold?"

"Not one." Tio looked as if he would truly throw up. "Our mole said it was a freaking *fleet*. Ten. Each one holds five guys."

Larger subs had been seized in other South American countries. The cartels were going high tech. What was next? Shipping the shit by space shuttle? He shuddered at the thought of orbiting cocaine.

"That's a lot of blow." He did some quick calculations in his head. "If they used the Colombians' building plans, the subs are a hundred feet. They could be moving as much as seventy-five tons of coke."

The color drained out of Isabel's face. "After they make that delivery, they'll come after me and my family. I have to get Sean and the kids out of Chihuahua, back to the US where they'll be safe."

Alejandro lifted his chin at Tio. "Did your informant give you any idea of when and what route they'd take?"

"They move out at midnight tonight. Taking the scenic route along the outside of the peninsula from Culiacan to Ensenada."

With two dozen marinas on the west coast between Ensenada and Huatulco, they could literally hide ten subs anywhere in plain sight. The best time for the combined ATFE forces to strike would be midnight, just as the subs left Culiacan.

"Tio, tell Pepe and the rest of the troops to get ready. We attack Edmondsville at dawn."

Tio looked to Isabel for confirmation.

She nodded, her long dark hair swirling in a light breeze. "Do what he says, Tio."

After the big man lumbered away, she confronted Alejandro. "What about the subs? If we don't take care of them, my family's in danger."

He grinned. "I'm gonna drop a dime."

"You're joking, right? The Mexican *federales* are a bunch of incompetent idiots. They don't have the ability to find their asses with both their hands, much less find and take out those subs."

"You're right. But the US does."

Her eyebrows practically flew off her face. "How?"

"When I was in prison, I received a lot of offers for deals if I'd roll over on some people." He shrugged. "I never took them up on any of their offers. Maybe it's time I did."

"I've got kids to protect." Brow furrowed, she chewed her lower lip. "You sure this will work?"

If all went well, his boss would earn extra brownie points for scoring an amazing piece of intelligence and making what might be the drug bust of the century. Best of all, they'd be out of his hair so Alejandro could focus on the job at hand—rescuing a dozen young Tarahumara women and a baby.

He gave her the thumbs up. "Your competition will never know what hit them."

Chapter Nineteen

Zeke Edmonds sat on his throne in the grand chamber, stared at the giant blue and white emblem of his congregation, and pondered his options. With the natives' bodies disposed of in a bottomless well, if any police ever showed up, they'd never find them. But what to do about the other Indians who got away? He couldn't assume they would run home to their little villages and stay there.

For all he knew, tens of thousands of natives could emerge from their caves, valleys, and mountains, and swarm Edmondsville—their sheer numbers crushing him and his followers. Zeke was a man of God, had never carried a weapon, nor had he ever served in the military. But he knew someone who had. He sighed and motioned to his security chief.

The man inclined his head and whispered, "Yes, Father?"

"Bring me Brother Aaron." He paused. The former army engineer might be more willing to help if he knew he was forgiven. "Let him put on clean clothes. Release his wife."

"Yes, Father." The big man hustled out of the meeting room.

"Sure you want to do that?" Miriam's voice rasped in his ear. She squeezed onto the seat alongside him. "I thought he was a traitor."

"Woman, what would you have me do? Keep one of the best minds in Edmondsville locked away, useless to us?" He eyed his wife. A hint of a smirk played on her lips. "What's so amusing?"

"Seems odd you'd release your mortal enemy so soon. He could be your undoing."

A frisson ran along his spine. He tried to shake off the chill. Zeke knew she meant to be spiteful, but there was a kernel of truth in her remark.

"Crises make for strange bedfellows. When this is all over, we'll see if he's loyal or a traitor."

"And?" She raised an eyebrow.

"I'll do what needs to be done."

Miriam was taking up too much space, filling up *his* throne. As soon as this was over, she had to go. There'd be no need for her in the End Days. Not when he had the Mothers of the Twenty-Four to attend to his—and the baby's—needs.

"Father," the chief of security called.

Zeke blinked. Bruised and battered, Brother Aaron stood before him in clean clothes.

Zeke raised his voice so all could hear him. "We had intruders this morning. I worry more may come."

With his gaunt cheeks, and haggard appearance, the man who once looked as if he could play football now resembled the walking dead.

"What is it you want me to do?"

Zeke lowered his voice. "You were in the military. We need a plan of defense."

Brother Aaron guffawed. "I was in the US Army Corps of Engineers. We *built* things. You're better off asking for help from your head thug. He was a sheriff."

"He deferred to you," Zeke spoke through clenched teeth. "Are you saying you won't help us?"

"I never served in a conflict. I dredged harbors, managed waterways, and built dams."

Zeke covered his face with his hands.

"I told you so," Miriam whispered, her hot breath scalding his neck. "He's useless."

"Go tend to the Chosen One."

"Sister Rose is with him." Miriam cackled. "I wouldn't miss this for the world. Pride goeth before a fall, Father."

He had to get away from her. "Brother Aaron, join me in my chambers please." He gave Miriam a pointed stare. "Alone."

He nodded to the security chief.

"I need your men to stand guard up top. Arm as many of our members as possible. We don't know when the Indians are coming, or how many of them there will be. But they *will* be back."

****

Two lanterns glowed atop the table Alejandro had dragged out of the cabin for planning the strategy session. Isabel, Tio, Pepe, Alejandro, Angie, Julio, of beer brewing fame, and Sister Teresa stood in a circle awaiting Alejandro's plans. The nun would not be entering into armed conflict, but she had been adamant about being in on the planning. Alejandro mentally shook his head at the motley crew.

Lord, if you exist, we need all the help we can get.

"Right now, I'm betting the old man is scrambling." He set a rock down in the center of the map of Edmondsville and the surrounding terrain.

"Edmonds has the advantage of the higher

elevation. We have the element of surprise."

Alejandro used a stick to point to their location.

"We're here, about fifteen miles away. We can't run there in three hours like our friend, Julio, but we can get there before dawn on our ATVs. With our camouflage, they'll hear us coming, but they won't be able to see us. We have more than enough handguns and long distance rifles for all thirty-six of our trained shooters. Plus a lot of ammo."

Angie interjected. "But we don't want to hurt Jake, the girls, or any unarmed members of the cult. So tell your men not to shoot unless they are in imminent danger. It's critical for them to understand this isn't a war. It's a rescue."

Isabel snorted. "A rescue with three dozen of us to a thousand of them. Great odds."

"You forgot about Julio's buddies." He nodded at Sister Teresa.

The nun picked up where he left off.

"We sent a dozen runners to the Tarahumara village and all the surrounding ranchos. They'll meet you tomorrow at dawn at the base of the Edmondsville bluff."

"Once we arrive, the three surviving scouts will lead us up the side of the mountain and through the caves that honeycomb the compound. That's how the scouts got into Edmondsville the first time."

"But this time," Tio said with a wicked grin, "they'll have friends."

Alejandro took some more questions and when it seemed all were satisfied, he closed the meeting. "Tell your men to try to get some sleep. We need to be up and out in two hours."

The group dispersed leaving Alejandro and Angie facing each other across the table. The flickering light from the lantern cast shadows on her face. He could see she was on edge and there was no way he was going to be able to sleep.

"Want to take a walk?"

She smiled. "Trying to take me to see your etchings again?"

"Maybe," he drawled. "Or maybe I just want to talk with you. Is that okay?"

"I hear the stream looks nice by moonlight."

Running over boulders and between the crannies of the hard surfaces, the water chuckled as if it had a private joke with the rocks. Alejandro took Angie's hand and helped her perch on a boulder next to him. "How are you feeling?"

"Excited. Elated. Terrified. All of my worst nightmares combined into one horrific sweaty mass."

She shook her head and covered her face.

"My mother is just as crazy as my father. Any illusions I had about her were shattered last night."

"What do you mean?"

"Do not tell Isabel I shared this with you. It's very private."

Angie began to recount her conversation with the tipsy Isabel during the *tesguinada*.

"Halfway into this, she asks me, 'Did your father ever touch you, you know, the wrong way?' All of the memories that I tried to keep under wraps and repress for years exploded. Not only did my father rape me on a regular basis, my mother knew what he was doing. She called me a liar when I tried to tell her."

A tear trickled down her face. He leaned over and

kissed the tear away.

"I'm so sorry. No one should be violated like that. And no one should have their reality invalidated. Your mother should have protected you."

Her shoulders shook. "Yes, she should have. That's why I really went into law. Not to support my father's insane idea of taking over the government. I wanted to put both of them in jail. Then I met someone." She paused. "I was a public defender. He was like you."

He kissed the top of her head and caressed her back. "How so?"

"A drug dealer."

Alejandro forced himself to relax. He was playing the role of a drug lord, after all. A *capo.*

"And?"

"I was already a heavy drinker. He got me hooked on coke." She shuddered. "I was high when I met Jake's father and got pregnant."

"But you got clean." He'd never seen her use any alcohol or drugs except aspirin or coffee. "You stayed clean and sober."

"Yes," she whispered. "As soon as I found out I was pregnant, I quit using. But, I'm afraid if I spend any more time with you, I'll fall back down that rabbit hole."

Right at that moment, he hated his job, hated being undercover, despised what he had to become to play the part. If only he could tell her the truth, maybe then she'd see the real man. When she looked at him, she saw a sleaze bucket. "What if I had a different job?"

Tears shimmered in her eyes. "You'd still be a murderer."

He dropped his hand. "What are you talking

about?"

"When I asked Tio if you killed Raul, he didn't deny it."

He could strangle Tio. Alejandro had told Tio what he wanted to hear. He could never tell the truth for fear of endangering his handler and his Mexican counterparts. In reality, he'd taken Raul into the desert where he'd been handed over to the joint US-Mexico task force. At this moment, the disgusting former cop and serial rapist was locked away in an underground prison, singing his heart out to the US and Mexican authorities in exchange for not having his nuts cut off.

"What else did my big friend tell you?"

"That was enough. I understand the urge to kill him, I really do. I wish I had the nerve." She sniffed. "I don't think I could do it unless my son's life was in danger. I'm not like you. Or Isabel."

He tried to digest what she was saying, but something wasn't making sense. "What does this have to do with the boss lady?"

"She told me if I was serious about getting my son back and ever having another moment of peace in my life, I'd have to do what she did."

"What's that?"

"She said I'd have to kill my mother and father. Kill them both."

The stars wheeled overhead and the stream, once cheerful now had a sinister sound. He felt as if someone had kicked him in the balls. The air whooshed out of his lungs, and he teetered on the boulder.

Ramon Mendez. Isabel's father. Dead. Was it true?

The man who murdered his nephew and maimed his brother was out of his reach for all eternity. At one time, Alejandro thought he'd be happy if he heard the news, but instead he was disappointed he hadn't had the opportunity to do the deed himself and watch the monster die.

Or was he?

"Alejandro, what's wrong?"

"If I tell you something, you can never reveal it to anyone else. If you do, I'm a dead man."

He had to tell her who he really was. He needed her to know he was a good guy, not the scum of the earth. It hit him all at once. Angie's love and approval were what mattered to him now, not killing Mendez.

She took his hand and placed in on her chest, over her heart. "I trusted you with the worst secrets of my life. Now you know I'm a recovering addict and alcoholic, and I was sexually abused. I'm about as damaged as anyone could be." She sighed. "Give me a peso."

"What are you talking about?"

"Give me some money." She put her hand out. "I'm serious."

Alejandro reached into his wallet, pulled out a bill and placed it on her palm. "Now what?"

"Now I'm your lawyer." She nodded. "I cannot be compelled to testify against you in a court of law."

"I'm not worried about a court of law. There are much scarier people, like Ramon Mendez and his daughter."

"He's dead."

"Exactly my point." He leaned over and said in a low voice. "I'm trusting you with my life because I love you. I want you to know me for who I really am—"

She put her hands on his head, yanked his lips to

hers and kissed him hard. He pulled away, breathless, confused. "What the—"

"Shut up and kiss me back." She whispered. "We're being watched."

****

When Angie's lips met his, her head spun. Rock climbing had prepared her for tumbling down the side of a wall. But with that she had a partner to catch her. Now she was free-falling without any rope to catch her. Why did he have to go and tell her he loved her? Why couldn't he have just kept it the way it was? They'd had a great sexual experience, a fling, and when it was all over, with any luck, she'd go home with Jake and cry her eyes out, because dammit, she was in love with him, too.

But no, he had to ruin everything, make her hope for more, and make her hate herself for falling in love with a drug dealer all over again. Only this time, he was even more dangerous and had scary friends, like the one watching them right now. She'd caught the big man out of the corner of her eye, noticed him just as Alejandro was about to reveal something to her. Whatever Alejandro had been about to tell her wasn't for Tio's ears, she knew that much. It had to be something terrible, but what? How could anything be worse than drug dealing and murder? Why did he have the sudden urge to spill his guts to her out here in the middle of the night just before they were about to launch the rescue effort? Wasn't she already strung out enough?

His hands stroked her hair pulling her lips tighter, drawing her back into the moment. She trembled at his touch. *Damn his wonderful lips and tongue.* She wanted them both on her breasts and thighs, nuzzling, sucking, and nipping. As he nuzzled her neck she arched her back, leaned into the kiss, and moaned.

Her mind went blank and a voice boomed in her head: "Sometimes you need a deputy angel, sometimes you need a warrior, and sometimes you need both. See with your heart, not with your eyes."

Angie gasped and knew without a doubt, that Alejandro was the one who would save her sanity, her soul, and her son.

Chapter Twenty

Holding the Chosen One on her hip, Miriam stood next to Zeke and watched the congregation stumble in. Midnight was the time this group of peaceful farmers and followers would normally be in bed, resting up for the next day's work. Couples whose marriages had been dissolved when they joined the community stood shoulder to shoulder and held hands.

Well, that wouldn't do at all.

When this emergency was over, they'd be disciplined. But right now, they were about to be attacked by infidels, and her husband had better come up with some inspirational words.

"Father, talk to our people, tell them about your vision from the Lord."

She had written the speech for him. He'd better get it right.

Zeke's eyes rolled up to the heavens, and he clutched the side of his head. *Nice touch. Show them his moment with the Lord.* A few more beats and a murmur of concern began to roll over the crowd.

She turned and smiled at the crowd.

"Fear not." Under her breath she said, "They're getting impatient."

He didn't respond. His hands shook, and he rocked back and forth. Enough with the theatrics. Time to get

Sharon Buchbinder

on with the show. The natives were restless.

"Father?"

Why wasn't he talking? What was wrong with him? For one horrifying moment, she thought he was having stroke. His eyes flew open, and he raised his hands in the priestly way.

"I've had counsel from the Lord. He has spoken."

Her heart leaped, and she gave a huge gasp of relief. Ever the showman, her husband had managed to surprise even her.

Eyes wide, voice low, Zeke began the well-rehearsed speech. "The Lord said he that overcomes, and keeps my works unto the end, shall rule the world. The Lord promised us the morning star."

Thrilled to hear him intone the words she had selected and transcribed, she stood transfixed by his voice.

He took a deep shuddering breath and his voice rose. "The Philistines are coming. They envy us our flocks, our crops, our Chosen One. The heathens sharpen their axes and prepare to cut us down as we sleep. The Lord says we must prepare for the coming attack and be strong. We cannot lose."

Women in the audience sobbed, and men flicked tears off their cheeks. Miriam had never loved her husband more than she did now. Once again, his green eyes blazed, and his voice swelled with confidence and enthusiasm. The man was on fire.

His voice boomed and echoed in the large chamber. "We will not allow our women to be sold into the hands of the Philistines. We will fight to the death, if needs be. Be with the Philistines so we can smite you on the battlefield and burn your bodies as you lay dying."

Tears filled Miriam's eyes. She particularly liked her last line about burning people alive.

"Who amongst you is with me?"

Cheering, foot stomping, and whistling erupted into a deafening roar.

"Who amongst you is with the Philistines?"

The crowd responded with hissing and booing.

"Brother Aaron, come forward." Zeke pointed at the still bruised and gaunt man.

That wasn't on the script. *What was Father doing?*

The engineer glanced around, a frown on his face.

"Yes, yes, come here." Zeke grinned and waved the man up the stairs.

Brother Aaron took a few halting steps toward the throne. Men slapped him on the back and women urged him forward. At last he stood alongside Father.

"Mother, give me the Chosen One."

What was he doing? This was totally unscripted and she didn't like it one bit. She handed over the wide-awake, kicking child.

"Look at the babe," Zeke chortled and held him up high. "He's excited, too."

"Brother Aaron," Zeke intoned. "We are entering into war. Anything can happen. I could be killed."

The crowd cried out, "No, no, no."

Where was the old fool going with this?

"In the event of my death, the community will need a designated leader."

Yes, they would. She was here to receive that honor. Her acceptance speech would be brief. She'd be humbled by the honor, ready to be a servant leader to take on this important role. She lowered her head, closed her eyes, and waited for the announcement.

Zeke took a deep breath. "I do hereby anoint you, Brother Aaron as the Leader of our congregation."

Her eyes flew open.

What? How dare he?

She was going to have words with Zeke—later, when they were alone.

Jake wailed, and the old man smiled and pulled him close to his chest. Zeke placed two fingers over the child's mouth and whispered, "Don't steal the show."

The baby chomped on the old man's finger. Zeke yelped and yanked his hand away.

In a trice, Brother Aaron snatched the child out of the air as he fell out of Zeke's grasp. Applause broke out.

Blood ran down Father's arm. "No worry," he gave a forced laugh. "It's just a flesh wound." He took Miriam's proffered handkerchief and whispered, "When did he get teeth?"

She whispered back, "He's had them for awhile. Fat lot you know about your grandson."

The crowd visibly relaxed, but Miriam fumed. *That's what the old man got for screwing things up.* The child knew better, why didn't the stupid old goat? The kid would be biting Brother Aaron next.

The engineer and heir apparent smiled and bounced Jake in his arms. The child cooed. Then to Miriam's horror, the baby placed his little hands on the big man's gaunt cheeks and began to pat them. Brother Aaron's pallid face turned pink, and his bruises began to fade.

The Chosen One was blessing Brother Aaron?

The final blow. She turned her face away. Disgraced first by her husband, and now by the Chosen

One, hot tears of humiliation ran down her cheeks. This was not the way things were supposed to go. *She* was supposed to be the designated one in charge, not the traitorous Brother Aaron.

Rage simmered within. Armed like all the others, Miriam clenched her fist around the handgun in her pocket. She could shoot both men right now, but the timing was bad. She took her hand out of her pocket, smoothed her skirt, and forced herself to appear calm in front of the adoring crowd. Timing was everything. Right now she couldn't fix things. But, in the not too distant future, one way or another, she was going to find a way to make things right.

****

Shortly after midnight, Alejandro gazed over the floor of the valley outside the little cabin. Right now, the US-Mexico task force was busy on the west coast of Mexico. Per instructions, he'd placed his beer and tequila orders at *El Hombre Loco* using the latitude and longitude of the competitor cartel's departure city. To indicate the presence of the fleet, Alejandro had also ordered ten bottles of whisky for "depth charges" the code word for drug subs.

He could have sworn he heard a gasp on the other end of the line, but perhaps he'd only imagined his handler's reaction. Right now, if all had gone well, the US and Mexican police and military cooperative task force would be making one of the biggest drug busts in history. No doubt, his handler and his handler's boss would receive awards and promotions. Best of all, they were far away from Edmondsville.

Lit by the headlamps on the ATVs and MUVs, the assembled troops resembled bug-eyed monsters ready to roar to life. The Tarahumarans had a head start. With their foot speed, they should be close to the base of the mountain, if not already there. The plan was simple—divide and conquer. As the Mexicans swarmed the outside of the mountain, the Indians would lead Alejandro and Angie through the mountain. He knew the tunnels could be tricky and hoped he had packed sufficient rock-climbing gear if they encountered any steep ascents. The scouts who had survived the attack were physically smaller than Alejandro and Angie. He prayed the passages would be wide enough to accommodate them. Otherwise, they'd have to go to the back-up plan—climbing up the steep side of the cliff.

With his voice already hoarse from speaking, he shouted out one last command. "Remember, this is a rescue mission. The lives of innocent women and children depend on you. Shoot only if you are shot at."

Sister Teresa shouted a blessing in Spanish, then in English. "May God bring everyone home safely." She turned to Alejandro. "Even the worst person has the breath of the Lord in him." She nodded in Isabel's direction. "Or her. God be with all of you."

Angie squeezed his hand. "I'll be right here with you, every step of the way."

The thought of her at his side encouraged and terrified him. If anything happened to Angie or Jake, he'd never forgive himself. He had to protect her and her child, at all costs. Tio had made it clear on several occasions that he wanted Angie. He was certain the giant had overheard him confess his love to Angie. The big man acted as if they were buddies, but information was power, and Tio was relentless when he wanted something or someone.

"I know." He pulled on his helmet. "Let's ride."

He snapped the visor in place and turned the key in the ignition. At his signal, two dozen ATVs and MUVs roared into life. The noise prevented any conversation. As the MUV jounced over the rocks, the moonlight revealed a gnarly trail pocked with holes, boulders, and pine trees. Even with shock absorbers on the vehicles, when this run was over they'd all be two inches shorter. He knew the lookouts for the cult would hear their arrival. He hoped the sound of a thousand giant lawnmowers in the night would make it seem as if they had three thousand men, rather than just three dozen— to strike fear into their hearts. If they had any sense, they'd hand over the girls and the baby. But based on what he knew of these zealots so far, he doubted that would ever happen. Right now, he had to focus on getting there and put the pedal to the metal.

****

As the night sky changed from black to light gray striped with rosebud pink, Angie clung to the side of the vehicle and thought about her son. He'd been just a year old when he'd been snatched out of her life. Now he was fifteen months old, a toddler. How big was he? Were his eyes still green, or had they turned brown like the pediatrician had predicted? Was he eating solid food? Was he healthy? Would he recognize her? The thought of him not knowing her made her chest hurt. Bad enough her parents had stolen him from her. But if they had also stolen his memories, she would kill them with her own hands. She wanted to confront them both, force them to admit all the horrors they'd thrust upon her. The litany was a long one—isolating her on the farm, not allowing her to have friends outside of the cult, killing Janice. Her father had stolen her innocence; her mother had stolen her trust. The beatings and starvation were nothing compared to the sexual and emotional abuse she had endured. Stealing her son, not once, but twice, had been the crowning blow.

Angie wanted to force them to confess their sins and to beg her forgiveness. She would be the judge and jury. If they threw themselves at her mercy, then maybe, just maybe she might consider telling Alejandro to spare their lives. She shook her head and ordered herself to stop obsessing. She'd deal with it when and if the time came. She had other worries. Like Tio.

Why had he followed Alejandro and her to the stream? She wondered how much he had heard. She knew the big man had the hots for her. She'd seen it in his eyes the first time she'd met him. Unlike Alejandro, Tio had stared at her exposed breasts that day in the police station. Every time she ran into him, he gazed at her tits as if they were still bare. After the incident on the shooting range, he'd come up behind her in the hallway, grabbed her by the waist, and pushed his erection into her butt. Then he'd whispered to her that he wanted to suck on her nipples like lollipops. She'd avoided being alone with him after that, but Angie still felt naked when she was around him.

Despite being very direct with Tio, he had never stopped hinting that that he wanted to have sex with her anytime, anywhere. She needed the big man's help, didn't want to piss him off, but if he heard her confessions about her addictions, he'd be sure to use that against her. She shuddered. The thought of him touching her made her want to take a bath. He was dangerous and persistent. If Tio got to Jake before they did, he might use the child as a bargaining chip. He knew she'd do anything, including having sex with him, to save her child's life and get him back safely.

Just then gravel and clods of dirt flew up around the MUV. Alejandro struggled to keep control of the vehicle and managed to get it behind a large outcropping of rocks. The sudden silence in the desert night was deafening. Angie strained to hear something, anything.

A spray of bullets hit the boulder closest to them raining rocks down on their helmets.

They were under fire.

And at least a mile away from the base of the mountain.

Chapter Twenty-One

Miriam walked behind Zeke into the bedroom and slammed the door. He whirled and gaped at her. The last time she'd seen that look on his face was right after she beat Janice to death with a shovel. Good. The handgun in her pocket, while not as satisfying a tool as a shovel, would take care of this matter—just as soon as he announced his mistake.

She spoke through clenched teeth, tried to keep her voice low so the hard of hearing Sister Rose and the sleeping child wouldn't wake up.

"How dare you anoint Aaron as your successor?"

Zeke's eyes darted around the room. "He's a good man. Smart. People look up to him."

"He's a traitor. You said so yourself."

"He didn't drug me. He and his wife were locked up the last time I had a strange vision." Zeke looked abashed. "I was wrong to accuse him."

"That's not the only thing you're wrong about." Deep in the folds of her skirt, the pistol felt warm and reassuring. One shot. That was all she needed. "Did you forget you promised to make me the next leader?"

He shook his head. "Miriam, please. Don't be silly."

"Silly? You think I'm silly?" She sneered. "Who's the man who runs away screaming and crying like a baby when I serve him fresh women on a silver platter?"

"That's not fair." Color rose in his face. "Someone drugged me."

"There aren't any drugs." She took two steps closer to him. "Whatever decisions you make are the ravings of a madman."

"You go too far. You're a woman, the weaker vessel. No man would ever follow you." He raised his fist. "You need to be taught a lesson."

Shaking with rage, she yanked the weapon out of her pocket, locked both hands around the grip, and pointed it straight at his chest.

"You like this decision, old man? I made it all by myself."

Ashen-faced, he stared at the pistol.

"Surprised? You shouldn't be. You told the head of security to arm everyone so they could fight the heathens."

"Miriam." Perspiration gleamed on his forehead. "Don't do this."

The smell of acrid sweat filled the small space. He really was afraid of her. *Good.* He'd made her beg for mercy for so many years, it was about time he had the pleasure.

"Get on your knees."

"Wh-what?"

"You heard me." She poked him with the gun. "Grovel. Beg for my forgiveness."

He knelt and clasped his hands.

"I beg of you. Don't shoot me."

She chuckled. "Don't worry. First you're going to tell everyone you made a mistake. What was the word you used? Oh, yes. You were *wrong*."

He sniffled and tears ran down his wrinkled cheeks.

"You think you may have Alzheimer's. Your judgment is impaired. Brother Aaron isn't the heir to your big throne. It's your wonderful wife and help-mate, the woman who knows everything about the congregation."

He bowed his head and sighed. "Yes, I will do it. But—"

"But what?"

"Didn't you hear the gunshots? I came down here to make sure you and the baby were safe."

"You came down here to hide. You're good at that." She pointed at the door with the gun. "Okay, fine. Get up."

He struggled to his feet. She backed up and opened the bedroom door.

"Before you die, you still have some work to do."

"I don't understand."

"Of course you don't, you poor demented creature." She poked him in the back with the gun. "Keep walking, straight ahead."

"Where are we going?"

"You'll find out."

He stumbled along the corridor and whined. "I don't understand."

Gun covered by the voluminous folds of her skirt, Miriam prodded him forward at each hesitation. Overhead, it sounded like firecrackers going off at a fourth of July picnic. At last, they arrived at the Crèche. Brother John, former pilot, eunuch, and Guardian of the Twenty-Four sat on a hard-backed chair in front of the door, a rifle across his lap.

He leaped to his feet. "Father. What is the news?"

Miriam poked her husband in the back with the handgun. "Tell him how well we're doing."

"It is End Days."

The man's face fell. "What should I do?"

Miriam spoke up. "Father needs to spend some private time with the Mothers of the Twenty Four to prepare the future generation."

Brother John nodded and turned to unlock the door. "Sacrifices must be made."

Zeke jerked around and stared at Miriam, his eyes wild with panic.

"Don't worry, Father. They're expecting you. Each of the girls has met and held the Chosen One. They adore him. They understand how important they are to God's plan."

Keeping one hand clenched around the pistol, she used her free hand to pull his head toward her lips.

"Time for the rooster to visit the henhouse."

Miriam pushed him through the door and slammed it behind him. Now she had him where she wanted him. She didn't need Zeke to dispose of Brother Aaron. She could do it herself.

"Lock the door, Brother John."

The bald man complied and turned around.

"Give me the key."

Frowning, he dropped it into the palm of her hand. "I don't understand."

"You don't need to."

At last her time had come.

"Don't let Father out, no matter what he says. It's for his own good."

****

The solid pine door slammed behind Zeke, and he had to wait for his eyes to adjust to the gloom. It was the first time he'd ever been in the Crèche. Miriam had attended to all the details.

He took a deep breath to calm his nerves and gagged. The room smelled like a latrine. A white bucket stood in the corner with a toilet seat on top. A roll of tissue and a bag of lime sat on the floor next to it. A dozen beds jammed one against the other along one wall. Along the other wall stood a basin, and a metal pitcher. A nearby table held a stack of towels. The girls wore long white nightgowns and huddled in the back of the room, their brown eyes wide.

He raised his hands to show his palms were empty. "*Hola.* I've come to say hello."

The largest girl spat at him and said something in Spanish. It sounded like a string of curse words, but then again, he could have been mistaken. Foreign languages had never been his forte.

He recognized the one who had turned into a demon. Daniella. She looked lovely, with that long brown hair, those beautiful teeth. Maybe Miriam was right, it was time for him to pay a conjugal visit.

"Daniella." He crooked his finger. "Come here. *Aquí.*"

The teenage shook her head. The big one stepped in front of Daniella, crossed her arms over her chest, and lifted her chin.

Was that the one whose father had shown up without warning?

"Mina." He waved her over.

She shook her head.

"You little bitch." He strode over to her and grabbed her by the arm. "I tell you to get over here, you come."

He threw her on a bed and she fell with her knees on the floor, her face on the blanket.

"I like you better that way." He unbuckled his belt and dropped his trousers. He reached for her nightgown, and a chorus of screams rose, took shape and swarmed over his head.

Bats, a thousand of them, dove at him, ripping his hair, and clawing at his face.

He stumbled, and Mina rolled over onto her back.

No longer a beautiful young woman, green scales covered her skin and her fingers tapered into talons. Yellow serpentine eyes bulged out of her head, and she licked her bright red lips with a long tongue of flames.

"Not again." He covered his face and shrieked. "Help, Brother John, let me out."

The chorus of screams became a singsong chant. "He can't hear you, he can't hear you."

Zeke fell to his knees and threw his head back in prayer. "Oh, Lord, hear my plea. I'm Daniel in the Lion's Den."

A hag with drooping tits and gray hair cackled. A troll with one eye in its forehead gave a low rumbling guffaw and drooled. A gray demon with black lips and nipples capered and pranced on a nearby bed. The dragon that had been Mina stood over him and showered him with green scales. The bats landed and grew larger, red eyes glowing, high-pitched shrieks bouncing off the stone walls.

He leaped to his feet, and the creatures danced around him in a circle. Wheeling slowly, he tried to gauge which one to grab first. He lunged at the smallest one, a bat with long fangs. Just as he got his hands around its neck, the shrieking grew into a deafening roar and he felt the first of many strikes to his legs, back, ribs. A large claw connected with his groin. He grabbed his balls, fell to the floor, and the world went black.

****

Alejandro zigzagged across the desert floor and pushed Angie behind a boulder. The weight of weapons, ammo, ropes, carabiners, and flashlights made the going slow, but using the ATVs was out of the question. Might as well paint big red targets on the vehicles. He keyed his walkie talkie.

"Tio? Pepe? Isabel? Anybody hear me?"

"Tio here. What's your location?"

"Angie and I are behind an outcropping of rocks, about a quarter mile southwest of the bluff. We're close, but no cigar."

"Stay put. I'll come to you. Go to radio silence. They might be listening in."

Crap. That was an unsettling thought. If the nut jobs tuned into their frequency, they really were in trouble. He turned his walkie talkie off.

Angie gave Alejandro a tentative smile. "You okay?"

"Fine," he lied. "You?"

"Great." Her chin quivered, and she blinked. "Never better."

After ditching their helmets, they both had donned black knit hats to reduce the opportunity for her father's lookouts to identify her by her bright red hair. A few wild red strands fluttered next to her big green eyes. He reached over and tucked them back under the material.

"You look good in desert cammies. Very becoming."

"You, too." She sighed. "So close. I'm itching to storm the castle. Get Jake."

He nodded. Boots scrunched nearby. Alejandro put his fingers to his lips. He looked up and relief flooded him.

"Bro, you nearly scared the crap out of me."

Tio grinned. And raised his Glock, aiming it at Alejandro's chest.

"Hey, man, that's not funny." Alejandro rose to his feet and motioned for Angie to stay put. This was no time to be fooling around. "Put the gun away."

"You think you're *so* smart." The big man sneered. "How's that computer gonna help you now, *Bro*?"

Alejandro ran through all the possibilities in his mind. Tio had been watching him ever since he showed up in Mexico. Had the thug figured out his real identity? Where had he gone wrong? Was it the satellite phone that tipped his hand? That time in the garage, Tio had looked as if he'd kill him if he even looked at him wrong. If it hadn't been for that bottle of liquid protein spilling in his pocket, he was sure the giant would have shot him. Be cool. Stay in character. "What the hell is wrong with you?"

"How long did you think you'd get away with it?"

Alejandro shook his head. *Think man, think.* "I don't know what you're talking about."

"Sure you do." Tio glanced down. "Drop the gun, coke whore."

Angie's weapon clunked as it hit the ground. Alejandro dared not look away from the big man, had to keep eye contact. It was like playing chicken with a psycho. His heartbeat kicked up a notch, and his fingers and toes tingled. He had to stall, talk the man out of doing something stupid. "Tio, you're like a brother to me, man."

"Yeah, right. A big dumb one you can boss around, get ahead of. After all the years I've worked for that bitch, Isabel, you come waltzing in and the next thing I know, I'm just a piece of dog shit on your shoe. Not happening, *bro*. You see, we're out in a battle field where *anything* can happen. Bullets flying all over the place, you get shot by one of those wackos, the slut is mine and I move up in the ranks." He grinned. "It's all good. Now, just back up a little, cuz I don't want no blood on me—"

There was a popping sound.

Tio's mouth dropped open in an "o" of surprise and he fell face down in the dirt. The back of his head oozed bright red blood.

Isabel stood a short distance away in a shooter stance. She nodded at Alejandro. "No one calls me a bitch."

She slid her .25 caliber automatic back into her pocket, walked over to Angie and helped her stand. "You okay?"

Gulping hard, Angie nodded.

Alejandro had never been so happy to see the head of a drug cartel in his life. He wanted to kiss her, but restrained himself. "How'd you know?"

"I didn't like it when he told you to go to radio silence." She pulled off her knit cap and fluffed her long black hair. "You were in charge of this operation, not him. I had a bad feeling."

Alejandro glanced down. A phone stuck out of the dead man's back pocket. "No cell towers out here. Why would he bring this with him?"

"Let me see." Isabel tapped the screen. "He wasn't just jealous." She held the phone up and showed him the recent phone calls, all with out of country area codes. "Looks like Tio was working for the Colombians. I bet he thought he was going to take over my operation, be a big drug kingpin." She kicked the corpse with the metal tip of her boot. "Asshole."

A horrible thought occurred to Alejandro. "What about his brother, Pepe?"

"Pepe's not really related to Tio."

He scrambled through his mental files trying to play connect the dots. Who was playing for whom? It was a bit like trying to figure out who was going to win the Super bowl without knowing all the players. "That doesn't mean he wasn't in on this with him. Aren't you worried he'll be the next one to try to take over?"

She shook her head. "Not at all. Pepe's *my* younger brother."

Before he could process this tidbit, Alejandro's walkie talkie crackled and Pepe spoke.

"Isabel? Alejandro? Tio? If you can read me, please respond."

Gunfire burst in the background.

"Soon would be good. We got a situation here. The scouts won't take us into the tunnels. They say they're haunted."

Chapter Twenty-Two

Zeke woke up with a pounding headache and blinked at a painfully bright light. He must have had another hellish vision. He blinked and looked into Brother John's worried face.

"Thank the Lord, you're okay."

Tears ran down the Guardian's cheeks. He had scratches and bruises all over his face and neck.

What the hell had happened to him?

"I got you out of there just in time. Those beasts were about to smother you with a pillow."

Beasts. Someone else had seen them. He grasped his follower's arm.

"You saw them?"

"Oh, yes, they were a bunch of harpies, kicking you and screaming."

"A dragon. Did you see the dragon?"

John looked confused and shook his head.

"What about the demon with the hooked tail? No? Surely you saw the troll? The hag? No?" Not again. He released John's arm. "Where's my wife?"

"I don't know. She left and took the key to the Crèche. I had a spare." Brother John's eyes went wide. "She said it was for your own good, but I couldn't stand the screaming. Please forgive me."

Forgive him? Zeke wanted to hug him.

"You did the right thing." He shuddered and recalled the vile room. "John, why don't the girls have running water and a toilet?"

The other man's eyes widened.

"Your wife's orders. Said they were brood mares, belonged in a stable."

His visions for the Mothers of the Twenty-Four had never included filth. In his dreams, they were all willing, wanton virgins waiting anxiously to serve him. He should have been more involved. Over time, they would have learned to love Edmondsville. Miriam had ruined *everything*.

"How long was I in there?"

"Twenty or thirty minutes?"

His wife couldn't have gotten far. He had to find her before she did anything else crazy.

****

Angie held her breath and raced behind Alejandro and Isabel during a lull in the gunfire. A crowd of natives and cartel foot soldiers squatted at the base of the bluff. The once jovial Julio stood with folded arms and a stony stare. The other Tarahumarans refused to make eye contact with Angie or Isabel. They would speak only with Alejandro, and only because Sister Teresa had told them to listen to him.

Alejandro nodded to the group then spoke directly to Julio. "What happened?"

After some awkward moments, followed by a volley of conversation back and forth, Alejandro shook his head and returned to Angie's side.

"He says there are three ghosts in there. Mina's father and the two dead scouts warned them to stay out of the tunnels, that it was too dangerous." He threw his hands up. "They were our only hope of going in through the back door."

Angie frowned. "Where did they see the ghosts?"

"That tunnel, over there. They won't go back in."

The natives had told them the tunnels were the quickest route to the compound and her son. She wasn't about to give up this easily. "That doesn't mean we can't."

Alejandro and Isabel exchanged glances. "Angie—" he started.

"No. It's not your son. Either of you. And it's not their son. It's my son. You said yourself the only other way was up the side of the mountain. With people shooting down at us." She turned on her heel. "You can stay here if you want, but I'm going."

"Angie—" Alejandro called after her.

Tears stung her eyes. She hadn't come all this way just to give up. She turned on her miner's headlight and walked into a long, dark tunnel. After twenty steps, a fetid miasma enveloped her. She stopped, covered her face with her knit cap and turned to go back. She'd heard of underground methane leaks. She had no desire to be gassed to death. That must have been what the Tarahumarans smelled. Fine. She'd leave, but there was nothing supernatural about a pocket of gas. Her light flickered, then went out. Crap. She hated being in the dark. Something dripped on her head. She jerked, slipped and fell onto a pile of rags. What the hell? Was this some kind of garbage dump? Suddenly her light came back on.

****

Alejandro stroked his beard. Why was Angie so stubborn? Couldn't she see how upset the

Tarahumarans were when she went into the tunnel? There had to be a way to get to the top of the fortress without spending all day climbing up the rock wall. Thinking back to the satellite maps, he tried to recall all the possible approaches and came up empty. Isabel stood off to the side speaking in low tones with Pepe. *Her younger brother.* Why hadn't that been in any of his intelligence reports? Where had he been all these years? Had he really been in the Mexican military or had he been in a safe house in another country?

He cocked his head and listened closely. The birds were singing. Odd. Had the shooting stopped? Come to think of it, he hadn't heard any gunfire since Angie headed into the tunnel, at least fifteen minutes. He'd better see what was happening with her. Maybe she *had* found a way in. Wouldn't that be a kick in the ass?

Alejandro turned to tell Isabel where he was going when an eagle dropped out of the sky, grabbed a rabbit and flew off. Had he been any closer, he could have reached out and grabbed the bird's tail feathers.

"Holy crap. Did you guys see that?"

Then it hit him. They needed an eagle. A big one to snatch their rabbit. He huddled with Isabel and Pepe, told them his plan. Then, over Julio's shouted protests, he started jogging toward the tunnel to tell Angie the good news. She, of all the people on this mission, needed to know there was a faster approach. She'd be so happy, he just knew it. They'd be in and out and Jake would be safe, along with the Tarahumaran girls. She wouldn't believe her good luck.

Just as he set foot inside the passageway, Angie slammed into him and shouted, "Dead. They're all dead."

Chapter Twenty-Three

Miriam tiptoed past the snoring Sister Rose, snatched up the sleeping child, and speed walked to the great room. She was sick and tired of this charade. She was in charge. Not that old goat and not Brother Aaron.

Jake whined and wriggled in her arms. She re-adjusted him on her hip. This "baby" was getting big enough to do his own walking. She was tired of waiting on everyone, being the slave, the go-getter and the whipping boy for Zeke. Tired of being dismissed because she was a woman. So what if she'd only had an eighth grade education. That didn't mean she was stupid. *Oh contrary*, as Zeke would say.

Her extensive street education had included picking pockets while Zeke held them spellbound, and helping people look for the thief when they discovered their losses. She'd never been suspected by the victims or the police as the real crook. Zeke on the other hand, with wild eyes and red hair had been pulled into countless interrogation rooms. Not once had the cops been able to prove a thing, all because his innocent-looking wife had hidden the goods. They'd saved up enough to move to the Eastern Shore and work on an ingenious long con.

Preacher and his wife.

The plan had been to tell the congregation all

contributions went to help poor people in Africa. They were supposed to pocket the money, show them photos of grateful natives, and share thank you notes from adorable "children." Cash in hand, they would leave town in the middle of the night, rich and happy. Miriam's unexpected pregnancy put those plans on hold. Zeke had been furious, telling her she'd done it on purpose, screwed up their timing. He beat her daily. Despite her earlier yearnings, her fear of Zeke outweighed the desire to have a child. She prayed for a miscarriage, but the tenacious child had held on for the entire nine months. Angie's birth changed everything.

The storefront became a real church, and they bought a chicken farm. Things were quiet. Until Zeke's seizures became more frequent, and the Lord began speaking to him. God told her husband to build a town in Mexico. He prophesied and foretold, and when Angie got pregnant and came home to get clean and sober, Zeke had a massive seizure. He awoke filled with the power of the Lord and a sense of urgency. They had to prepare for their move to Mexico. End Days were coming, and Angie was carrying the Chosen One.

Miriam shook her head. How had that old goat recognized the child's special powers? Yes, she saw the marks on the baby's hands, the stigmata. But palm lines could be interpreted however you wanted. Until the baby healed her on the plane ride, she had not believed he was really the Chosen One. And he belonged to *her*. With Jake at her side, she would rule Edmondsville and eventually, the world.

But right now, she had to take care of Brother Aaron.

****

Zeke paused at the entry of the great room and clung to the wall. When he took a deep breath, a painful stitch shot through his side. Bitches must have broken his ribs. He took shallow panting breaths and glanced up at the stage. What the—

Brother Aaron stood in front of the throne. Next to him was a growing mound of rifles, handguns, and ammunition.

"That's right, it's time to lay down our arms."

A woman placed a handgun on the stockpile. "Thank you for saving us from this insanity."

Insanity? What were they talking about?

Sister Anne took the stage alongside Brother Aaron. "We are farmers, not warriors. We want to live here in peace."

Miriam was right. Aaron *was* a traitor. He tried to shout out, to tell his congregation to pick up their guns, fight the Philistines, but his voice came out in a hoarse whisper. "Stop."

The former Sheriff of Wicomico County and Edmondsville Chief of Security mounted the steps, his rifle in hand and his handgun still holstered. A wave of relief washed over Zeke. *Thank God.* Soon all would be right again.

The former lawman placed both of his weapons on the stack. "Let us beat our swords into plowshares."

"No," Zeke whispered. "Not you, too."

"Is that everyone's weapons?" Brother Aaron asked.

"No." Miriam climbed the steps, the child glued to her hip. "I have one and I know how to use it." She whipped the gun out of her pocket and pointed at the big man. The gun clicked. Nothing happened.

A hush fell over the crowd.

She shook the weapon and raised the gun again.

Zeke found his voice, "Miriam, don't!"

She spotted him in the back of the room. "This is all your fault."

Brother Aaron rushed off the stage, pushing his wife ahead of him.

"Grab her," Zeke ordered. Panicked, the crowd surged past him, buffeting him like a tidal wave.

Jake wailed and Miriam took aim at Zeke.

The bullet whizzed by his ear. He ducked behind the wall and hobbled down the corridor to the outside. He hoped to find a place to hide out by the solar panels, somewhere, anywhere away from his insane wife.

Chapter Twenty-Four

Angie gasped and clutched at Alejandro once she was out of the tunnel. She couldn't get the sight of the dead Tarahumarans out of her mind. Piled up like broken dolls, the men's white loincloths were covered in slime and their bright colored shirts were splattered with dried blood. And the smell, she'd never get that smell out of her nose. She gagged, turned her head, and vomited.

Alejandro held her hair away from her face and rubbed her back. "It's okay. I'm here."

When she stopped retching, he handed her a canteen of water. "The missing man, Mina's father, I think he may be in there with the scouts. There's a blanket. Rolled up. Smells awful."

"Julio," he shouted. "Your missing men. Their bodies are in that tunnel." He turned to Angie. "I have no idea of what they do with their dead, but at least they should know where they are."

Angie finally stopped shaking and took a swig of water. It was as if she'd found Janice all over again, only this time there were three bodies. She shuddered. "Their instincts were right. There are ghosts in there."

A *thwup-thwup-thwup* sound overhead alerted everyone to the arrival of Isabel's private chopper. As it set down, wind from the propellers blew up dust and dirt, forcing everyone to cover their eyes.

Alejandro shouted. "Our chariot awaits us."

The pilot threw the door open. "Storm front coming in," he bellowed. "We gotta move now."

Crouching low, Angie ran and leaped into the vehicle.

Alejandro leaped in behind her, followed by Isabel. The boss lady jumped into the seat next to the pilot and grabbed a set of earphones.

Angie looked around the cabin. "Is this thing safe?"

Isabel smiled and yelled, "*Chica*, this is a military grade Huey, combat ready."

The sky became slate gray and lightning crackled in the distance. "Let's roll."

The Huey lifted, and Angie's stomach lurched. Lucky it was already empty. She put on the headphones, and Alejandro showed her how to key the mike. "How will we land?"

"We won't," Isabel said. "We're getting dropped in by the solar panels. It's the flattest spot. You'll have to climb down a ladder."

Angie closed her eyes and prayed.

God, if you really exist, I need your help now.

****

Zeke hid behind a solar panel. If he could just catch his breath. The wind began to rise, and electricity crackled in the air. Lightning streaked across the sky, moving closer to the bluff. He huddled under a panel. A baby howled.

Shit.

She was nearby.

"Zeke, I know you're out here," Miriam called.

"Come out, come out, wherever you are." She giggled, a high crazed laugh. The hairs on the back of his neck stood on end.

The baby wailed, inconsolable.

He attempted to become one with the pole. A bullet whizzed by, missing him, but pinging off metal a few feet away.

"If you come out, I'll tell you a secret."

He'd talk to her. From behind the post. "What secret?"

"Betcha want to know why you've been having those strange visions."

"It *was* you!"

Miriam laughed like a hyena. "Think again."

Jake wailed. "My love, please, you're upsetting the Chosen One."

"Don't worry about him. Actually, maybe you should be worried about him."

He nearly jumped out of his skin. She was closer.

"You *really* want to know this secret." Miriam snickered and shifted the baby on her hip.

"I don't want to die for it."

"Think about it. Why did every woman except me turn into a demon that only you could see?"

She was plucking at his last nerve. "Was it LSD? Peyote? Some other drug?"

"Idiot. It was the baby. Every one of them had held Jake before you tried to breed with them."

Was she saying the Chosen One had turned all of Zeke's desires inside out and created demons before his very eyes? *Preposterous.* Everything he'd done had been for the Chosen One.

His wife was stark, raving mad.

Time to turn on the charm and get the gun and the baby away from her. He put his hands up and stepped out from behind the pole. She was ten feet away and stared right at him.

"Miriam, please. Be reasonable. "

She waggled the handgun at him and spoke to the sobbing baby. "Hear that, Jake? He wants me to be reasonable." She shot at the ground by his foot. "How's that?"

He jumped, grabbed his ribs and moaned. "My darling."

The sky roared with the sounds of a helicopter. Miriam looked up. He raced behind another pillar. With each move, it felt as if someone was stabbing him in the chest. He had to keep going. Or he was a dead man.

****

Alejandro saw Miriam with the baby and motioned to the pilot to let them down as close as possible to the forest of solar panels. He dropped, rolled, and came up with his weapon drawn, taking aim at the woman. But she held the baby right in front of her. He couldn't take a shot without risking the child's life.

Angie fell to the ground beside him, and a thunderclap shook the solar panels. The helicopter lurched, lunged sideways, and finally rose. The pilot banked away from the top of the bluff, leaving the two of them alone facing off with Miriam and the baby.

Angie froze in place beside him. "What are we going to do?"

"Well, if it isn't my darling daughter and some new beau. Nice of you to drop in, Jezebel." She pointed the gun at Angie. "Don't even think of trying to shoot me."

"Mommy, please don't hurt Jake." Angie threw her

weapon down. "I'm unarmed."

"What about lover boy?" Miriam shouted over the rumble of thunder.

Alejandro tossed his weapon on the ground. The moment gunmetal hit a rock, Zeke materialized out of the forest of solar panel posts.

"Miriam, stop—"

She wheeled on her husband and pulled the trigger. The gun roared. His face a mask of shock and surprise, Zeke looked down and grabbed his chest. Blood spurted between his fingers. His mouth opened and closed, and he fell face down on the ground.

"Now who's in charge?" She cackled, and Jake wailed. "Who's next?"

Alejandro jumped in front of Angie. The muzzle flashed. He caught the bullet in his shoulder, flew backwards, and landed on the ground. To his horror, the muzzle flashed again. Angie collapsed on top of him. Thunder roared and the sky turned white.

****

A thick quilt of silence enveloped Angie. Alert and pain free, she opened her eyes and floated over the earth. It felt as if she could reach down and touch the players in the scene below. Her father lay covered in blood, her lover was pinned under her own mortal body. This was it. No more hallucinations, no more religious delusions—she was dead. And had failed to extract her son out of her psychotic mother's clutches.

Angie choked back a sob and slid deeper into her well of despair, the black walls surrounding and closing in on her. What happened to her guardian angel, Metatron? Was God punishing her for her sins? Her logical self, her lawyer's brain objected to the notion of *any* God, much less one with enough time on his hands to single out one poor addict in recovery who wanted to save her son's life. If there *was* a God, why wasn't he here, at her side, smiting her mother? If God was all powerful, why couldn't he help her up, not hammer her down? Hadn't she paid with her miserable childhood? Why, oh why, did Jake have to pay for *her* sins? She wailed in grief, but no sounds emerged.

Lightning flashed, and Metatron appeared before her. Sparks crackling off the top of his head and flames shooting from his flapping wings. He grabbed Angie by the arm and pointed below.

The baby struggled, grabbed his grandmother's arm, and chomped. His grandmother shrieked, dropped the child, and grabbed her bleeding wound. Up on both feet, Jake toddled toward his mother's corpse, wailing. He threw himself on Angie's chest and began patting her pallid in death face.

The crazed woman raised her weapon and took aim at her grandson.

Metatron roared.

A ball of lightning struck the gun, knocking it out of her hand.

A second bolt struck her on the chest. Angie's mother fell to the ground and lay still.

A moment passed, then another. Just when Angie thought it was all over and Jake was safe, she got up to her knees and reached for Angie's loaded Glock.

Blinding light shot across the dark sky and struck the older woman on the side of her head, lifting her off her feet and throwing her into a metal post. She fell to the ground like a ragdoll. Death settled over her features and wiped the rage off her expression, leaving nothing but a pathetic husk of an old woman in its place.

With Jake safe at last, Angie knew her job on earth was done. Her life for Jake's. A good trade.

Thank you for saving my son's life.

She surrendered and turned to follow Metatron into the light. Darkness fell and unseen hands grabbed at her arms and spun Angie into dizzying gyrations. Her bearings lost, she no longer knew up from down, nor could she see any sign of Metatron's lightning bolts or sparks. Where did he go? What was happening to her? Was she being sent to hell? She closed her eyes and prayed for her son and for forgiveness for all her sins.

When she opened her eyes, ecstasy surged through her. Saved, she was saved, and oh dear God, she was back in her own body. Back on earth with her darling baby boy. She looked up at the light gray sky, took a huge gulp of air, and shouted, "Jake!"

Her son knelt on her chest and leaned over her head. "Pat-a-cake, pat-a-cake."

Hot tears trickled down the side of her face. Her son was alive, well, and he was speaking.

"Oh, Jake," she whispered. "Thank God, you're okay."

But what of Alejandro? Had he sacrificed his life to save her son?

The man beneath shuddered and took a great gulping breath. "Angie?"

She rolled over and could barely believe her eyes. "You're alive. I'm alive. And my son is—" She grabbed her baby and Alejandro and squeezed them both as hard as she could. "I don't care who you are or what you do," she sobbed. "You saved my son's life and that's all that matters.

He pulled her face close to his. "I'm not a drug lord."

"You don't have to lie to me. I love you. You're my deputy angel, my warrior. I know that now. My heart sees you and knows you for who you really are."

Alejandro gave a shaky laugh, hugged Jake and kissed Angie on the forehead. "I love you too, babe. Just to be a devil's advocate, do you think you could handle being married to a good guy?"

Metatron had told her that she needed a warrior and an angel. That Alejandro was her deputy angel. If she told him that, he'd never believe her. He'd think she was crazy.

"You're a drug lord, a *capo*. You killed an evil man, a corrupt cop who was about to rape me. You did the world a favor. You got rid of that scum and protected other women."

Alejandro sighed. "I am not, nor have I ever been, a drug dealer, a drug lord, or a killer."

Was the man dense? She was accepting him for who he was. "I told you, you don't have to lie to me. I love you. All of you."

"Angie. Please. Can you keep a secret?"

"I'm your lawyer, remember?"

Alejandro looked her straight in the eyes and said, "I swear on my nephew's grave and my step-brother's life, that everything I'm about to tell you is true," He took a deep breath and pulled her closer. "It's a long story, but I think we have some time."

Sharon Buchbinder

Epilogue

One Year Later, Baltimore, Maryland

Angie sat on the sofa and watched the throng of well-wishers greet Sarah and Dan, then deposit more birthday presents on the growing pile. Foil balloons bobbled each time the front door opened and closed, as if threatening to make an escape from the house. Her husband carried a plate of appetizers in one hand and a soda in the other. He placed both on the coffee table in front of her. Even after a year, she sometimes slipped and called him Alejandro, instead of his real name, Josué or Joshua in English. When she found out he was Jewish, not Roman Catholic, she laughed so hard she cried. What was it with her and Jewish men and Jewish angels?

"Can I get you and the baby anything else?"

She felt a kick. "The baby says you can sit down and take a rest."

Joshua placed his mouth close to Angie's belly button, "Come out, come out, wherever you are."

"Stop, you're tickling me," she giggled. "The baby will come out whenever he or she's good and ready."

"You're sure you don't want to know if it's a boy or a girl?"

"Yup. At least we've picked out names. Zackariah

270

if it's a boy, Rachel if it's a girl."

"That's a good name," Dan said leading a red-headed boy over to his mother. "Jake told me he likes that name. He also likes his little sister's presents and wants to open them for her."

"She asked me to," Jake said.

"Yes, of course." Dan rolled his eyes. "She's not as advanced as you were at that age. Your little sister isn't even talking yet."

"Yes she *is,* Daddy. Leah talks to me all the time." He pointed to his head. "I hear her in here."

Angie exchanged a glance with her husband. *Did Jake really mean that?* She thought about Metatron's revelation that her son had powers handed down from generations of healers in his father's family, powers that had been foretold in scrolls still to be discovered in caves in Israel.

"Dan, I have to ask you, has your family always been physicians?"

Jake's biological father shook his head. "Not every generation, but close. My great-grandmother and grandmother were midwives. Some called them witches because they always knew the gender of a baby *before* it was delivered. It was one of the reasons my ancestors moved around a lot. My grandmother and my grandfather fled the country because their neighbors didn't care for Jews, much less Jewish 'witches'."

Jake climbed on the sofa next to his mother's lap and patted her belly. "You okay in there?"

The baby kicked in response.

"Don't tease your sibling." She leaned against Alejandro/Josué. "Dan, where's your wife?"

"She's wrapping up a meeting on the computer.

Sarah's volunteer work with not-for-profits is coming in handy. She's been giving Isabel advice about how to set up a foundation for the Tarahumaran boarding school and orphanage." He sipped a glass of wine. "She should be done shortly."

"Well, between the grape vines, coffee groves, and apple orchards that Sister Teresa set up with the gold Brother Aaron gave her," Alejandro/Josué said, "they should be able to get out of the marijuana growing business soon."

Angie couldn't believe how remorseful the entire Edmondsville Community had been. With their homes and former lives in the US gone and their cult leader dead, the congregation had decided to elect Brother Aaron as their leader. The first thing he'd done was to release the Tarahumaran girls from captivity and escort them down the mountain to their families. On behalf of the entire congregation, Brother Aaron had also pledged to assist the natives in whatever way they could. They said it was the least they could do to make reparations to the Tarahumarans for their losses.

The gold, as Angie had thought, was out in the open the whole time. Painted white with a blue star, the two-foot wide shield hanging in the great room had been solid gold. Zeke had seen it every time he sat on the throne.

"Isabel swore to Sarah that she was getting out of the trafficking business. She's talking about building a casino in Chihuahua." Dan shook his head. "I have a hard time believing she's telling the truth and really going straight."

"It's only a matter of time before the US and Mexican governments get sick of these drug wars."

Alejandro/Josué said. "Isabel has a family, wants to protect them. She's diversifying her portfolio, investing in legal activities, keeping her money and staying out of jail. The boss lady is a smart woman."

Angie pinched his leg. "Stop calling her that. I'm your boss now."

"Ouch. You should be grateful. Isabel didn't bat an eye when I told her I was moving to the US to set up my own business. She was happy to have a 'friend' across the border who might be able to help her guys out in a pinch. Of course, my new supervisor at the Baltimore ATFE thinks it's great. With her as my buddy, we get all sorts of intelligence on the other cartels."

His cell phone rang. "Natasha. How are you?" He nodded. "That's great. I'm so glad that worked out. And your daughter, does she like her new school? Yes, we'd love to see you when you come to Washington to testify. It's a date." He pressed the off button and glanced at Angie. "What?"

"You're a chick magnet, that's what. It's a good thing I trust you. Otherwise I'd worry about you with that Russian bombshell."

He kissed her cheek. "Strictly business, my love."

"Better be."

"Besides, I fixed her up with my step-brother, Luis. Now *that* man is a chick magnet."

A little blonde girl in a frilly pink dress crawled over to the couch and pulled herself up to stand. She smiled, patted Angie's knee, and babbled.

"Well, hello, Leah," Angie said. "How are you today?"

Jake said, "She says she's fine, Mommy. She wants

273

to play with Rachel."

"It's going to be a while before the baby comes. And, we don't know it's a girl, Jake."

Angie smiled at the adorable blonde. A contraction took her off guard. She gasped, then relaxed. *Braxton-Hicks contractions.* The doctors had warned her they were a possibility in the third trimester. Another cramp, this one harder. The obstetrician had been positive she was due in a month. *Maybe a phone call was in order.* This wasn't her first child, and these contractions were coming fast. *Remember the mantra. Puff, puff, blow.*

Alejandro/Josué grabbed her hand. "Are you okay?"

"Think—we'd—better—get to—the hospital."

The room exploded in a cacophony of advice, and questions, but Jake's beet red face had her undivided attention.

"Rachel's coming out!" Jake screamed. "Rachel's coming out *now*!"

A word about the author...

After working in health care delivery for years, Sharon Buchbinder became an association executive, a health care researcher, and an academic in higher education. She had it all—a terrific, supportive husband, an amazing son, and a wonderful job. But that itch to write (some call it an *obsession*) kept beckoning her to "come on back" to writing fiction. Thanks to the kindness of family, friends, critique partners, Romance Writers of America, and Maryland Romance Writers, she is now published in contemporary, erotic, paranormal, and romantic suspense.

When not attempting to make students and colleagues laugh, she can be found herding cats, waiting on a large gray dog, fishing, dining with good friends, or writing.

You can find her at www.sharonbuchbinder.com